UTTERLY EXPLOSIVE

PAULINE MANDERS

This second edition (paperback) published in 2019 by
Ottobeast Publishing
ottobeastpublishing@gmail.com

First edition published 2012

Cover design Rebecca Moss Guyver.

ISBN 978-1-912861-05-7

A CIP catalogue record for this title is available from the
British Library.

Also by Pauline Manders
Utterly Fuelled (2013)
Utterly Rafted (2013)
Utterly Reclaimed (2014)
Utterly Knotted (2015)
Utterly Crushed (2016)
Utterly Dusted (2017)
Utterly Roasted (2018)

To Paul, Fiona, Alastair, Karen and Andrew.

PAULINE MANDERS

Pauline Manders was born in London and trained as a doctor at University College Hospital, London. Having gained her surgical qualifications, she moved with her husband and young family to East Anglia, where she worked in the NHS as an ENT Consultant Surgeon for over 25 years. She used her maiden name throughout her medical career and retired from medicine in 2010.

Retirement has given her time to write crime fiction, become an active member of a local carpentry group, and share her husband's interest in classic cars. She lives deep in the Suffolk countryside.

ACKNOWLEDGMENTS

My thanks to: Janet Bettle, who set me on my way; Beth Wood for her positive advice and encouragement; Pat McHugh, my mentor and editor; Rebecca Moss Guyver, for her enthusiasm and brilliant cover artwork and design; the Write Now! Bury writers group for their support; and my husband and family, on both sides of the Atlantic, for their love and support.

CHAPTER 1

The midday sun shone down on Utterly Academy from high in a cloudless sky. It should have been a perfect summer day, but the peace and tranquillity of the Academy, nestling amongst the rolling Suffolk countryside on the outskirts of Stowmarket, was about to be shattered. For cocooned within the darker recesses of the Academy ovens lay a small cartridge of liquid propane gas. It had lain there for several hours, slipped into place by a malicious hand, undetected by the kitchen staff. The perpetrator had guessed, with some perspicacity, that the cooks rarely looked into the large greasy ovens before switching them on to gas mark 7, ready for the trays of Yorkshire puddings. And as the ovens got hotter, the liquid gas inside the small pressurised cartridge slowly vaporised, expanding and straining against its seams.

Whilst the temperature in the kitchen inexorably climbed, Mr Blumfield, the carpentry course director, was drawing his morning teaching session to a close. He looked around at his students, scattered untidily through the spacious carpentry workroom, like flotsam and jetsam beached on his workbenches. He glanced up at the pallid ceiling for inspiration. He was proud of this modern prefabricated unit, its pleasingly simple lines in stark contrast to the yellow brick Edwardian mansion from which it spawned. He sighed deeply as he scanned the class again. Would these fledglings be able to fly?

He had taught carpentry and furniture making in this peaceful backwater for three decades. His former pupils hadn't moved far; they'd even lived long enough to produce a second generation of students for him. God; by the time he retired he would be teaching the sons of sons. This particular bunch had been trained in the safety of the classroom for the past year and in ten days' time they would venture out into the real world for their apprenticeships. But he sometimes wondered if laid-back Suffolk resembled today's world, with its static population. Most people seemed to live in picture-book villages, hidden between undulating fields of sugar beet. Still, his students were a promising bunch, at least most of them would be, once they'd got the idea there were twenty-four hours in a day, not twenty-five.

'Now just settle down a moment and listen. I'll pin up the apprentice placements on the noticeboard at two, after lunch. Everyone has an apprenticeship. Yes Matt? You have a question?'

Matt shook his head and blushed. Mr Blumfield sighed and pulled himself to his full five feet five. He'd leave the difficult one for later.

'May I remind you they're non-negotiable. Chrissie, Chrissie Jax; come and see me about your placement. Five past two this afternoon should be fine.' Without looking back, Mr Blumfield turned on his heel and walked briskly out of the workroom.

•••

Matt Finch stared at Mr Blumfield's receding back. He felt his cheeks burn as his plump face flushed beneath his dark sandy hair. The tutor had singled him out. He'd looked directly at him and said *yes Matt*. There could only be one explanation. Old Blumfield must have read his thoughts, seen the question in his eyes. 'He must've meant the Willows apprenticeship,' he whispered under his breath, 'It's mine! Who'd a thought?' Granted, he might not be the class high flyer, but he was better than Chrissie, at least. OK, he was clumsy. His mother called him a grut lummox in her strong Suffolk accent. Others called it dyspraxia; it sounded better that way, as though it wasn't his fault. But he listened, followed instructions to the letter, and turned up for most of the classes. That must have paid off. Matt glanced at Chrissie, the only girl on the carpentry course, and grinned. Strictly speaking, "girl" conjured up someone much younger, whereas Chrissie was definitely past the first flush of youth. But they were friends; two misfits, really. Chrissie, middle aged, blonde and tiny; Matt, nineteen, overweight and clumsy. Together with Nick they had stuck together from the word go.

Matt sighed and looked at his watch. 11.50 am. He'd chosen his clothes with care: tee-shirt, slightly too tight; jeans, designer shabby - and trainers. He tugged at the cheap cotton fabric, straightening the logo *Umbrella Assassins* emblazoned across his chest. It was proof he followed a local band due to feature at the Ipswich Music Day in a few weeks' time. He ambled to the main stairs. The canteen and kitchens were up on the first floor in a new wing, jutting out from the main body of the old mansion building. Why they hadn't been put on the ground floor, he'd never understand. Hmm, roast beef and Yorkshires today.

By the time he arrived, most of the carpentry year had gathered around the service entrance, along with some of the music and performing arts students. Matt could always pick them out; musicians and actors took such care of their hands. A few had drifted further in and were seated at Formica topped tables near the window, well away from the service counter. The modern plate glass looked out over the well-manicured gardens where lavender beds, roses, and tall blue and pink stocks reassured and soothed the eye. The students were too early; lunch wasn't ready to be served. There were still eight more minutes to wait for the Yorkshire puddings to cook, and all the while a small queue formed at the canteen entrance.

Matt could see that Chrissie and Nick had got there before him. They were already slumped at a table, deep in conversation. As he approached, Nick gestured towards the empty plastic chair at the table and grinned. His pleasant round face seemed at odds with his lean frame and long legs, and even if Matt hadn't known, it would have been obvious from the wood glue still clinging to his fingers that he wasn't a musician.

'I bet you'll get the Willows & Son apprenticeship,' Matt heard Chrissie say.

Matt stood by the chair and smiled. Blimey; maybe she was right? 'Yeah, I think I'm in with a chance on that one.' His Suffolk accent always got stronger when anxious or excited, lengthening the a and rolling the i, like a stone at the back of his mouth.

'No, I didn't mean you Matt; Nick is Blumfield's favourite.'

'So?'

'So if Nick's the favourite, then it's odds on he gets the best apprenticeship, and that's Willows & Son.'

'Hmm,' Matt grunted. He wanted the Willows apprenticeship, and he wanted it badly. Hadn't he just heard old Blumfield say, y*es Matt?* He frowned. Could he have misunderstood? He tried to sound off-hand, 'Not sure I'd go there. Not after the trouble last year.'

'What trouble?'

4

'Didn't yew know?' He preferred to say *you* in the Suffolk way, drawing out the end of the word so that it sounded like a w. When no one answered he continued, 'John Willows' son died horribly at the workshop last summer.'

'That would be the "& Son" of John Willows & Son, I take it.'

Matt thought for a moment. That's what he liked about Chrissie - she was always clear and precise. He knew what she meant. No double meanings. He nodded slowly, 'Yeah, John junior.'

'So what happened?'

'The poor bugger was found with a nail in 'is neck. A six inch nail, by all accounts. And fired from a nail gun. They say 'e tried to pull it out an' that just made it worse. There was blood everywhere. He choked on 'is own blood.'

'But that's ghastly.' Chrissie's face paled beneath her short blonde hair.

'It must have been a freak accident, surely?'

Matt took his time. He should have guessed Nick wouldn't see anything suspicious about a six inch nail sticking out of someone's neck. 'What I'm sayin' is - was it foul play?'

'But why would anyone want to?'

'Don't know.'

'You seem to know an awful lot about it, Matt. But foul play?' Nick shook his head.

'Hmm, it could mean a permanent job with prospects for the right apprentice, though.' Chrissie glanced across at Nick. 'And the right apprentice might just be....'

Matt leant in closer to catch Chrissie's last word, hoping it would be his name, not Nick's. But as he watched her mouth open, all he heard was a tremendous bang. A deafening blast ripped the words from her lips as the gas cartridge exploded, blowing the oven door off its hinges and launching the Yorkshire puddings into orbit.

'Oh my God,' Chrissie seemed to mouth, as a ball of burning gas shot from the kitchen.

Matt felt the pressure wave punch him from behind. He was knocked off balance and propelled forwards. Instinctively he threw himself into a dive. For the first time in his life he felt weightless. He travelled through the air, unaware of the rolls of fat surrounding his midriff - he just sailed forwards. And for a few brief seconds he was a comic-book hero with arms outstretched. That is until a superior force took charge and gravity weighed in.

He yelled as his hands collided with the unyielding floor. Unable to pass through, he stopped dead. The rest of his body fell like a stone and his wrist buckled. Landing heavily on his chest, he fought to breathe - but no air would pass. For a moment he thought he might die. Motionless and detached, he lay amongst broken plates and cutlery. Food from the service counter was strewn on the floor. Chips and ruptured ketchup sachets took on a ghoulish appearance to Matt's oxygen starved brain. He knew something bad had happened. He'd felt it when his wrist snapped. Matt closed his eyes as a fuzziness descended, shutting out the Armageddon that had unleashed itself on the Utterly Academy canteen. All he could hear was a high pitched screaming in his head.

He must have blanked out for a moment because the next thing he felt was moisture trickling down from his head. The air smelt of rubble-dust and smoke. Something was shaking him, but it was just too much effort to open his eyes. He lay still and hoped whatever it was would go away. The shaking changed to a sharp prod.

'Argh!' he cried out, opening his eyes as a jolt of stomach-lurching pain shot through his right arm.

Chrissie spoke as she bent over him, but strangely no sound came from her mouth. The screaming noise in his head just ratcheted up a notch. Nick's face came into view. He too was moving his lips but there were no words. Matt frowned as he watched his friend. Why had he lost his voice? His whole manner seemed urgent and the debris in his dark brown hair looked pretty real. So why didn't he speak? Matt shrank back as Nick reached out to shake him.

'No, don't touch me. It's me wrist. Get off! Shit, I must've bust it.' He knew he'd spoken because he'd formed the words. But he couldn't hear himself. It was weird. The stomach-lurching pain certainly felt real enough.

He watched Chrissie cough and choke as smoke billowed from the canteen kitchen. Cold water showered down from the ceiling sprinklers above, mixing with the ketchup and producing pools of red tinted liquid on the marble-effect floor tiles. Matt felt Nick's firm hand slip beneath his uninjured arm and the other grab at his tee-shirt. The flimsy cotton strained as Nick tried to haul him up off the floor.

'What you all sayin'? All I can hear is a load ol' squit!' He'd reverted to pure Suffolk-speak.

Suddenly Chrissie's face was right up close, almost touching his nose. Anger leapt from her eyes as her lips moved. This time he could make out faint words above the screaming in his head. He might be wrong, but he was pretty sure she'd just sworn at him.

'Well why didn't you say it were time to get goin'?'

Chrissie said something more and looked heavenwards as Matt felt his body lift upright. Blimey, she'd summoned up the Almighty. But it was Nick, from his height of six three, who had finally heaved him off the ground. Matt found himself propelled, part carried and half dragged, towards the exit. Chrissie led a path between upturned tables and chairs as smoke caught at his throat and stung his eyes. Finally they stood for a moment, side by side precipitately at the top of the main stairs leading to the ground floor.

Matt gazed down the steps. He could see the fire escape doors already thrown wide open. Somewhere beyond there would be fresh summer air and the Academy gardens. But stretching across his path were the glinting metal strips that reinforced the edge of each step. For a moment his fuddled brain transported him to the film set of Indiana Jones. He was searching for the Cup of Life. A penitent man can pass this way, he thought and lowered his head, curled into a ball and threw himself forward. Nick, taken unaware and supporting his weight, flew with him. Downwards they travelled, barely touching each step and gaining speed. By the bottom Nick was taking three steps in a stride. They hurtled through the open fire escape doors, Nick still holding on to Matt.

'Argh!' Matt yelped.

'Are you OK? What in God's name possessed you back there?' Nick shouted as he untangled himself from Matt. 'You just threw both of us down the bloody stairs.'

'Argh! Me friggin' wrist, it….' But Matt stopped. He'd heard Nick, or at least he'd heard part of what Nick had said, certainly the *what in God's name*, bit.

'It's OK, mate; there'll be ambulances soon. You'll be OK.' But Nick's voice sounded strangely distant and tinny.

8

It reminded Matt of how things sounded for a while after the music festivals in Ipswich. Back then his ears had felt blocked. But why now? Of course, an explosion. That's why Nick's voice was muffled.

•••

Matt's head felt heavy as he stirred. He had no idea where he was. It was as if he'd never been. There were no thoughts, no memories, no emotion – nothing, just a blank; like going to sleep and waking without dreaming. And as consciousness crept into those first groggy moments, he tried to place where he was, to recall the last few hours. But they'd gone. Where? He was too deep to open his eyes and too tired to move again, so he lay motionless as his hearing slowly connected with his stupefied brain. He became aware of a gentle hissing. What was it? Had it been there before? He couldn't remember but he needed to know.

'I'm afraid he must be oversensitive to morphine, we don't normally see a reaction like this,' a kindly voice explained, strangely distant.

'Ah, I see. Thank you, nurse.' A deeper intonation.

Matt rolled his head sideways, keeping his eyes closed as he surfaced from the void. It was strange but he hadn't guessed his head was on a pillow. The plastic covered, regulation NHS microfiber was so firm it bore no resemblance to a soft, comforting cushion. He had a crick in his neck and his mouth felt stale and dry. Still in a trance-like state, he opened his eyes hoping his mother would be there. A blurry figure took form, but he didn't remember her wearing navy blue trousers and a white shirt with epaulettes before. He struggled to focus. Where was he?

'Mum….'

'Is he waking up?' the masculine voice asked.

'I think so.'

'Mum?' He'd started to doubt. When in any of his nineteen years had his mother ever been there when he'd needed her? She didn't do the touchy feely stuff; she wasn't one to give a spontaneous hug, or even hold his hand. He'd never understood why.

'Mum?' He hoped that if he opened his eyes wide enough, he'd be able to see her concerned smiling face. But of course that might prove difficult. His mother had never been concerned and she certainly didn't smile much. She would have needed to feel affection for him before she could show concern.

'Ah good, you've woken up at last,' a gentle, far-away voice harmonised with the soft hissing in his head.

'Where am I? Why…?' Matt struggled to gather his thoughts as he looked around, slowly absorbing the sounds and smells of a hospital ward. He saw pastel patterned curtains half drawn around his bed, a drip stand with a bag of clear fluid, and a nurse standing nearby holding a chart. When his gaze finally settled on the policeman near the end of his bed, he gasped in horror. 'Argh!'

'It's OK. You're in hospital now.' It was the gentle voice again.

Matt stared at the policeman. If he closed his eyes, maybe he'd disappear.

'Is this the young man you called us about?'

'Yes, he was acting strangely. The staff were suspicious, what with the explosion and, well I'm sure Sister's explained.'

Strangely? Acting strangely? Matt closed his eyes - that way the voices seemed more distant and nothing to do with him. Now where was that hissing coming from?

'We came straight away. It's not really our responsibility; we have to hand it on to the counter-terrorist lot. They've been informed and as soon as they arrive, well we can leave it with them. I'm just here in case he tries to leg it in the meantime.'

Leg it. Leg it? Why would he want to leg it? The hissing changed to a whine. Matt kept his eyes shut.

'I doubt he'll do that. Just look at him. And he's attached to a drip stand.'

That was too much; he had to look. He raised his right arm and peered at a crepe bandage. Christ, what had they done to him? And then something seemed to come back, a vague memory: someone pulling at his hand, a tight tourniquet biting into his arm, an injection of something and then a blissful nothingness tingling down to his fingertips.

He looked up into a pair of hazel eyes, wide with alarm.

'It's OK, it's OK. You can put your arm down.' The finely striped blue and white tunic suited her. 'You've been in an explosion and you've broken your wrist. No, no it's OK; it's been put back, splinted. But we'll need to keep you in overnight. You were acting a bit strange and, well we had to alert the police - what with the explosion.' The nurse let her voice trail away as she looked across at the policeman still standing at the end of his bed.

He followed her gaze. Behind the policeman a man approached, his heals clipping on the hard flooring. The sound was strident to Matt's sensitised ear drums. Clip, hiss; clip, hiss. He wore his shirt unbuttoned at the neck, no tie and five days growth on his clean shaven head. There was no mistaking him, he was fuzz – plainclothes fuzz. 'Shi-t.'

'Hello.' He flashed his identity card at the policeman and smiled at the nurse. 'Counter Terrorist Unit, Martlesham Heath. I got here as soon as I could.' The smile died on his lips as he turned his attention on Matt. 'You've caused a bit of a stir, I'm afraid. Could you confirm your name for me?' There was a long pause before he added, 'sir.'

'Um, Matt Finch, but….' *Shit! Counter Terrorist Fuzz. What the hell's going on?*

'Good; I understand you wouldn't give your name before. So it's Matt Finch.' He wrote the name in his notebook. 'It's purely a formality, sir. We need a few details, if you feel up to speaking?' But he didn't look at Matt for confirmation; instead he smiled at the nurse.

Matt nodded. He reckoned the bloke must know the nurse, otherwise why would he keep smiling at her? Of course; he was making a play for her, and at the end of his hospital bed.

'Could you confirm your address, please?'

As Matt went through his details he noticed his own left hand, his good hand. Strange – he was clasping something. He couldn't think why he'd be holding onto….

The plainclothes followed Matt's gaze. 'If you could just open your hand slowly, please?'

Time seemed to stand still as Matt uncurled his fingers. The plainclothes tensed as something glinted in the unnatural overhead strip-lighting. The links of a metal strap started to appear and then a disc. Matt let it fall onto the pale blue linen bedcover. It was a Rolex watch.

'Well they said you were unnaturally attached to that.' The plainclothes glanced at the policeman and smiled. Matt noticed the smile – the way he raised his eyebrows made it feel threatening. He hadn't smiled at the nurse like that.

'Me brother, he brought it back from Bangkok last summer. It's a present; not a real one.'

'So why's it so special you wouldn't hand it over to the nurses for safe keeping? You wouldn't even let it out of your sight. A false watch, you say, and imported. I think we'll take it for the time being, if that's OK with you, sir. I'll give you a receipt.' The plainclothes leant across and scooped it into a plastic evidence bag with his pen.

'What you…?'

'There's been an explosion and you were there. By all accounts you were acting suspiciously. You even have *Assassins* printed on your tee-shirt, I'm told. And now you're holding onto – well, what you say is a false watch. I know this isn't London, and Utterly Academy isn't a typical target, but… terrorism. Can't be too careful.'

Matt groaned. Something started to come back; a vague memory of a nurse reaching for his watch. It needed to be removed. He'd thought she was stealing it - the only present his brother Tom had ever given. The pain and fear had crashed through him, and then the memory blurred. He had no idea what had happened after that. Clearly they must have given it back, why else was he clasping it? What had the plainclothes just said? Terrorists?

'You're talkin' a load ol' squit!'

'No need to be offensive.' The policeman leant forwards and glanced at the nurse before adding, 'Ah, that's Suffolk for, silly talk, isn't it?'

The plainclothes shook his head. 'Detonators and micro transmitters can be very sophisticated these days.'

'A detonator? You mean there was a bomb?' Matt felt the sweat breaking out on his forehead. The man must be joking, surely? He stared at the plainclothes. Was he wearing tights under his creased chinos? Was he about to break into song and tap-dance around the bed? Judging by the sound he'd made when he clipped his way down the ward, Matt reckoned he could probably do a passable tap-routine. This was a madhouse; madder than a box of frogs. 'But I was blown up,' he whispered, shaking his head.

The plainclothes fell silent while he considered this. 'But so are suicide bombers.'

Matt cast about, pulling at the bed clothes. He had to get away but he was flanked by the policeman and the nurse. The plainclothes stood at the end of his bed. Suddenly a familiar shape caught his eye as it hurried up the ward. He froze, hardly able to believe it. Surely things couldn't get any worse? 'Mr Blumfield, what you doing here?'

'Hello, Matt. Found you at last.' Mr Blumfield's face glistened with perspiration in the warm oppressive air. He breathed heavily.

'Are you the father?' the policeman asked.

Mr Blumfield stood, resting his hand on the back of a hospital chair. It was greyish-pink, designed to look as if covered in plush upholstery but in reality was wipe clean plastic. It gave an illusion of comfort, a bit like Mr Blumfield's visit. 'Of course not,' he snapped before smiling briefly at Matt and then turning his attention back to the policeman.

Matt gave up the unequal struggle and feigned unconsciousness. Mr Blumfield's voice sounded comfortably distanced until a tap on his shoulder jolted him back.

'Come on Matt, I think I've cleared up a few queries with the police. They've got your details. They want to speak to you again. Here, it's written down. You're to present yourself at the police station in Ipswich, just off Civic Drive, in the next 48 hours - to give a witness statement, maybe answer some questions.' He shook his head, the age showing in the deep lines around his eyes. 'I can't think why they needed a counter-terrorist officer.'

'Thanks, Mr Blumfield,' Matt sighed. 'About me watch–'

'What's your watch got to do with anything? Now try to concentrate. I understand you've only broken your wrist. They've pushed it back into place; reduced it I think the nurse said. So that's good. It could have been worse.'

'Ah, that's why–'

'No doubt.' He cleared his throat. 'Your apprenticeship has been arranged at Hepplewhites. But you'll have to wait a few weeks before starting. I'll ring them later.' Mr Blumfield paused, acknowledging Matt's weak smile. 'As soon as you're all plastered up properly, you can come into the Academy to do some work on the Project Planning & Communication module instead. You won't need both arms for that.'

Matt groaned and closed his eyes.

Mr Blumfield stayed a few moments longer before leaving Matt to the administrations of the hospital. Matt had experienced a taste of what might be termed the caring side of the Academy.

CHAPTER 2

Utterly Academy had been closed for the rest of that Friday, the day of the canteen explosion, and also for the weekend. But by Monday, Chrissie had expected it to be open; business as usual, apart from the canteen, of course. So she was surprised to find her way barred by some coloured tape and a man from the fire service standing at the main entrance to the grounds.

She stopped her red, open top, 1973 MGB roadster and looked across the barrier. A wide gravel drive stretched beyond the tape, curving gently to a forecourt in front of the old Edwardian mansion building at the heart of the Academy complex. Fire appliances, vans and police cars were parked haphazardly, spilling onto grass verges and churning up the neatly mown lawn. Chrissie scanned the yellow brick façade for evidence of the explosion. It didn't take her long to spot the canteen windows. They were the ones on the first floor with smoke-blackened brick above the broken glass. It looked pretty dramatic from where she was sitting. Even the once fashionable chequered pattern of red brick was lost beneath the grime.

Chrissie got out of her car. She wanted a better view but she was shocked when she saw the formal flowerbeds and herbaceous borders hemming the main drive. For a moment she thought some huge animal had lain there, its massive weight crushing and flattening the plants before rolling on its back and then cavorting away. Purple lavender lay trampled and rose heads hung broken, weeping petals. But of course this wasn't the work of a primeval beast; this was the result of the student exodus, possibly eight hundred trainer-clad feet stampeding out of the buildings. And as she surveyed the muddy, waterlogged area beneath the canteen windows, she imagined how powerful the fire hoses must have been. A shard of broken glass glinted in the sun and instinctively she put up her hand to shield her eyes. Her movement triggered a reaction from the fire service official manning the coloured tape barrier.

'I'm sorry, miss. No one's allowed through unless you've got a special pass.'

'But I need to get into the Academy. I won't go near the canteen or kitchen.'

'Sorry, miss. No one's allowed in yet.'

'But…'

He puffed out his chest and squared his shoulders.

'But I can see people walking around the buildings over there.'

He tapped his helmet. 'Hard hats; they're wearing hard hats, miss.'

She smiled sweetly.

'It not just falling masonry, miss. It's hot spots.' He drew out the vowels and emphasised the t, making the words sound hot. 'And then there's gas; maybe pockets of it. We can't have you walking around in your clippy-cloppy heels. Just one little spark, and well… boom!'

Chrissie looked down at her sensible soft pumps. 'Haven't they turned the gas off yet?' She took a step back.

'Of course. Those people, as you call them, are fire investigators and structural engineers. They're professionals.'

Chrissie bristled. 'Have you any idea how long before we're allowed back into the Academy?'

'No, miss.'

So no surprises there then. Chrissie swallowed her irritation; no point in saying thanks and thanks for nothing. Better to maintain her dignity. The officious little man was only doing his job, after all. It was probably best to get back in her car and drive home. There were bound to be updates on the Academy's website and besides, she could make a mug of tea while waiting for further news. She caught sight of her reflection in the rear view mirror as she reversed her MG back onto the road. Her short blonde hair had whipped into a frenzied mess, her trademark blue mascara was smudged across one lower eyelid, and her yellow sunflower motif tee-shirt had attracted a cloud of thunderflies – tiny black insects that blew in from the fields across Suffolk at that time of the year. She pulled a face. No wonder the fire official hadn't let her pass the barrier; she looked positively deranged.

Chrissie took her time driving back to Woolpit, the sleepy Suffolk village she called home, just north-west of Stowmarket. She thought of her modest cottage as her refuge; it was somewhere to bolt the door and lie low when the outside world got too much for her. If she'd ever stopped to think about it, she would have said it was the emptiness and hurt she shrank from rather than the world itself. She'd lived at No. 3, Albert Cottages for nearly ten years, the last two alone. The stone plaque on the front wall proudly declared the year 1876, the year her end-of-terrace cottage was built. Unfortunately that sense of permanence hadn't applied to Bill, her husband of ten years. Well, eight years, if she didn't count the two since he'd died.

It was always a pleasure to open her front door and step into the cool interior. If she'd felt happier, she might even have smiled to think her cottage was built with bricks baked from the same chalky clay as the Utterly mansion. She flung her car keys on the hallway table. They skidded across the polished surface, clinking against an old photo-frame – large and heavy, made of pewter but pretending to be silver. Bill smiled back at her, the wind lifting his dark hair as he sat, captured by the camera lens, forever astride a stile somewhere near Aldeburgh. She remembered that day. They'd walked on a steeply shelving beach of shingle, and later, when they got home, Bill emptied his pockets.

'You've collected half the beach,' she'd shrieked, laughing as he produced, like a conjurer, yet another and then another pebble from his jacket. She'd wanted to toss them all into the garden but he'd insisted at least one should be saved. She chose the creamy-golden one, and so there it had rested on the table where she'd just thrown her keys. Idly, she ran her fingers over its smooth, rounded surface and without thinking, picked it up and pressed it into her palm. It was somehow comforting to think the warm sandy limestone in her hand might contain a fossil shell – something preserved for eternity.

Still holding the stone, she walked into her tiny kitchen. It was time to make that mug of tea she'd promised herself. Her laptop sat lifeless on the scrubbed-pine counter; there would be time enough to switch it on. Let the kettle boil first, she thought. But it wasn't easy making the tea one-handed while holding Bill's stone in the other. 'I must let go and move on,' she murmured, but she still held the stone. And that was the whole point – moving on, keeping busy; it was the key but easier said than done when you felt more at ease with the past and with old things.

Flash! The sunlight suddenly blinded her as it reflected off the aluminium toaster. For a moment she was back in the explosion. She closed her eyes as she braced herself, but there wasn't a thunderous bang or smell of rubble dust, and just as quickly as she was in the explosion, so she was out of it again and standing in her kitchen, breathing fast and sweating.

'Get a grip, Chrissie Jax,' she whispered, 'the canteen – it was no more than a scaled-up version of being slow to light the grill while leaving the gas flowing. Bang! Eyebrows singed but nothing more. Get over it.' Of course Matt would need a little longer; probably six weeks for a broken wrist, she reminded herself. It wasn't so easy getting over Bill. How long for a broken heart?

She switched on her laptop. Its carrying case was balanced on a kitchen shelf above a stack of unused cookery books. It reminded her of her previous life with the daily commute to Ipswich. Had she been right to make the change? To throw up her old life and make a fresh start after Bill died? God it was hard, this business of swimming alone against the tide of life. She shook her head and read the notice posted at last on the Utterly Academy website.

'So the structural engineer has finally given the OK for the buildings to be reoccupied tomorrow morning. Yes!' she said, punching the air and smiling.

She skimmed on, 'But the *canteen kitchen and dining room are to remain off limits - closed.* Well I can cope with that. The food was bloody awful anyway.' Chrissie smiled again. One more day and she'd know which apprenticeship she was going to get.

And so on Tuesday morning she was among the first in a group of excited carpentry students clustering near the departmental noticeboard in the main corridor of the Academy building. In reality, it was more of an open hallway than a passageway, taking up a large area on the ground floor at the heart of the old mansion. Mr Blumfield had finally pinned up the list of apprentice placements.

Chrissie, standing near Nick, looked up at the typewritten list. She grinned as she saw Nick had got the Willows & Son apprenticeship. She'd guessed he would. Right again. But as she looked on down the list, she found her name but there was nothing written against it. She checked again. No. Just a blank space. She felt her face redden. Embarrassment, then anger. They'd just ignored her. Just because she wasn't male, wasn't tall, wasn't able to manhandle the huge planks of timber they worked with. But then she hadn't joined the carpentry course to get closer to wooden roofing supports and heavy floorboards; she was interested in cabinet making and furniture restoration.

'Well, that's bloody strange, Chrissie. Your name's up there, but nothing's written against it.'

Nick must have seen the tear at the corner of her eye. She knew it, could feel it in his tone. Damn them all. She'd thought she could retrain, use the lump sum from the widow's pension and finally do something she loved after all those years as an accountant. But how the hell could she even start when they just ignored her, like she was just some inconvenience to them all? They wouldn't confront her, refuse her a place. They'd just overlook her until she went away.

Nick gently touched her shoulder. 'Don't you remember? Old Blumfield said he wanted to see you in his office at five minutes past two last Friday, but the appointment kind of got blown away.'

Chrissie nodded. Nick was right; she'd completely forgotten, what with all the drama of the explosion.

'Perhaps you should go and see him today and he'll explain what's going on.'

'Yes, good idea. Thanks, Nick. Oh and well done.'

She smiled mechanically. 'You've got the Willows apprenticeship. I guessed you would. Did you get the impression Matt thought he might get it?'

Nick looked heavenwards and shrugged. 'God knows.'

Chrissie laughed, 'No doubt he'll tell us.'

'Poor bugger.'

Chrissie tried to gather her thoughts and control her emotions. If she barged straight off to Blumfield's office now, she'd lose her temper, or worse - burst into tears. She needed to decide on an approach. Ice cool, acidic? No. She was still too cross.

Twenty minutes later, Chrissie approached Mr Blumfield's office, hidden away on the first floor of the old building. The staircase and first floor corridor had been cleaned since the explosion, but she couldn't fail to notice the smoke-stained paintwork as she passed the coloured tape barring access to the canteen. Chrissie's pulse raced. For a moment she could smell the smoke and rubble again, and then irritation replaced the olfactory flashback. Typical, she thought. No chairs outside his office, just a bare corridor with a stark notice on the door: *Mr Blumfield, Director Carpentry Department*. The solid wooden door was ajar.

'God, he'd better be here.' She raised her hand to knock.

'What's that you said? Are you absolutely sure?' Mr Blumfield's voice floated out, angry, questioning.

Chrissie froze, her hand mid-air.

'That's the preliminary finding? I suppose the fire inspector knows what he's doing?'

Only one voice, she thought. He must be speaking on the phone.

'Alien material? I know it was an unusually lively batch of Yorkshire puddings, but you're not suggesting a UFO started the explosion? .... No, I am taking this seriously.... Oh I see. Shrapnel embedded in the oven door, not baking-tin metal.... Yes I know; the ovens had been on for a while before the explosion.' He lowered his voice. 'You mean this was a deliberate act? .... No, no. Matt Finch? Surely he couldn't have had anything to do with it?' His voice sounded louder as he walked towards the door.

Chrissie stepped back.

'Good God. Just when we thought we might get university status. This is all we need; police crawling all over the place. And the press....'

As the door slammed shut, she just caught his last words; 'A counter terrorism security adviser? I've got to see a counter terrorism security adviser?'

Chrissie stood, her face inches from the closed door. Now what? She waited, almost putting her ear to the solid wood. This was a conversation, or rather a half conversation worth hearing. But the sounds were too muted; she couldn't catch what was being said and besides, she was wasting time. It might not be the best moment to see Blumfield but she couldn't be put off any longer. She smoothed her short blonde hair with a quick nervous movement. Today at least she looked smart and business-like. Yesterday's sunflower tee-shirt had been replaced with a blue broderie anglaise short sleeved blouse. It complimented her grey-blue eyes and of course the blue eyeliner, already starting to smudge. But no thunderflies on her today! She raised her hand again to knock just as the door was flung open. She froze, foolish with one fist still held in the air.

Mr Blumfield stood in the doorway and stared at her for a moment. 'Oh it's you Mrs Jax. Come in, come in.' He turned back to his desk and sat down. He looked rather flushed.

'My name on the list. There was nothing written against it.'

Before she could continue he waved his hand. 'Please sit down, Mrs Jax.' He indicated an elegant copy of a Mackintosh chair, an over ambitious project from a previous course many years before.

Chrissie settled on the uncomfortable high backed chair. She was sure he kept it in his office for that very reason. It would never do to encourage students to linger longer than was absolutely necessary. She tried again. 'There was nothing written against my name.'

'I know, I know.' He paused, choosing his words, 'That's because, Mrs Jax, I have arranged a rather special placement.'

She raised an eyebrow. Special? God.

'I have an old contact in Wattisham. I've been waiting for a student; a special student to complete our Millennium project.'

'What? But it's 2010.'

He nodded carefully. 'We've been waiting for the right student, as I say, Mrs Jax. How do you feel about totem poles?'

Chrissie had never been asked this question. Not in forty-two years. She had no views about totem poles.

'Totem…? But what's that got to do with…? What project, Mr Blumfield? Why a special…?' Her tongue stuck to the roof of her mouth as her thoughts raced on.

'I've just said; a totem pole, eighteen feet high.' He beamed at her expectantly.

Chrissie paled as she imagined the height of three doors standing on end.

'It will depict local events over the last one thousand years.' There was no stopping him now. 'You can construct the project during your apprenticeship with Ron Clegg.'

'I can construct…? Are you serious? Who's Ron Clegg?'

'Do pay attention, Mrs Jax. Ron Clegg is my contact near Wattisham. I've already told you that. Now the totem pole, that's the exciting thing.'

Chrissie gathered her thoughts. 'You're saying the important events affecting the… the Tribe of East Anglia over the last one thousand years? Has enough happened? I mean, will we need all eighteen feet, Mr Blumfield?' Chrissie fought to keep her face straight. 'After all,' she continued, her voice catching, 'East Anglia has always been a bit of a back-water, even after it was drained.'

'Yes, yes,' he said waving his hand. 'I'm sure you'll think of something, Mrs Jax.'

Her eyes twinkled. 'Yes I'm sure I will Mr Blumfield.'

'Now, we've already got the tree trunk - well once you've found it. There's a receipt somewhere. When you've tracked down where it's been stored for the past ten years, all you'll need to do is transport it over to Ron's workshop. Simple.'

'All I…? Simple?'

'Wonderful isn't it? I knew you'd be pleased.'

Chrissie almost choked as she suppressed a cough.

'But why me?' She paused to control her voice, 'There isn't much demand for totem poles in the UK. How will this, I mean how can this train me?'

'Ah, I should have explained. Old Ron Clegg runs a cabinet making and furniture restoration business. He's never had an apprentice assigned to his workshop before, but he could do with some help. Arthritis, I think. And he's always been a bit of a recluse, but I'm sure you'll do fine. He'll be a good teacher. Now–'

'So I'm to be apprenticed to Ron Clegg? But why wasn't his name on the notice?'

He put up his hand. 'No, no; you don't need to thank me.'

Thanking couldn't have been further from Chrissie's mind.

'You're not built for heavy construction, Mrs Jax. This will suit you better.'

'What? I'm not built for…?' Was the man serious? People didn't talk like this in 2010, surely.

He smiled at her again. 'Well, I knew you'd be pleased. It's just a matter of how to present things. That's what I always say, Mrs Jax.' And with that he looked back down at his desk still smiling. The interview was over.

Despite Mr Blumfield's rather idiosyncratic interpretation of people skills, Chrissie was surprised to feel an overwhelming sense of relief. She had an apprenticeship, thank God, and as long as she made it through the next year she'd be trained. But why hadn't his name been on the typed list? And why was she being placed with someone who had never had an apprentice before? Did that mean none of the local firms were willing to take her on? And if those weren't enough questions, she asked herself, who had told them she was small with no head for heights, a liability on a construction site? She straightened her broderie anglaise blouse. No, she could be as butch as the next person if she put her mind to it. But if anyone had stopped to ask, she would have happily confessed that cabinet making and bench carpentry were where she saw her future. So old Blumfield had actually done her a favour, though she'd bite her tongue rather than admit it. But a totem pole, now that was something else. Nothing on the course had prepared her for that. Hell might freeze over before she acquired sufficient skills to carve eighteen feet of figures and faces. Oh God!

Chrissie sighed as she went to look for Nick. He was bound to want to know how she'd got on and what old Blumfield had said, but to be honest, she needed to sort it out in her own mind first. How much to tell? Not the bit about Matt Finch. Best not to repeat things overheard through doors. She counted herself lucky when she considered her two young friends and she certainly didn't want to worry them. They had been so important during her first year at the Academy. Matt, in particular, took what she said on face value, never intuitively sensing any inner sadness, never asking probing questions; and kindly Nick, well he was sufficiently confident and at ease with himself to accept others, warts and all, and that included her age. Living in the here-and-now was for her a process of healing. She didn't want to be asked about her past, at least not until it stopped hurting.

It didn't take Chrissie long to find Nick. He was where she'd expected; in the carpentry workroom passing a board through the thickness planer. At first he didn't hear her above the noise of the machine.

'Hi!' she yelled.

Nick switched the machine off.

'Hi! Take your ear defenders off,' she yelled, this time cupping her hands to her mouth.

'What did Blumfield say?' Nick pushed the earmuffs up from his ears onto his head. They stood up like an arch, reminding Chrissie of a Viking helmet. He looked ridiculous and she tried not to laugh.

'Well he said quite a lot actually, well a lot for Blumfield.' Chrissie frowned as she remembered the bit about the explosion.

'And?'

'He's organised an apprenticeship for me at Ron Clegg's cabinet making and furniture restoration workshop. That's somewhere over towards Wattisham.' Chrissie couldn't keep the sudden smile from her face as the implications sank in.

'Good for you. So why didn't he put it up on the noticeboard?'

'Probably to make me sweat a bit. You know he doesn't like me. I didn't have the nerve to ask him where it was exactly.'

'It'll be somewhere close to the Wattisham Airbase. You know, where they repair and service the army helicopters. You must have heard of it. Even I've read somewhere that Prince Harry is probably going to be sent there for pilot training.'

'Wow, cabinet making and Prince Harry; I can hardly wait.' She'd keep the bit about the totem pole for later.

CHAPTER 3

Nick Cowley had never been so happy in his life. He stood up straight, stretching to his full height of six foot three and gripped the top scaffolding rail surrounding the three-storey house. A breeze ruffled his work clothing and the air caught and pulled at his dark brown hair. It felt strangely calming; nature's head massage. Explosions, smoke and canteen debris seemed remote from this height. The umbilical cord linking him to Mother Earth strained to hold on to those memories, already two weeks old. He smiled. Better put the yellow hardhat back on before the foreman noticed, and with that action the yellow plastic effectively clamped the cord. The past had been separated. The here and now was all that mattered.

'What the hell you doing up there?'

Nick waited as the foreman clambered along the wooden staging one storey below. He could feel the vibration of heavy footsteps transmitted through the exoskeleton of scaffolding poles. He guessed, from all the banging and clanking, that it would only be a moment before Alfred's head appeared above the third-floor staging, like Neptune rising from the ocean but crowned with yellow protective headgear. Nick watched anxiously as the aging foreman climbed the ladder to stand beside him, gasping with the effort.

'What you doing up here on your own? You frightened the bloody life out of me.' Alfred Walsh had at last found his breath.

'Sorry.'

'I should bloody think so. Haven't done a complete week with us yet and already you're scampering around like a bleeding monkey. What if you'd come over dizzy or missed your footing? What then? Could have a horrible accident if you fell from here.' As if to emphasize his point, Alfred looked over the top rail to survey the landing area below.

Nick followed his gaze and stretched over the rail. A well-manicured lawn stopped short of the house wall and an angular impressionist sculpture reached towards the sky. Or perhaps it was an upturned wheelbarrow.

'For God's sake, Nick; keep back from that rail.' Fine beads of sweat broke out on the foreman's face.

'I'm really sorry. I just wanted to have a look. It's… it's exciting.'

'Huh,' Alfred wheezed.

They stood on the top staging surrounding the seventeenth century house, deep in the Suffolk countryside - so hidden that the area was called World's End. Nick was still in his first week with Willows & Son. He'd been excited when the foreman wanted him there that morning - needing his young legs. The firm had been contracted to effect major repairs to the roof timbers and Nick in his enthusiasm had scrambled up the ladders to look at the rotten roof joists - except he'd been distracted by the height. He could see the wooden truss beams supporting the old peg tiles were already caving in. But the strength of breeze up there, well – he could imagine how sudden gusts might rip away loose tiles, hurling them into the air.

'We don't need excitement at this height. I couldn't cope with another body.' Alfred blinked briefly and then looked into the distance.

'Another body? What d'you mean?' Nick gave the foreman his full attention. No one had mentioned bodies before. He was pretty sure Alfred meant the dead sort, not vibrant voluptuous female ones.

'Over there,' the foreman said, ignoring Nick's question, and pointing, 'that's Wattisham Airbase. It's difficult to see from here, but at night the runway lights are so powerful the sky's all lit up. You can see it for miles.'

'A bit like Ipswich.'

'No, there's no runway in Ipswich, Nick. Ah, I get what you mean; the lights at night. It's too far away to see from here though.'

For a moment they stood companionably with their backs to the roof and gazed out over the gently rolling countryside, lush and peaceful, stretching into the distance. This was high for Suffolk, at least 250 feet above sea level, and when standing on the top staging - well it must have given them another twenty feet. They could see for miles.

'Whose body, Mr Walsh?' Nick couldn't help himself. The question just slipped out again, separated from reality by three storeys height and gently buffeted by wind. He bit his lip. Perhaps he shouldn't have asked.

A long silence stretched between them. Alfred kept his eyes focused on the horizon, and Nick shuffled uncomfortably. His movement finally jolted the foreman back from wherever the question had transported him.

'John junior, the boss's lad - I can see it as clear as day.' The foreman shook his head before continuing, 'Must've been about a year ago, I reckon.'

Nick held his breath and waited for more.

'Yup, I was first to arrive and there he was on the floor in the workshop. At first you can't take in what you see;

don't recognise it as someone you know. God, it was horrible.' Alfred lowered his gaze and studied his hand. 'I tried to do something; rolled him over to see if he was alive. But I should've known. He was so cold. Blood - it was everywhere; on my hands....'

Alfred looked down over the scaffolding rail. 'Christ, if you fell from here. Blood – it would be....' He shook his head. 'I always thought it strange, the punnet of strawberries in the workshop. He hated strawberries. He was allergic to them.' Alfred's voice faded.

'I'm sorry Mr Walsh. I had no idea you....' Nick frowned. He thought he remembered Matt saying something about a nail gun, but then maybe he'd got it wrong.

'Did he fall on a punnet of strawberries then?'

'Just stay away from the edge and do what you're bloody told. Understand?'

'Yes, Mr Walsh.'

Nick felt humiliated. He hadn't meant to irritate the foreman, though quite what he'd said to make him react so strongly was a mystery. So how had John junior died? Nail gun or strawberries? Mr Walsh hadn't said, but either way it was in the past and the foreman had made it clear he wanted to leave it there. Nick's irrepressible happiness resurfaced and he grinned. It had been worth a ticking off just to be up on the top staging near the roof. Yes, it had definitely been worth it all: dropping out of the Environmental Science course at Exeter; coming home to Barking Tye; spending the rest of the year trying to decide what to do; and then finally enrolling on the carpentry course at Utterly Academy. He thought back to the arguments with his mother.

'Don't get me wrong, we're pleased to have you back home but you're a clever boy, Nick. You could've got a good degree in Exeter, then a good job. If you throw it away now all your efforts will have been wasted. You'll have nothing. Just depts. Remember, there's a student loan to pay back.'

'It's no good, I've had enough. My mind's made up, Mum,' he'd replied.

'But why?' she'd asked, pulling and twisting at her fingers.

He'd found it hard to explain. He'd always wanted to work with wood, not as a designer, but with his hands. It gave him an inner calm and pleasure that words couldn't describe adequately. And so he'd simply given up trying to explain it to his bewildered parents. When he'd found his first year at Utterly Academy more difficult than expected, he'd kept it to himself. *I told you so* can be said in many different ways, and his mother would have found a thousand. He'd never had trouble making friends before, but for some reason he didn't quite fit in at Utterly. Most of the students on the course were suspicious of his easy charm and quick brain, apart from Matt who hadn't noticed and Chrissie who was probably brighter than him. But now that he was out in the field, or to be more precise, up some scaffolding and an apprentice with the best carpentry firm in the county, he knew it had been worth it all.

So for the rest of the day, while two other carpenters worked with the foreman up on the top staging with the roof timbers, Nick carried and stacked tiles. He was too busy to give nail guns and bodies, living or dead, another thought. Any spare attention was spent in trying to impress Alfred Walsh.

'When you've cleared up here, Nick, you can knock off. We won't see you on Monday, will we? You're on that Academy release day. Every Monday isn't it? God, you youngsters have it easy.'

'It's not a day off, Mr Walsh - Mr Blumfield works us pretty hard.'

'Hah!' The foreman shook his head and smiled, 'You youngsters.' A thought seemed to strike him as his smile faded. 'I read about the explosion. A couple of weeks back, weren't it?'

'It was only the kitchen oven. No one was seriously injured. No bodies.'

The foreman didn't smile. 'You seem to live dangerous. Just watch out, Nick. Just watch out,' he said as he turned away.

Nick shrugged. What was old Alfred Walsh talking about? But it was Friday and Nick's mind was on other things. He'd arranged to meet up with Chrissie and Matt at eight that evening in the Nags Head, Matt's local pub. Since Matt had fractured his wrist, it was easier for him to walk to his local than organise any transport, and anyway - it had a great local brew, the Land Girl.

•••

Nick arrived early. Chile was playing Spain in the World Cup late that afternoon and someone had told him the match would be showing on the pub's massive flat TV screen. He didn't usually follow the football, but as it was the main topic of conversation at Willows, he decided to catch the end of the match. That way he'd be able to say he'd watched it without lying, maybe even remember some of the players' names.

The noise hit him like a wall as he walked into the small crowded bar. Everyone's attention was on the flat screen, the excitement and buzz almost palpable now that the match was in its second half. He looked around at the tired and faded décor - red quarry tiles on the floor near the old fireplace and the rest bare floorboards, stained and worn. Old scrubbed pine tables and an assortment of chairs completed the furnishings. It smelt of stale beer. Nick caught the barman's attention and ordered a pint of the Land Girl. He gulped down the first mouthful as a cheer went up and someone jolted him from behind. He needed space if he was to fully appreciate the hoppy brew, and he slowly inched to the back of the crush and watched from the corner. Could life get any sweeter? And then his mobile beeped at him.

He thrust his hand into his pocket and pulled out his phone. He frowned as he read the text message. *Hi. What u up 2? Mel.* He slipped the phone back into his pocket. There was no way to hold his glass, watch the match and use his free hand to text back a reply. Something would have to give and for a change it could be Melanie.

He closed his eyes for a moment. The message was in his pocket, but his irritation was still out there in the bar with him. Not even a pretence of affection, he thought. She's just checking up on me.

It had been a rollercoaster of a relationship. He'd fallen for her in Freshers' Week in Exeter, almost a lifetime ago. They'd been an item for the first six weeks, but then he'd become disillusioned with the course and soon after that he dropped out. Mel had been very demanding at first, not wanting him to go, then later blowing hot, then cold. The distance eventually proved a bit of a damper when he found it difficult to make the frequent trips back to Exeter. Now he rarely visited. He never knew where he was with her. One moment her pale green eyes sparkled with warmth as her pale lips promised love; the next she seemed distant with cold anaemic skin and a sharp elfin haircut. Well, for the moment she could wait. Chile was playing Spain.

As he upended his glass almost an hour later, he drained the last few drops and glanced above his head. Oak beams straddled the ceiling, like ribs on a giant ribcage. He peered up at the ancient wood and for a moment scrutinised it for evidence of death-watch beetle damage. The sound of people chatting and drinking ebbed and flowed in the background.

'Sorry I'm late.'

Startled, Nick looked across the bar to see a rather flustered Chrissie.

'The headlights on that bloody MG are useless. Probably two candle-watt power, set low, one on each front wing and blowing in the wind! At one point I thought I wouldn't find the pub. Where's Matt?' Still catching her breath, she glanced around the bar.

'But it's not dark yet. You didn't need your headlight, sorry, headlights. If you will drive that old heap of rust it's surprising you got here at all.' Nick couldn't understand why she was so attached to the old 1973 roadster and braced himself for an acid reply.

'Why were you looking up at the ceiling when I came in? I thought you'd be watching the match.'

He laughed. He obviously hadn't been rude enough about the old rust bucket. 'Just thinking about today and yes, I have been watching the match but it's over now.'

'So, how did it go, and what's with the ceiling?'

'Chile – one; Spain – two. It's just the post-match discussion. A bit tedious.'

'No, I meant how did your day go?'

He took his time before continuing, 'Today was just… well just great actually.' He looked at Chrissie. How much to say? Her apprenticeship over with Ron Clegg had been a bit of a surprise to everyone and he still hadn't worked out if she was genuinely happy about it or just putting on a brave face. Best not to say too much about his day, it might be rubbing it in a bit.

'Come on, tell me more.'

'OK. Well, there's lots of clearing up, dogsbody stuff. But just to get up there – well I had to climb up on scaffolding and some joists.'

Chrissie shuddered.

'Sorry. You don't like heights.' He grinned as he remembered her fear of ladders. Just at that moment he spotted Matt, trying to look cool as he negotiated the swing door into the pub.

'Hi. What kept you?'

'No watch. Remember I told you… me Rolex. The fuzz took it, the wankers.' He drew out his a, and rolled the i to the back of his mouth, as the Suffolk in him surfaced.

'The fake Rolex Tom brought back from Thailand last summer?' Nick remembered Matt being very proud of the watch, though why he couldn't use the time feature on his mobile now the Rolex was gone, he couldn't imagine.

'Yeah… 'cept I told 'em it were false. Should've said fake an' that's probably what set 'em on it.'

'Shite Matt, it'll be in a thousand pieces by now. They'll be looking for a micro-transmitter or something.' Nick laughed as he spoke. Matt couldn't even load a screw onto a magnetic screwdriver without dropping it. Surely the police hadn't thought he could do anything as fiddly as rig a watch micro-transmitter detonator.

'Still, I suppose it could have been worse. They could have thought the nipple stud was a detonator.' Chrissie's clear voice cut through the air as background chatter drifted around the bar.

Matt raised his plaster cast to protect his chest. The barman looked across briefly and then back at the flat screen. No one else in the bar paid Matt any interest, except for a man in jeans and green sweatshirt who seemed to watch them as he quietly sipped his beer. He glanced away when Nick looked at him, turning his attention back to the screen. Nick gave him a cursory glance - probably early thirties, and thought no more about him. It was time for another drink.

'Mine's a pint of the Land Girl, and Chrissie? Your usual ginger beer? Oh, and while you're up at the bar, Matt - better get some cheese and onion crisps.' He cleared his throat, eyes watering. Matt's reaction protecting the supposed nipple ring had been priceless.

'Tom, it were Tom. 'E was the one come back from Bangkok with the stud.'

'Well let's hope that's all he came back with - apart from the Rolex, of course.'

'What you sayin', Chrissie?'

'Oh sit down Matt. And Chrissie, leave him alone. Remember he's injured.' Nick stood up. 'I'll get the drinks in. Usual, everyone?'

A few minutes later the three friends were happily settled with their drinks in the dimly lit snug bar. Nick thought Chrissie looked a bit sad and distracted, and Matt freely admitted that the Planning & Communication module was doing his head in. So while the other two slowly unwound, he happily recounted some of the foreman's tales from his day out on site with Willows & Son.

'Well it was the wind. Clean lifted the tiles and one flew through the glass conservatory roof – nearly had the owner! He reckoned it was safer up on the roof than down on the ground.' Nick could tell Chrissie wasn't listening. Her smile was mechanical and she hadn't noticed when he'd stopped speaking. But Matt leaned forward, hungry for more.

'Yeah, but did 'e mention John junior?'

'Well yes, but why're you so interested?' Nick knew what Matt was like when he got fixed on something. Dog and bone hardly did it justice.

'Come on, what did 'e say?'

'OK, OK. He was the one who found the body. He still seemed upset; didn't really want to talk about it. Didn't really say anything other than there was lots of blood. Oh yes, he said something about strawberries. There was a punnet of strawberries in the workshop and that was unusual because John junior didn't like them. In fact he was allergic to them. Then he went a bit strange – the foreman, I mean.' Nick frowned as he remembered the foreman's reaction. 'I don't think he's got over it yet.'

'Strawberries? But what's the relevance of that? I mean, did he think someone had been there with John junior before he was found? It's a bit – well tenuous isn't it? Anyway, why's it so important to you Matt?' Chrissie put her ginger beer on the table and studied his face.

'Well, we're kind of related – 'is mother was one of me father's cousins.'

Shite, Nick thought. 'You've never said before. So what does that make you then?'

'Not sure. A second cousin, maybe?' Matt scrutinised his glass. 'We never met. Me dad didn't have much to do with anyone. I mean 'e left us when I was five an' I don't think 'e had much to do with 'is own family either.'

'That's really sad.'

'So is that why you wanted the Willows apprenticeship?' Now Nick understood.

'S'pose so. I'd hoped they'd know I'm family an' just want me as the next apprentice.'

'But did anyone know you were related?'

'No.'

'Oh Matt.' Nick patted his shoulder.

'I aint pulliking.'

'Pullicking?'

'Complainin'.'

'I might have guessed. Suffolk speak.' Chrissie looked heavenwards.

Matt smiled. 'But the explosion - it dosselled me.'

'Dosselled? No don't tell me. I don't need to know.'

Matt struggled to reach the last crisps in the packet. Nick had noticed how Matt always seemed to do that – fill his mouth with food just as he was about to say something important. Unfortunately his fingers were hampered by his plaster cast. There was no way he could reach those last crisps. Matt thrust his left hand deep into the packet. It took flight, upending and discharging the greasy fragments onto Chrissie. The man in the green sweatshirt quickly looked away as Nick caught his eye. He'd been watching Matt again. Strange, Nick thought.

'Shit!'

'For goodness sake, Matt.' Chrissie brushed at her lap.

'Sorry. Didn't even know I'd any cousins till a year ago. Mum spotted 'is name in the paper. That's when 'e was found dead. An' then in the canteen, just as I'm telling you, there's this explosion. Well can't you see it has to mean somethin'?'

'So if you talk about it now, a barrel of Land Girl will explode?'

'Chrissie, don't talk a load ol' squit.'

Nick caught Chrissie's eye and shot her a warning look.

'How did you get on with your police interview?' Chrissie's tone had softened.

'I just told 'em what I remembered, an' that was that. They're sayin' some joker, or maybe a terrorist slipped a… a cartridge, you know - of camping gas into the canteen ovens, maybe over the weekend when it's quiet.'

'That's sick.' Nick screwed up his face and looked into his almost empty glass. He thought back to the smoke-stained paintwork outside the canteen. 'But who hates the place enough to burn it down?'

'Don't terrorists announce when they've done something? It was two weeks ago and nothing's been said. I mean why do it if you can't advertise your cause? As you say, Nick, it's more likely to be arson. And with arson, well it wouldn't have been anyone who was in the canteen at lunchtime. I mean you'd make damn sure you were well out of the way when the bomb, sorry cartridge, went off, wouldn't you?'

That's what Nick liked about Chrissie. She was always logical. Cool and logical. The conversation died for a moment.

'Well that certainly lets you off the hook, Matt.' Chrissie's eyes twinkled.

'Can't get it out of me mind. I think the explosion an' John junior are somehow connected.' Matt leaned forward. 'We can't do nothin' about the explosion. That's police stuff, but....' His voice faded away.

They waited. Nick could tell from Matt's face he wanted to say more. Thank God there were no more crisps left to try and fill his mouth with.

'Before the explosion I felt I'd be connected to me relatives if I got the Willows apprenticeship. But since the explosion I feel as if it were like a message from John junior 'imself.'

Oh no, Nick thought and looked at Chrissie to see how she was taking this.

'I'm absolutely convinced there's somethin' not quite right 'bout killin' yourself with a nail gun.'

'Well I'm not sure about messages from beyond the grave, but I agree; it's not quite right to do it with a nail gun.' Chrissie caught Nick's eye and shrugged.

'But why would anyone want to kill John junior? None of the firm's carpenters have an obvious grudge. I mean there's nothing to stop any of them leaving and starting up on their own if they wanted to. No; it has to be suicide or a freak accident.' Nick had a sense of foreboding. This was Matt in a dog and bone situation again.

'Let it go.' Chrissie's voice sounded sharp.

'Can't. Don't mind anymore 'bout not getting the apprenticeship. Fact is, I'm pleased you got it, Nick. But I... I feel a connection with John junior. Don't you see? I owe it to find out more.'

'Oh dear,' Chrissie sighed.

'OK, if it helps at all,' Nick paused, kicking himself for what he was about to offer, 'I'll ask a few questions next week at Willows.'

'Oh would you? Thanks mate.'

'That man over there, green sweatshirt – he's just leaving but he's been watching you all evening, Matt.' Nick felt it was time he mentioned him.

'What man? No, I didn't see 'im.'

'Yes, in jeans; about thirtyish. I noticed him too - short sandy hair, broken nose, perfect teeth. You don't think he was tailing Matt, do you? If they're suspecting terrorism… I mean after the business with the watch?' Chrissie frowned.

'What? A snouty cop?'

'Do you know, I sometimes think if we combined the three of us we might come up with one normal sized person with a vaguely normal personality that everyone could understand.'

'I doubt it,' Nick said under his breath, and for once he'd had the final word. Well almost. There was a sudden beep from deep in his pocket. He still hadn't replied to Mel's text.

CHAPTER 4

Matt settled into his chair and smiled at the blank computer screen. He'd been looking forward to this moment, the switch on moment. It was already well after nine and no self-respecting student would be seen dead or alive in the library at this hour, especially on a Monday morning. In terms of style, this hit the depths of uncool. The library, Utterly Academy's finest room, was deserted and Matt guessed that he would be alone, apart from the library assistant, of course. Matt flexed his fingers, limbering up for the keyboard. A little over 48 hours ago he hadn't known what to think. His mind, a jumble of half-baked thoughts and emotions, had been directionless. But the evening spent in the Nags Head with Nick and Chrissie had crystallised things for him – that, and the third pint of Land Girl. He was a man with a mission, but where to begin?

Chrissie had suggested finding out what John junior had been working on around the time of his death. As Matt saw it, only Nick might be able to find that out. But Chrissie had said no, the Academy kept a record of all the apprentices' work projects, a kind of catalogue for any interested student to look through.

'But John junior wasn't an apprentice,' Matt had reasoned.

'OK, but the Utterly student who was the apprentice at the time wouldn't have worked in isolation. Other carpenters from Willows would've been involved, perhaps John junior.' Matt wasn't convinced, but he'd been unable to come up with anything better.

He switched on the computer and within seconds was on the Academy website and then the carpentry page. *Apprenticeships* – he was sailing now. Bottom of the list with the W's and then 2009 and... nothing. Well no, there was something. *Accommodation huts for fruit pickers*. But where and when? Hmm, Matt closed his eyes to concentrate. Fruit pickers? Maybe from Eastern Europe? Nick could make some enquiries.

'The local press! Why aint I thought of them before?'

Matt glanced around the library. The morning sun streamed in through windows placed at regular intervals along the south-facing wall. Bookcases, magazine racks and computer desks jostled for space, but the room seemed deserted. What was it about librarians? Why could you never find one when you needed one? He'd noticed her when he'd arrived, the young assistant with long auburn hair, legs that stretched up to her armpits and a short skirt. A library pass hung around her neck and she had a smile to die for. But where...? And then he spotted her near the entrance door to the library, leaning suggestively across a desk. He smiled, and catching her eye, mouthed the word HELP. He knew he was pushing his luck by not getting up to go over and speak, but hey, he was a man on a mission; on the edge.

'Are you OK? Is something wrong?' The library assistant was all concern as she hurried soundlessly across from the entrance door. 'Are you in pain? Your face....'

'I was smilin'.'

'Ah well that's OK then. I thought, well I thought....' She looked down at Matt's plaster cast. Then flushing, quickly continued, 'Was there something?'

'Well yeah. I'm workin' on me Planning & Communication module. I really need to get on the local newspaper websites. You know, for me module.'

She was pretty, even up close and Matt observed her intently as she took a small notebook from her pocket and leant across to use his keyboard. He pushed his chair back to make space for her, but instead of looking at the screen she stared down at his foot.

'What's that on your ankle?'

'Wha'd'you mean?' He followed her gaze. And there it was; a not-so-white plastic ankle band with writing and a number. It bridged the gap between the top of his rumpled sock and his jeans. Oh no, he thought, my identification tag from the hospital admission. Over the weeks he'd come to think of it as his lucky talisman and now she'd spotted it. She probably thought he'd escaped from somewhere. With any luck, she might just believe he'd bought a charity bracelet.

'Oh that. Didn't know where to put it an' didn't want to look boastful. So, what you sponsorin' then?' It was a long shot.

'I… I ran the marathon.' She blushed again and turned her attention back to the screen as Matt shifted, trying to ease his denim jeans down to cover his ankle.

'Eastern Anglia Daily Tribune and the Eastern Daily Press OK for you?' She kept her eyes fixed on the screen.

'Thanks.' Matt watched her. It was a gift. He had no problems memorising sequences of numbers and letters, and now unbeknown to her he had the Academy ID access codes. She smiled and was gone. Rosie, the name on her library pass, had left the Eastern Anglia Daily Tribune site up on his screen. He found the search box and typed in June

21st 2009. Let's see what happened a year ago, he thought as he smiled to himself. He felt it had gone rather well with Rosie. Yes, she might even be watching him. But before he had time to look, the page had loaded. For the next hour or so, he scrolled and clicked, all thoughts of Rosie forgotten as he worked through 2009.

'Now that's more like it,' he sighed. The headline was hidden on an inner page, June 5th 2009.

Local Man Falls Foul to Nail Horror.

Matt read on. *The body of a young man was found early yesterday morning at the premises of Willows & Son, a well-known carpentry firm based in Needham Market. Staff discovered the body when they arrived for work. Ambulance and police were called to the site and a spokesman for the firm said workers had initially tried to give first aid resuscitation. He was taken by ambulance to Ipswich hospital where he was pronounced dead on arrival.*

The police searched the scene and took a nail gun and air compressor for further examination. They were unable to make any comments at this early stage. It is understood that the name of the dead man will be released later today.

Matt pursed his lips and shook his head as he read on. The reporter had followed with a short article about nail guns, no doubt to fill column space. A brief introduction and then straight in with safety issues; gory details about finger injuries; a nail shot into the heart; and difficult to imagine, a nail shot into the skull. Wow, grisly stuff.

'That's a bit… well….' Matt frowned. Most nail guns needed to be light and portable for use on building sites. Battery or small gas cylinders could fire short nails of up to one and a quarter inch length maximum, and there were smaller spring loaded versions. But why the air compressor? That suggested an industrial strength nail gun for long-er nails, not practical to use on site and more suited to the workshop. Matt scrolled on: June 6th 2009.

Dead Man Named.

The dead man discovered on Wednesday morning, 4th June at the premises of local carpentry firm, Willows & Son, has been named as John Willows (junior). He was aged 26, the only son of John Willows, and had worked for the family firm for several years. Cause of death is not yet known but may be the result of a tragic accident. It is un-derstood there will be a coroner's inquest.

Matt typed *Coroner Inquest* in the newspaper's search box and waited. After a little more click-and-scroll he found what he was looking for.

'Yeah,' he hissed, punching the air. Then remember-ing where he was, he looked around self-consciously. Per-haps she'd pretended not to notice?

September 24th 2009.

Local Man in Nail Death Inquest. Coroner Records Open Verdict.

'Open? What's that s'posed to mean?'

Matt read on. *The inquest into the death of John Wil-lows, known as John Willows junior was opened on Mon-day September 21st. The Coroner, Mr Judd, explained that a jury was required to comply with the Health and Safety at Work act of 1974.*

God, this was heavy stuff, Matt thought and scrolled on. He was impatient to know more, his heart racing as he read the pathologist's findings. *A four inch nail penetrated a main artery and windpipe.* The words seemed to jump off the screen. He hurried on, skimming and flying over whole sentences. The poor bugger had tried to pull it out.

Matt couldn't imagine drowning in a torrent of blood, but the pathologist definitely said that *as the nail was withdrawn, it unplugged the holes it had made and blood gushed into the windpipe*. Matt took a moment to picture it. 'Sh-i-t.' It was little comfort that *death would have been rapid*. The pathologist was probably trying to be kind. He'd never heard blood loss described as *catastrophic* before.

The report was surprisingly detailed. Even the family doctor gave evidence, saying there was no history of depression and no on-going medications, and as if to back this up, John Willows senior said his son had been looking forward to buying a new car.

'Any suicide note?' Matt whispered, and then the words *no suicide note* leapt off the screen. So, are they saying he was in his right mind when he fired the nail into his own neck? Matt shook his head. The rest was pretty boring; a whole paragraph about safety issues and the jury's visit to the accident site. Matt lingered over the nail gun manufacturer's words. *If fired into a material with little or no resistance, such as flesh, then the nail would be driven more deeply. It was therefore possible that a 4 inch nail could penetrate further than if fired into wood.*

He imagined the scene from the film The Day of the Jackal, when a bullet is fired into a watermelon. The graphic image of the exploding pink water-laden flesh burst into his mind and his stomach heaved.

Matt sat back in his chair. This was heady stuff. Poor John junior. And the pathologist? God, what a job. Well, that explained why an apprentice hadn't been assigned to the firm last year. The inquest hadn't been held by the time he'd been due to start. Matt sighed. He couldn't imagine his own mum being upset if he'd died. She'd hardly mentioned his broken wrist, apart from reminding him that he was a "grut lummox".

Wow, but reading all that stuff was so much better than working on the Planning & Communication module. He couldn't remember looking for information with such all-consuming commitment before. Matt smiled as he visualised the list of ingredients on the back of a crisp packet. He used to think that was absorbing but it didn't touch this computer search. If school had been half as interesting he might even have stuck out his A-levels. Instead he'd got bored and somehow lost his way, given up in the first year.

Meanwhile the sun streamed in through the large library windows with the intensity of a spotlight. Matt basked in its warmth, the sun adding to his feeling of general wellbeing. He stretched and imagined himself as a stealthy panther, a panther stalking his prey, a panther full of low cunning, a panther - with a plaster paw, he remembered as he caught sight of the plaster encasing his wrist. The chase, if a computer search could be described in big cat terms, had been totally riveting.

'He was goin' to buy a car,' Matt said out loud, deep in thought.

'Who was going to buy a car?' Chrissie whispered just behind him. He hadn't noticed her slip into the library a few moments earlier. No doubt she'd spotted him sitting in front of a computer screen with legs out straight and the temptation to tiptoe up behind him must have proved irresistible.

'Whooa!' He abandoned any attempt at a library whisper as he jumped. 'What you doin' creepin' up on me like that?'

Of course - it was Monday, the apprentice release day. He'd been so absorbed in his own thoughts that he'd been oblivious to everything else. He'd even forgotten Rosie, the auburn-haired library assistant, for a moment.

'Shush, keep your voice down. You looked pretty relaxed. I thought you were asleep, you know like Wilkinson the armchair cat. What's that you said about a car?'

Matt paused before letting a word escape, almost inaudible, floating on the warm library air. 'Panther....' He was still in the space midway between daydream and reality.

Chrissie frowned. 'Well now you're fully awake, who's going to buy... did you say a Panther? Weren't they retro-styled cars from the seventies? Sure you didn't mean Jaguar?'

The soothing tones of her soft voice failed to work their magic. Matt bristled. Only a moment before she'd likened him to a fat tabby cat. Wilkinson, for Christ's sake!

'I've been lookin' stuff up. John junior's dad said at the inquest 'e was lookin' to buy a car. Didn't say what kind.' Matt emphasised the last words.

'So why say Jaguar?'

'Didn't. I said panther.'

Chrissie frowned. 'I don't really see....' She glanced quickly in the direction of the library assistant. 'Shush, we're going to get chucked out of here.'

'Rosie won't chuck me out.'

'Rosie?'

Matt paused briefly before continuing, 'At the inquest the coroner asked if John junior was suicidal, an' his dad said 'e was about to buy a car. So 'e couldn't have been. D'you see?' He stabbed his plaster cast at the screen which still displayed the inquest report.

'Not really. Let me….' Chrissie pushed his plaster cast out of her line of vision and leant forward to look at the screen.

'No, no. It'll be easier if I print it out an' then Nick can read it too.' Matt could hardly contain his frustration, all attempts at whispering now abandoned. He clicked on *print*. How could she take this so calmly? The coroner had recorded an open verdict. It had a whiff of the not-quite-right. In fact it stank. It was his cousin, well second cousin, for God's sake! He watched impatiently as Chrissie went to pick up the paper from the printer and started to read.

'Well?'

'I thought you said it was a six inch nail,' she whispered.

'Four inch, six inch, whatever - it was a bloody long nail. Anyway, you're missin' the point. We use nail an' staple guns all the time. How can you fire one into your own neck, for God's sake?'

'Good question,' Chrissie replied frowning.

'There's more to it I reckon, an' I've got a nose for these kinds of things.' As if to emphasise his nasal expertise, Matt moved to tap the side of his stubby nose. It was short and slightly upturned, small and unimposing in the centre of his rather flushed face. As he swung his plastered right wrist upwards, he realised its extra weight and quickly changed his mind. It made more sense to use a clumsy left forefinger instead. Unfortunately both arms were now moving and it was too late to abort. Forefinger and plaster collided just short of his nose. Crack!

Chrissie bit back a laugh. 'Oops, I think you've been in this library too long, Matt.'

'Hey, don't laugh. Serious now, I've drawn a blank on the carpentry jobs last summer. Do you reckon Nick'll help on that one?'

'Yes, why not?'

'So what you up here for, Chrissie?'

'To look up something on totem poles but after what you've just said….' She fell silent and gazed down at the report in her hands. 'Come on, it's a wonderful sunny afternoon. I'm going home. Want a lift?' Chrissie glanced at her watch and then at the sun streaming in through the windows.

'Reckon so. I've spent most of the day in here,' Matt said, logging off the computer. He gathered up his papers with surprising efficiency and glanced round for Rosie. He managed what he hoped was a suitably winning smile as he passed the auburn-haired beauty near the Returned Book station. He quickened his pace as he followed Chrissie out of the library.

Chrissie strode on, her footsteps silent in the soft pumps she habitually wore. It reminded him of his earliest days at Utterly when he'd walked into the carpentry workroom for the first time. He'd stood nervous and unsure of himself as the other students moved around the workbenches, massing like blind worker-termites. At first they hardly noticed Mr Blumfield wearing his heavy linen work-apron and holding a register, until he called, 'Order!' And like a game of musical chairs, Chrissie and he were the only two students left standing without a place at a workbench.

She had been wearing pumps and Blumfield's eyes flashed and his expression froze when he'd caught sight of them. 'Please wear sensible shoes, preferably with steel toecaps in future,' he'd hissed. And Matt remembered her face flushing. But she wasn't the one forever dropping things; that was Matt's trick.

He shrugged away his memories and hurried to keep up as they reached the top of the main staircase. Fine beads of sweat broke out on his face and he hesitated. The image of dust and smoke, so real only two weeks earlier, seemed to billow around him. Chrissie was already striding down the steps so there was nothing for it but to follow.

'Come on, keep up. Goodness, you're sweating and we've hardly walked fifty yards. You need to take more exercise,' Chrissie said, throwing the words over her shoulder at him with the accuracy of a darts champion.

If Blumfield hadn't placed them next to each other on the far side of the workroom that first day, would they have become such firm friends, Matt wondered.

They slipped out through a side entrance on the ground floor and skirted round the Academy buildings, all the while Matt's pulse racing like a hamster on a wheel. Chrissie finally slowed down as she reached the student and visitor car parks, a hundred yards off to one side from the main entrance and neatly edged with small shrubs.

'Remember where you parked the car this time?' Matt puffed as he caught up. This was a common routine; as often as not she had to pause to remember where she'd parked her beloved red MGB. He stood beside her, catching his breath. The cars, mainly an assorted mix of silvers, greys and metallic colours were squeezed into the parking area. Most were only a few years old with huge bloated bumpers merging into their curving bodywork. The 1973 MGB was lower and smaller than a modern car and easily hidden amongst its bulky, but more roadworthy neighbours. Matt was only slightly taller than Chrissie, but the few extra inches gave him the advantage.

'There!' he shouted as he spotted her car. The soft top hood was down and the black leather seats were hot to touch when they reached the car. Chrissie hadn't bothered to lock it. Anyone interested in stealing it could simply have stepped over the doors and into the car – well not Matt, of course. He found it almost impossible to lower himself down into the narrow passenger seat, even with the door open. He was just too broad to fit comfortably into the space designed for a smaller young man of an earlier generation. Sweating as his slightly too tight tee-shirt rode up his back, he gasped as bare skin stuck to hot leather, 'Shite.'

There were no air bags or safety features apart from the seat belts, and the buckle was blisteringly hot against his side as he clicked it into place. 'Don't ever get a silver car. You'll never find it.'

And then he remembered. He'd been standing at the Academy bus stop close to the student car park on the previous Monday waiting for a bus home. His attention had been drawn to what he'd assumed was a student with a goatee beard and wearing a sweatshirt and jeans, which wasn't particularly remarkable. But his behaviour was decidedly strange. He'd walked around the car park looking intently at the cars. Then he'd stopped, taken a notebook out of his pocket and started writing. Matt assumed the goatee was writing a message for the car owner, but instead of tucking the paper under a windscreen wiper, he circled the car as if it was prey. The weirdest thing though, was that the car attracting all this attention had been Chrissie's red MGB. Matt had intended to mention it to Chrissie but somehow it had gone clean out his mind until now. He didn't seem to fit the description of the man in the Nags Head, but then he hadn't noticed his teeth.

'Chrissie....'

'Strawberries – there was nothing in the inquest report about strawberries.'

'No.'

'Hmm....' Chrissie turned the ignition, revved on the throttle and accelerated out of the car park. The noise from the engine and turbulent air was deafening, all attempts at further conversation hopeless. Each bump in the road jarred up through the worn suspension which then rocked and swayed as wind whipped through Matt's hair. Every rural smell and exhaust fume assaulted his short, sleuthing nasal passages. He looked at the wood veneer dashboard with chrome surround to each instrument gauge. The speedometer needle pointed to 40mph. It felt like seventy as Chrissie steered the car away from Stowmarket.

The rolling Suffolk countryside was bathed in afternoon sunshine and it didn't take long before all thoughts of the goatee stranger were buffeted away by the wind. When a field of free-range pigs with their corrugated metal shelters shot by, Matt found himself wondering if pigs could get sunburn. He was distracted further as he imagined applying sunscreen factor thirty to a pig.

Five minutes later and they were entering Stowmarket from the north, passing the Nags Head. Matt was almost home. Chrissie turned into what was locally known as the Flower Estate. Each small road and cul-de-sac had been named after a different flower. The small estate had been built in the 1970s for rural council housing and was surprisingly pleasant. Most of the houses had gardens with vegetable plots and looked out, either front or back, onto fields.

Matt's home, where he lived with his mother and older brother Tom, was a semidetached bungalow on Tumble Weed Drive. Someone must have thought tumble weed was a flower.

'Sorry I took the long route round rather than drive through Stowmarket. I needed to clear my thoughts. It struck me, the date of John junior's death and the canteen explosion – one's the anniversary of the other. See you at the Nags Head, Friday night,' Chrissie said as she watched him climb out of her car.

'Yeah, you're right.' Matt hadn't thought about the date of the explosion before. June 4th 2010.

He felt stupid as he tried to get out of the car, struggling and floundering like a seal out of water. Gravity had aided his short rounded body when he got in, but trying to exit, well that required strength and technique. He tried to heave himself up from the low seat without the aid of his splinted right wrist. As he stepped out, the car door swung closed, catching at his shins. He had never felt less like a sleuthing panther. For a moment he imagined his legs as those of a different noble beast, maybe a bison – yes a bison, dangerous and snorting, but with disproportionately thin bony shins. Now you wouldn't want to shut a car door on that. He knew Chrissie would only liken him to the Bison Chevrolet, a heavy-duty truck from the 80s, if he said anything so he kept the image to himself.

'Hmm, one's the anniversary of t'other!' he echoed, 'Shite.'

CHAPTER 5

Chrissie's memories of the canteen explosion were now effectively banished to the distant recall area of her mind. She no longer suffered flashback images or sudden panic when a car misfired; in fact she didn't think about it at all unless prompted by a specific question or a direct reference. 'Was it really only three weeks ago?' she would have re-marked.

Even she was surprised by the speed she'd settled into her apprenticeship, although her first day had been less than auspicious. True to form, her sense of direction had let her down and she got completely lost trying to find the turning to the workshops close to the Wattisham Airbase perimeter. Eventually, late, flustered, and with her short blonde hair whipped into a frenzy, she rocketed up the potholed track that led to Ron Clegg's furniture and restoration business. Chrissie could still recall the pleasure she felt as she got out of her red MGB roadster and gazed at the workshop com-plex for the first time; relief that she had found it and amazement at its ramshackle timelessness. It consisted of an old wooden barn and a series of brick outbuildings sur-rounding a roughly concreted yard. Ron explained, in one of his talkative moments sometime in her first week, that the buildings had originally belonged to a farm before being sold to him as workshops for his business. The assortment of outbuildings had been variously converted for his use.

She had been curious to meet Ron Clegg, and also a little apprehensive, but was quickly reassured by his greet-ing. He held himself rather stiffly and when he extended a warm, gnarled hand in welcome, she shook it firmly, determined to appear confident and business-like. He seemed amused by her appearance and her car but made no comment, a faint smile never leaving his eyes as he watched her organise her toolbox on a cluttered workbench near the main barn workshop door – one of her first jobs.

'So, Mrs Jax, tell me about yourself,' he finally said towards the end of her second week. He waited quietly for her reply, his manner correct and polite. If she'd had to describe him she supposed she would have said he was old-fashioned, always addressing her as Mrs Jax - quaint really. And he moved slowly. It gave an impression of calmness which probably had more to do with his arthritis than his nature.

'Well....' She didn't know what to say, where to begin. She'd been grateful that he hadn't seemed too interested – happy to talk about himself and of course, carpentry and cabinet making. She guessed by his greying hair and the lines on his face, that he must be close on sixty. But he didn't mention any family so she assumed he was alone. He certainly spent most of his time at his workshops. She suspected he lived only for his work. But what to say about herself? Now that was a question.

'Well, Mr Clegg,' she eventually answered, 'I've been assigned the ten-years-late millennium apprentice project for the Academy's carpentry department. It centres round a totem pole. Actually, I was hoping Mr Blumfield had already spoken to you about it.' Chrissie paused as she stared at the floor. 'And I really have no idea where to start with the project,' she finished in a rush.

Ron Clegg didn't answer for a moment and Chrissie began to wonder if he'd heard her. Finally he spoke.

'I asked you about yourself, Mrs Jax. The totem pole can wait; after all, it's already waited ten years. I can't help but notice you're not typical apprentice material. No. No, let me finish,' he continued as Chrissie tried to object. 'Tell me, what makes you at this stage in your life want to become a cabinet maker?'

Chrissie felt her face flush. *At this stage in my life*, Chrissie parroted to herself. Since when had forty-two become a life stage? She was about to launch into an angry tirade but the words *cabinet maker* slowly penetrated beyond her auditory cortex and spread deeper into her brain. She was being classified as a potential cabinet maker rather than as a failed jobbing carpenter. Now that was something special. As always, she seemed to find herself distracted from the main question, her thoughts going off on a tangent. 'You really think I can become a cabinet maker?' she asked by way of an answer.

'Yes of course, if you're motivated and willing to learn.'

Thank God he hadn't added any riders, she thought, like the pigs are fuelled and ready for take-off.

'Well,' Chrissie said as a surge of optimism swept through her, 'where to begin?'

'The beginning is usually a good place, Mrs Jax.'

She took a deep breath. 'After leaving school I trained to be an accountant.' She paused as she noticed the surprise on his face.

'An accountant?'

'Yes, you see I'm good with numbers. And initially I was happy working for a small firm in Ipswich. In fact I met my husband through my work.'

Ron nodded slowly. 'So why now? Why cabinet making now, Mrs Jax?'

Chrissie ignored his question. Her thoughts were running on, and she knew if she didn't articulate them, she might lose the thread and not make any sense of the turmoil in her head. She found it difficult to think of herself as a separate entity to Bill, and in order to explain her current situation, she had to explain Bill. His death had turned her into the person she now was.

'Bill was one of the clients. He ran a small business recycling rubber from old car and tractor tyres.' Chrissie paused as Ron nodded again. 'He was good at his job. He was doing something useful, putting something back, rubber in fact.' Chrissie fell silent as she thought back to those office years; the growing disillusionment with her own work, the tedium of other people's accounts. 'I wanted to do something useful too. I wanted to do something with my hands.'

'I shouldn't think there's much demand for a craftsman's skill in accountancy, Mrs Jax.'

'Not unless you want to count beads on a lexicon. Accountancy doesn't give any outlet for manual dexterity. Lateral thinking and inventiveness, the so called creative accounting, yes; but I wanted to be able to do something honest and tangible. To be able to look at something and say I made that. And then fate stepped in. One of the rubber recycling plants moved to Czechoslovakia. Bill had to travel there regularly. It seemed sensible to take advantage of the cheaper labour costs and there was less red tape around the environmental controls, not to mention masses of old car and tractor tyres left over from the communist days.

There was plenty of rubber to recycle.' Chrissie paused as she chose her next words.

'Unfortunately he died in an accident.' In her mind she thought of him as falling foul to a rubber related incident. The phrase had a rhythm and softness, almost poetic; much less harsh and final than the sound of the word accident. Besides, if she said rubber related incident, most people blushed and didn't ask more. It was a conversation stopper.

'I'm so sorry.'

Chrissie walked over to her toolbox and rummaged about, crashing the tools around in the bottom of the box – anything to distract herself, to get her emotions back under control.

'What happened, Mrs Jax?'

Chrissie turned to face Ron. 'Bill developed a severe latex allergy.' Chrissie fought back the tears as she sent a metal ruler skidding across the workbench. Crash! It collided with a try square. 'He became sensitive to rubber.' Thump! She dropped a screwdriver back into the box. 'He used to come up in red lumps and a rash if he touched any rubber, or latex as the doctor called it.'

'Like hives?'

She nodded. 'Two years ago when he last visited the Czechoslovakian rubber recycling plant, he inhaled an un-expected release of rubber fumes. Well that was it. He went into anaphylactic shock and died, right there, out in Czech-oslovakia. I was devastated.' Chrissie paused, biting back a sob. 'One moment he was making plans for the future, our future, and the next he was gone... dead... nothing. Just memories.'

'But that's terrible.'

Chrissie turned her attention back to her toolbox. 'It set me thinking. Made me take stock, so to speak. The life insurance payment was very generous but it doesn't bring someone back. I realised I needed to leave something behind when I've gone, Mr Clegg. You know, after I'm dead. And if not children then… a change of career before I'd left it too late.'

'You're not intending on leaving us - to die just yet, are you Mrs Jax?'

Chrissie smiled. 'No, and the totem pole doesn't count as a….' She felt she'd said enough.

'Well,' he gave a little shiver, 'all this talk of after we're gone, it sets you thinking. Sometimes it's better to concentrate on the present. And talking of the here and now - time to be getting on Mrs Jax. That next coat of French polish can't wait any longer.'

Chrissie was pleased to have an excuse to get back to her work and avoid any further talk. It didn't really help. Her ambition to restore furniture was supposed to be the healing medicine but it was proving slow. She hurried out of the barn workshop and across the corner of the courtyard to a small brick outbuilding. It was low ceilinged with rough yellow Suffolk clay bricks on the floor. Pieces of old wood and furniture were stacked and balanced haphazardly against the walls. Shelves were crowded with pots and jars of oils, varnishes and polish. It looked, smelt and felt like a haven from the outside world.

She busied herself with applying the third layer of French polish, shellac dissolved in methylated spirit, to a flat mahogany board she'd left drying on a workbench. Ron had asked her to practise her French polishing skills on cast-off wood before letting her loose on a restored table top. No easy acrylic varnish in Ron Clegg's workshop, she thought, as she poured more French polish onto her special rag. Utterly Academy taught both oil and acrylic based varnishes, but working with shellac and methylated spirit was like a journey back in time. The grain and colour of the wood came to life as she worked on the mahogany, just as a dry colourless sea shell glows pinks and blues when submerged in water. She inhaled happily and deeply. Perhaps the meths fumes were getting to her head.

Chrissie gazed across at the fireplace, disused and dusty, the chimney breast almost as wide as the room. It had a curious old copper tank placed high in the back of the hearth, making up part of the fabric of the wall. Strange, she thought, I must ask Mr Clegg what that is. I don't think I've seen anything quite like it before.

Ron appeared silently in the doorway as if he was a genie summoned by the lamp, or in this case an old copper tank. 'How's the French polish going?' he asked as he walked across the room to inspect her work. 'Don't forget what I told you. If the wad you're applying the polish with starts sticking to the surface, you can use linseed oil to lubricate it, but not too much or it'll leave streaks.'

Chrissie knew the wad of cotton wool wrapped in cloth was called a rubber. Ron would also have known that, so she was grateful he'd avoided using its correct name. It might be a different type of rubber but, rubber was rubber. And rubber was a word she wanted to avoid for the moment – a painful word association. There, she'd thought of the word four times in trying not to think of it at all.

'You can remove the streaks if you wring out the wad with a little methylated spirit and then wipe the surface again,' Ron said helpfully.

Chrissie stood back to look at her handy-work. She could see she had indeed created streaks. Tramlines in fact.

'I don't suppose that counts as a "satin" finish?'

Ron shook his head, smiling. 'Wire wool and then wax polish will give you the "satin look", but you need a high gloss finish first.'

The harmony was suddenly interrupted by a loud rumble from the outside world. At first Chrissie thought a motorbike was roaring up the track, but the noise had a vibration and beat that was unmistakably rhythmic. As the noise grew louder, it became almost palpable, and the walls and ceiling resonated like a giant sounding-box.

'Helicopter,' she said, raising her voice above the juddering sound, and then felt rather stupid. She'd stated the obvious again. She wondered if she would ever get used to the noise of the rotating blades that heralded the monster dragonflies overhead.

'Wattisham Helicopter Base; they're busy today.' Ron had waited for the helicopter to pass before speaking.

'They'll be training for search and rescue, I expect. Hovering and winching.' Ron looked up at the ceiling briefly, as if he might be lifted into the sky by an errant Sea King. 'We're pretty close to the airfield here. You'll get used to it after a while.'

Chrissie nodded, but she had to know, 'What was this building used for before it became a workshop, Mr Clegg?' She looked in the direction of the curious old copper tank in the fireplace.

Ron followed her gaze. 'You mean that old copper tank? That was part of a still used for distilling. The condenser part is missing but that copper tank was like a copper kettle, heated by the fire in the grate underneath.'

'Ah.'

Ron thought for a moment. 'I don't know exactly what they used to distil here. Maybe it was to extract essential oils such as lavender or clove.'

'And alcohol?'

'Doubt it. Mainly beer drinkers in this part of the world and you don't need a distillery to brew beer. No, I think lavender or clove oil is more likely.'

Images of lavender filled Chrissie's mind. Her mother had always grown lavender and she could still remember as a youngster cutting and drying the flowers to put in sachets. But of course that was years ago. Long before her parents sold their modest family home and moved away to Southampton. They wanted to be nearer to her older brother Simon and his young family. Chrissie had been so independent, so un-needy, and when she hadn't provided the longed-for grandchildren, there just wasn't enough to counterbalance the pull to Southampton. And so they had gone. That had been four years ago.

'Now try not to get distracted, Mrs Jax, and just concentrate on the job in hand. You're meant to be learning French polishing, not the art of distilling essential oils,' and with that Ron left to return to his own work in the barn workshop.

Left alone once again in the old outhouse, and not just any outhouse but a former distillery, Chrissie tried to picture herself running a *parfumerie extraordinaire*, the official "nose" of the House of Jax and making perfumes from Suffolk herbs and flowers. She imagined hints of honeysuckle and lavender with undertones of beeswax and methylated spirit. Hmm, such a scent would probably be more suited to wood polish than a sophisticated perfume, but she liked to dream.

Another helicopter rumbled overhead and Chrissie looked at her watch. The morning had flown away and it was almost lunchtime. If she was quick she might be able to see the Sea King helicopter while it still hovered overhead.

Aviation fuel? That could be a secret ingredient, she mused as she stepped out into the bright midday sunshine. Oh yes, she thought, the House of Jax could certainly come up with highly original and unusual perfumes to suit the discerning nose of anyone, from plane spotter to lumberjack.

She had to shield her eyes as she looked upwards. The sun was directly overhead and the dark underside of the helicopter looked exposed and vulnerable from her position directly beneath it on the ground. It reminded her of a monstrous dragonfly but lacking the grace of its short-lived relative. She walked through the small courtyard between the barn and various outbuildings that made up the Clegg workshop complex. She was concentrating on the helicopter and hardly noticed the young man loitering near the main entrance to the barn workshop. She assumed he was a customer, but he hurried away as she approached.

Strange, she thought, why would he rush off? He looked quite young, and his only distinguishing feature was a goatee beard. The man in the pub the other night had looked like an undercover policeman, but this one looked too young, too…. Maybe that was the whole point, he was a better agent. But then it was Matt they were interested in, wasn't it? She shook her head. This was silly. There was no reason for anyone to be tailing her. She needed to pull herself together.

Chrissie walked up the track leading from the work-shops to the perimeter lane running close to the edge of the Wattisham Airbase. There was no sign of the visitor. He appeared to have vanished into thin air. But how had he got there? She supposed with all the helicopter noise, it was possible she hadn't heard a car engine; but maybe he was a plane spotter who'd got a bit misplaced. She'd noticed some when she'd driven towards Wattisham village. Only last week she'd turned right instead of left and driven past the Wattisham Airbase War Memorial. She couldn't help noticing someone sitting in a van near the perimeter fence with a notebook and thermos. Had to be a spotter, he was wearing an anorak, after all.

Her search for the goatee stranger led her up onto the Wattisham perimeter lane. It was lunchtime so there was no immediate need to return to the workshop; a forty minute midday break was permitted. It seemed to Chrissie that physical work required a longer rest than brain work.

She ambled along the lane. There was a broad grass verge with a ditch and hedge between the high wire fence and lane. The hedge was overgrown and thick with many different shrubs and small trees. She counted the different species as she walked. Accountancy had left a deeply im-bedded instinct to count and she found herself mentally adding and dividing as she walked. There were at least sev-en different species in ten yards of hedgerow: the hawthorn had grown to tree size; there was a small crab apple tree and wild hedge rose; huge brambles with blackberries forming; sloe thorn shrubs laden with unripe sloes; and small beech and birch. Those were the species she could identify, but there were plenty which she couldn't name: large leafed shrubs with flowers bearing poisonous looking red berries; small scrubby bushes with green current-like fruit; and weeds with feathery leaves.

The high wire perimeter fence was visible above the lower sections of the rough hedge. It bore a yellow notice with large black print; WARNING: DOGS ON PATROL. She smiled as she imagined a pair of helmeted dogs wearing army flak jackets walking past.

A thousand acres of cut grass, concrete runway and airbase buildings stretched beyond the wire.

Chrissie tuned back towards the Clegg workshops. At least she now had an idea for one of the carvings on the totem pole. Instead of an American eagle with outstretched wings, she could carve a World War II plane with outstretched wings - so then she wouldn't have to carve any feathers.

CHAPTER 6

Nick had almost completed the second week of his apprenticeship at John Willows & Son. It was Friday morning and he was looking forward to the weekend. As a first year student at Utterly Academy he had not valued his leisure time, but after only two weeks of starting work promptly at 8am he relished the thought of a lie-in on Saturday morning.

The routine was always the same. The workforce arrived at the Willows & Son workshop at 8am sharp and those who were working off site would then travel to the "job" in one of the works vans; white vans with bold green lettering both announcing and advertising the long established carpentry firm.

Unfortunately the rather fancy lettering chosen by John Willows senior made the double L in Willows look like a D, and consequently most of the travelling workforce referred to themselves as the *Green WiDows*. Mr Willows had red / green blindness. Both colours looked the same to him. He had intended to choose bold red paint for the lettering on his white vans, but by the time his mistake was discovered it was too much trouble and expense to change the green paint. So at 8am on that Friday morning the *Green WiDows* were preparing to leave the workshop in the white vans with fancy green lettering.

'Someone needs to go over to Damson Valley Farm this morning,' Mr Walsh, the foreman, announced to everyone and no one in particular. 'The boss had a call last night from one of the Farrow boys. They're having trouble with the wooden huts we made last year. Something 'bout doors and windows jamming. Hopefully not too big a job. The

Farrows are good customers and the boss wants someone over straightway to fix it before the weekend. So who can we spare?'

The foreman cast a speculative glance at his workforce. 'Dave, you could go there today. Take young Nick with you. He's a good tall lad. He'll help you rehang those doors. Good experience for him. Now get what you need and get going, before we have another call from the Farrows.'

Nick looked at Dave. He was a slightly tubby, middle-aged carpenter who enjoyed a pint of beer, or three, at the end of a hard day's work. His slightly portly waist suited his affable nature; he enjoyed nothing better than a good natter, and all the better if he had a pint in his hand at the same time. Mr Walsh was right, Dave would find him a help. There was a definite advantage to being six three if you were hanging doors, and now that Nick was also building up some muscles from the physical work, he was the ideal assistant.

It hadn't always been that way. Nick remembered being embarrassed by his skinny build at school and coupled with his height, it made him acutely aware he cast a very long shadow - a stick-man, like the illustrations in his childhood story-book of Don Quixote. But at least he'd never tried to stoop to disguise his height. His mother sought to reassure him by saying he'd thicken out in time, and looking back on it now, he wasn't too certain how to take that. It might have sounded better if she'd said he'd develop his muscles when he started a more physical lifestyle, and hanging doors fitted that bill.

Nick threw his toolbox into the back of a white van as Dave climbed up into the driver's seat. It was the only one left; the others had already been commandeered or were already on their way to the various job locations in the county. As Nick banged the van's rear doors shut, he noticed the smashed near-side tail lights. Better tell Dave, he thought as he stepped up effortlessly into the passenger seat. He started to speak but Dave slammed the van into reverse and all Nick managed was a grunt as the words were jolted out of him. He put out a hand to save himself as he lurched forwards into the dashboard. He'd just about steadied himself when Dave thrust the gears into first and accelerated forwards out of the workshop yard. Nick landed in a heap on the front passenger seat.

'Come on lad, stop messing about and put your seat belt on,' Dave said as he turned out onto the lane, looking neither to right nor left. 'You may already have guessed I wanted to be a rally driver when I was your age.'

Nick noticed that Dave didn't attempt to use the indicator at any turning, so it probably didn't matter that the near-side tail lights were smashed. They were redundant on this particular journey. Dave drove the van like a man possessed, all the while keeping up a constant flow of conversation. At least he keeps one hand on the steering wheel, Nick thought as the van swept over a humpback bridge and Nick's stomach dropped before lurching up into his throat. He'd just about recovered from that when he was pulled sideways by centrifugal forces greater than his own weight. He closed his eyes as the van sped around the blind bend. Nick didn't need a seat belt; he needed a harness. Meanwhile, Dave seemed unaware of the near misses as passing cars squeezed into the side of the lanes to make way for the van. Later, Nick would describe it as a white-knuckle ride.

'Damson Valley Farm. Now there's a name for you,' Dave chuckled. 'So called because they don't grow damsons and there's no valley. The Farrows have farmed there for generations. There was always a small orchard but more recently they've dropped the sugar beet, corn etcetera and instead concentrated on expanding the fruit side of the business. They've planted more fruit trees and put up those huge poly-tunnels for soft fruits. You know, like raspberries and strawberries.' Dave paused as he took a bend almost on two wheels. 'Now they have to get fruit pickers over from Eastern Europe every summer, and of course the fruit pickers need accommodation. Lucky for us, Willows got the contract last year to build some accommodation for them, well, wooden sheds more like. We weren't allowed to build anything more substantial.'

Nick couldn't believe it when Dave started chanting, 'Picking - peeling - packing - planting,' in time with each swerve as he flung the van around the corners. Nick was about to add *pruning*, but Dave had started a tuneless rhythm – beating out his words on the steering wheel with his hand:

'That's what they say.
That's what they do.
Picking all the produce just for you.'

'The rapping rally driver,' Nick joked, despite his churning stomach.

Dave smiled, pulling up briefly at a T-junction.

'Why do the fruit pickers come? I mean it doesn't sound a very attractive job?' Nick managed to get the question out before Dave roared off again.

'Well they're promised the basic hourly rate and they reckon if they're picking for eight, ten or maybe twelve hours a day... well that's good money. Trouble is there's not good picking every day, what with our weather and the ripeness of the fruit. So, if you only pick for four hours, you only get paid for four hours work, not the eight or more you'd expected. By the end of the week you may have only worked 20 hours, and that doesn't add up to much. No one tells them that till it's too late,' Dave replied.

'And to learn the language, some must come for that,' Nick added. There was a lot to take in and Nick fell silent while he digested it all. He also knew that he'd promised Matt he'd ask about John, the boss's son. But he didn't really want to. Let sleeping dogs lie, his mother always said; but his father would have countered, don't put off till tomorrow what can be done today – and he couldn't put it off any longer. A promise was a promise. Besides, he was meeting Matt and Chrissie at the Nags Head that evening. He couldn't turn up and not have tried to find something out. So was he a sleeper or a doer?

'Did the boss's son work on the dormitory sheds last year?' There, he'd asked.

The van slowed as Dave negotiated another road junction. 'Yes, I'm pretty sure he did. I think he was mates with the oldest Farrow boy. Old Mr Farrow has three sons; two of them still work in the business. If I remember right, the youngest was always a bit of a tearaway. Heard he got into some sort of trouble with the police, not sure what. Think he was called Francis, no Phillip – yes, that's right, Phillip.' Dave stopped talking for a moment. He was concentrating on turning into the Damson Valley Farm entrance.

Nick watched Dave's hand rest on the handbrake. Oh no, Nick thought, not a handbrake turn. Please God, no. There was a squeal of brakes as he was thrown forwards against his seat belt. But the van stayed straight as it juddered to a halt. Dave switched off the ignition and applied the handbrake. A dog started barking.

'Have I ever shown you my legendary handbrake turn Nick?'

Before Nick could think of a suitable reply, a young man with fair hair and dressed in clean blue overalls appeared from one of the outbuildings. He walked over to investigate their arrival and looked at the name emblazoned on the side of their white van.

'Good morning, Mr Widows.' He spoke in a clipped, precise way.

'No, no, I'm Dave and I work for Mr WiLLows,' Dave said, emphasising the l in Willows. 'This is our new apprentice Nick. Good morning.'

'Ah! Well I am Jan; Jan Kowalski and I work for Mr Farrows. Good morning. Follow me please.'

Ah, that's it, Nick thought; with all those Ks in his name he has to be Polish.

Jan turned on his heal, and not waiting, strode off across the courtyard leaving Nick, still thinking about Ks, and Dave to hurry after him. He walked in a rigid erect manner, his clean blue overalls giving the impression of a military uniform. He led them briskly past old outbuildings that had once been pig pens and milking sheds, but were now disused. They were a reminder of the time before Damson Valley Farm had turned to large scale fruit production.

'Here,' he said, pointing to the door of a smart new wooden shed with windows at regular intervals along its length. It was one of three almost identical sheds Willows & Son had constructed the previous year.

'Door sticks. Problems opening windows. Fix please! Our pickers will be out all day so no one getting in your way. Valko will stay with you here if you need anything,' and with that Jan turned and left.

'Chatty isn't he,' Dave remarked as he gave the door a shove.

The door suddenly unjammed and flew open. Nick almost jumped in surprise. Standing in the shadows on the other side of the door was a short stocky man with dark features and swarthy skin. Despite the sunny summer day he wore a leather jacket. He didn't make a sound, but appeared to examine them for a few seconds before speaking. Nick tensed. He felt as if he was being sized-up by a guard dog deciding whether to attack or let them pass. The man's eyes flickered, and then he suddenly smiled with his mouth, but the smile never reached his brown eyes.

'*Dobar den*. Let me introduce myself. I am Valko and I will stay with you while you work.' He spoke perfect English but his body language didn't reflect his easy manner of speaking. He exuded menace.

Nick wondered why Jan had wanted someone with them while they worked, but, if these were the accommodation huts, then maybe it was to make sure they didn't nick anything. He smiled at his subconscious pun and turned his attention back to the door that was sticking.

'So, Velcro, where did you pop up from?' The name had slipped out before he could help himself. He should be more careful.

'It's Valko. I'm from Bulgaria.'

'That's a long way from Suffolk,' Nick replied, smiling again.

'*Da*.' The word sounded flat. Impassive.

'Stop chatting, Nick and get me the battery powered screwdriver,' Dave interrupted. 'This door's going to have to come off. Maybe we'll only have to adjust the hinges but I think we'll end up planing off the bottom - can't do that while it is still hanging.'

Nick nodded. Dave's voice sounded sharp but he couldn't think what he'd said to upset him. It was probably best if he just hurried back to the van and fetched whatever Dave wanted before he got really irritated. Or was it simply the Valko-effect? He certainly made Nick feel edgy.

'Where're you going?' Valko asked before Nick had taken more than a few steps.

'Back to the van to fetch the battery powered screwdriver. OK?'

Valko hesitated. He seemed torn between staying with Dave at the shed door and accompanying Nick back to the van. In the end the pull of the shed must have won because he nodded slowly.

Nick smiled and started walking. It had been straightforward when he'd followed Jan. He'd just walked from the van, through the yard, past some old disused farm buildings, round the corner, and then there in front of him were the three long wooden sheds. Unfortunately finding his way back past the unfamiliar landmarks in reverse order was not so easy. He took a left turn rather than a right at the old pig pens and then he was lost. He found himself walking past some medium sized warehouses which he assumed were used for packing and storage. He took another left turn and found himself coming up behind what he assumed was the old milking shed and then, after negotiating a pile of discarded fruit crates, he was back on track.

It would be easy to hide or "lose" something here, he thought. At least he wasn't quite as bad as Chrissie. He knew where the van was parked; he just couldn't find it, whereas Chrissie wouldn't have remembered where she'd parked her MG in the first place. There were too many out-buildings and yards.

'Thank God,' Nick sighed as he finally entered the front courtyard and spotted the van. 'And it's exactly where Dave parked it earlier. No; correction - did an emergency stop.' Nick walked around the van to open the rear doors.

'Argh!' he gasped, nearly bumping into Jan who ap-peared to be looking at the near-side tail lights.

'Where's Valko?' Jan asked. Surprise flashed across his eyes, but his tone was sharp and accusing. 'He's meant to be watching after you.'

'Valcro's with Dave in the accommodation hut. We needed some tools we'd left in the van. Is that a problem for you?' It was time to get his head around this Velcro / Valko tongue twister before it caused trouble. 'So what's your interest in the van?'

Jan didn't answer immediately. He looked from Nick's face back to the smashed tail lights and then his frosty manner thawed half a degree. 'I am liking all cars and vans. You need to get that fixed. You don't want police stopping you. I am good at fixing motors. Mr Widows should get that fixed.' Jan fell silent and watched Nick as he selected the tools he needed.

'Follow me!' he commanded, and just as when Dave and Nick had first arrived, he led the way back to the long wooden huts.

'You've taken a while getting those tools,' Dave said, greeting Nick with a smile. Valko hovered deeper in the hut, well within earshot, and watched. Nick looked from Valko to Dave and raised his eyebrows, questioning.

'Just ignore him,' Dave whispered. 'The sooner we get on with this, the sooner we'll be out of here,' and then raising his voice back to normal volume, he continued, 'I've checked the windows while you were gone, and it shouldn't take us long to sort the one out in here. The window at the end of the hut though could do with a replacement sill. Someone's been standing on it to climb through the window. That's the only way it could've split off like that.' He paused before continuing, 'But we can make it back at the workshop and fit it later. That'll be a good job for you.'

Nick and Dave worked steadily over the next few hours and tried to ignore Valko. Every time they turned around or looked up, he always seemed to have them in his eyeline. Dave was a bit tetchy but Nick chattered away, trying to keep him at ease. As Valko watched, Nick learnt how to adjust the door and window hinges. He helped to plane back the wood where the door and windows were catching on their frames. He'd done it all at Utterly in his first year, but that was in theory. Dave had the practical tips old Blumfield had never mentioned. It was always different "out in the field", so to speak.

Dave even extended his teaching to include the theoretical techniques required in rally driving. At one point he swung his arms enthusiastically in various directions to illustrate the correct line to take a corner. Nick, crouching as he worked on the lower door hinge, caught a glimpse of Valko standing behind Dave, his dark eyes boring into his back. Suddenly, Valko stepped forwards.

'Dave, behind you!' Nick hissed under his breath.

'That's a nasty cough you've got there Nick. You were choking when we set out in the van this morning. You OK?' Dave asked, concerned.

Dave may not have heard his warning, but Nick was pretty sure Valko had caught every word. Why else, Nick wondered, would he have slowly looked from Dave, back to Nick and then smiled at him, showing his teeth, his cold brown eyes as expressionless as a shark. He could have sworn he even licked his lips.

'You like driving. You were a rally driver, Dave? Cars – they're my passion. In Bulgaria I used to drive. I was good. Valko Asenov! No one drives faster!'

Nick and Dave were so surprised that for a moment they didn't know how to react.

'I didn't know they made cars in Bulgaria.' Nick laughed and then thought it was probably best not to joke with Valko.

'You mean those old Czechoslovakian Skodas from the communist days? A tractor has more power. Pah!' Valko almost spat out the words. 'It may surprise you there are fast cars, but not made in Bulgaria. *Da* - now there are some fast cars in Bulgaria. But go on Dave, I like hearing you talk about driving.'

Nick glanced at Dave. His arm hung limp by his side, the best line to drive a corner forgotten as he looked at the door hinge. Words seemed to have deserted him as he gently pushed the door, gauging its clearance from the ground as it clicked shut, Valko still on the other side.

'Nice one,' Nick breathed.

'Now come on Nick, let's get on and finish up as fast as we can.'

By mutually unspoken agreement they worked on in silence, determined to finish as swiftly as possible. It wasn't long before Valko was escorting them back to the van, their tasks completed there for that day.

'We'll come back next week with the wood for that sill, Valko. I've measured up. Should be a quick job,' Dave said as he climbed into the van.

'Please be sure to phone and tell Mr Farrow the day you'll be coming and then we'll be expecting you, *do pro-kasno*,' Valko replied in a silky voice.

Nick slammed the van door, pleased to be sitting on the front passenger seat in relative safety. Maybe a fast get-away would be good, he thought. Burning rubber might not be such a bad thing after all, and he buckled his safety belt, ready. 'That was….'

'I know, tense,' Dave said.

Nick looked back at Valko. He stood with feet slightly apart and arms crossed - solid, his eyes never wavering from the van.

'Time to get going, Dave,' Nick muttered.

'Good lad - got your seat belt on? You're learning fast.'

Dave pressed the ignition, the engine leapt into life and Nick gazed at the view across the flat land of Damson Valley Farm, his head firmly pressed into the headrest as they accelerated away.

•••

Nick was, as usual, the first to arrive at the Nags Head that Friday evening. He'd been brought up to be punctual and hated being late for anything. Good time keeping had been drummed into him from an early age by his father, a senior planning engineer with British Rail and latterly, the Great

Eastern division. By timely chance, Nick even started life by arriving exactly on his predicted delivery date, and that was before the era of caesarean sections on demand. His father said he'd inherited his punctual gene, but Nick suspected timeliness was more down to nurture than nature.

Nick was looking forward to having a drink with Chrissie and Matt and bought himself a pint of the Land Girl. It had been a rather strange day over at Damson Valley Farm, and he just wanted to relax. He settled into his customary corner seat in the snug bar, stretched his legs out under the small table and savoured the first few sips from his overfull glass. Two of the World Cup quarter finals had played out earlier that evening and the drinkers were no longer interested in the end of match commentary post mortem. Their main interest was reserved for tomorrow when Germany played Argentina. Germany had already knocked England out of the last sixteen, and feelings would be running high – but that was tomorrow and for the rest of Friday evening, drinking was the order of the day. The barman switched off the flat screen TV and someone put a coin in the jukebox.

The speaker boomed out a melody and the words drifted across. Nick sipped his beer, hardly following the lyrics, unaware he was really listening and as the chorus played on, some of the phrases seemed to echo his own emotions. He began to realise something he hadn't wanted to admit to himself for months. Mel was like a pair of boots weighing him down. She was in Exeter and he was hundreds of miles away. He felt... but what was that last line? Is that how he felt? When he thought of her, he was filled with nothing but guilt and frustration. Did he love her? All he knew was he needed to break free.

Suddenly a commotion disturbed his quiet thoughts. It all happened pretty fast. One moment the pub door was closed, the next it was half ajar. There was a flurry of limbs, a shriek, and then Matt lay spread-eagled across the bare floorboards, surrounded by paper strewn in every direction. At first Nick thought Matt had been attacked, but as he took in the scene, he realised – well, judging by the mess scattered on the floor - he must have been carrying a large sheaf of A4 paper and simply misjudged the door. No doubt, six foot of solid wood had swung back and taken him by surprise. The result lay there for all to see. Conversation in the bar stopped as drinkers and barman stared at the spectacle near the door. The words swimming with boots on floated out on the air and then everyone started moving and talking again, just as in a film when a single frame freezes for a couple of seconds. Another customer, trying to enter the pub behind Matt, caught the swinging door, stepped over his legs and asked, 'You OK?'

Matt groaned and struggled up onto his knees, trying to collect everything together, grasping at his papers in a rough and random order.

With a sigh, Nick put his glass down and walked over to help. He couldn't but notice that the A4 paper was covered with photocopied newspaper articles. Strange, he thought, whatever is Matt doing with this lot? He couldn't remember when he had last seen Matt reading anything, let alone a newspaper. 'Are you OK, mate? Here, let me help.'

Matt nodded as he checked his wrist plaster cast.

'Come on, you great wally. You look as if you could do with a pint.'

'Yeah, since you're askin' – Carlsberg.'

This time Nick didn't bother to buy any crisps. He shook his head in disbelief as he sauntered over to the bar. It was like having a younger brother, well sometimes. But that was the whole point. Nick didn't have any brothers or sisters and occasionally he caught himself thinking of Matt as if he were that brother missing from his life. He should have felt irritated or embarrassed by Matt's clumsiness, but instead he was amused. What surprised him most was the feeling of protectiveness that seeing Matt in a heap on the floor awakened. Of course he knew Matt already had a brother Tom, but relationships in Matt's family were complex; much too complex for Nick to understand. He returned with a pint of lager and smiled as he passed it into Matt's outstretched hand.

'Woa! Careful,' Nick yelped as a splash of Carlsberg slopped from the glass. He turned his attention to the paper strewn across the small table. Matt had been attempting to shuffle the sheets of A4 into some sort of order. Unfortunately they were now covered in a fine spattering of lager.

'So, what's this about?' he asked.

Matt set his pint down on the table, his face still flushed from his fall. 'I wanted to show you some stuff, but it's all jumbled up now.'

'Show me what stuff?'

'I've been in the library. Blumfield thinks I'm workin' on his bloody module. Well I aint… well not all the time. I've looked up some stuff an' I wanted to show you. Seemed best to print it off.'

'Come on then, let's have a look,' Nick said as he gathered up the slightly damp paper and started to read. It didn't take him long to realise Matt had photocopied articles covering the coroner's case and the discovery of a dead body at the Willows site. As he read, an idea started to take form. He supposed it must be his subconscious at work, making sense of something niggling at the back of his mind. Firstly, Dave had told him that John junior and the oldest Farrow boy had been friends. That linked him to Damson Valley Farm in some way. Secondly, before he died, he had been working on the fruit pickers' accommodation at Damson Valley Farm. However something else nagged at him. He'd met Jan and Valko at the farm and their interest in cars and vans was – well, unsettling. There were just too many coincidences. Damson Valley Farm seemed to be a common thread.

Nick looked up as he finished reading to discover Chrissie had arrived. 'Hi,' he said. He had been so engrossed in his own thoughts that he'd been oblivious to everything around him. He smiled a welcome as she sat down with a glass of ginger beer. She must have been here a while, he thought; I didn't even notice her come in or buying her drink at the bar.

'Matt showed me all that on Monday,' Chrissie said, inclining her head towards the sheaf of papers in Nick's hand. 'Of course it wasn't covered in beer then. It seems his cousin was going to buy a car before he died.' Her neatly styled blonde hair caught the light as she threw her MG car keys down on the table.

'Top up this evening when you drove?' he asked, grinning. Why she drove that old relic, he'd never understand. He took a sip of his neglected beer, before continuing, 'I think Matt's maybe on to something.'

'See, said I'd got a nose for this sort a thing.' Matt's plump face glowed as he shot a quick glance at Chrissie.

'Well my nose is picking up hints of barley and hop from that wet paper – nothing sinister or suspicious. I just don't see how buying a car has anything to do with anything. Explain.'

Nick tried to gather his thoughts into some kind of order. 'I went over to Damson Valley Farm today to do some work for Willows. It may not be relevant, but Matt's cousin worked there last year. You see,' Nick paused to take another sip of beer before continuing, 'Willows won the contract to build accommodation huts for their seasonal fruit pickers.'

Matt nodded slowly as Chrissie frowned. 'And?' she asked.

'And that tells us where he was working. There were these two weird men there today. One looked kind of military, a Polish chap I reckon, and then there was this short Bulgarian Rottweiler in a leather jacket. They were like "the master and his henchman". There was something very strange in the way they wouldn't let us out of their sight.'

Chrissie started to laugh.

'Now come on, tell me what's so funny about that?' Nick asked.

'Ah! The mystery unfolds. Are you sure they weren't from Transylvania? Maybe the military one was a vampire. Count Dracula with his fly eating servant Renfield. Eying up your throats were they? And of course the nail in John junior's neck was a failed attempt at a stake through the heart.' Chrissie suddenly looked serious. 'Did you by any chance catch a view of their teeth?' She stopped when she caught Matt's expression. 'Sorry Matt, only joking.'

'No, you're missing the point. They were both extremely interested in cars. They were obsessed. It's all they spoke about. If Matt's cousin was looking to buy a car, well he was working there after all, he could easily have got involved with them in some way. And they were really creepy.' Nick looked over at Matt to see how he was taking it.

'See I knew there were somethin' up. But... a second cousin, he were me second cousin, Nick. And, Chrissie, shouldn't a stake through the heart be wood?'

'Good point.' Chrissie seemed to be enjoying the vampire theme.

Matt nodded. 'I could look 'em up on the internet. Facebook an' Twitter? If you've got some names I could type 'em in, then somethin' like cars, convictions, fruit pickin'.'

'Vampires?'

Nick could see Matt wasn't laughing. It was time to rein her in. 'Stop it Chrissie, that's enough. Now tell us what you've been up to over at Ron Clegg's this week.'

'There's a limit to how much you'd want to hear about French polishing. Let's just say I'm all polished out.' She paused while she seemed to think for a moment before adding, 'I still haven't done anything about the totem pole yet - except worry a bit.'

'Yeah but have you seen the helicopters up close, Chrissie? You're near Wattisham, aint you?'

Nick laughed. It was just like Matt to miss Chrissie's undercurrent of angst and ask the techie questions.

'Yes, some great yellow thing with its side door open - hovering up there with a winch or wire dangling down.'

'Reckon that'll be a Sea King practising search an' rescue. Any Apaches or Lynxes?'

'Crikey Matt, how would I know?'

'Well….' Matt put his glass down so that he could use both hands to illustrate the shapes. 'If you look at 'em from below they're more angular than Sea Kings. And they aint yellow, see? There should be loads Apaches and Lynxes. 'Course durin' the Second World War the American Air Force were there.'

'Ah well that explains the war memorial on the perimeter lane,' Chrissie said. 'I couldn't understand what AAF Station, followed by some numbers meant.'

'Yeah, AAF. America Air Force till 1945, then the RAF took it back,' Matt explained.

'And then what happened?' Nick asked. This was becoming interesting.

'The army's what happened. Their Air Corp grabbed it from the RAF a few years back.'

'I'm sure I've read there's a gliding club based at Wattisham, as well.' Nick couldn't believe it when Matt nodded. How much did he know about the airbase? But then he'd always been full of surprises; an encyclopaedic memory for numbers and trivia, but not always joined up or cross referenced. Sometimes Nick likened it to pushing a button and then ping, out came the information.

'Gliders don't sound very high tech for the army. Are you sure Matt? Do they train pigeons to send messages as well?' Chrissie asked.

'Now you're taking the piss. I'm only tellin' you what I know. It's helicopters mainly, with some glidin' on the side. Even the police, I think.'

'The police?'

'Yeah, the Suffolk Police 'copter unit's based there as well. So: RAF, that's those yellow ones for coastal rescue;

and then there's Army Air Corp with their Apaches; and… glidin'!' Matt counted them off on his fingers in turn.

Nick and Chrissie exchanged glances. Nick was stunned. Matt must be a closet plane spotter, he decided. There was no other explanation.

'Ron remembers when that dirty great wire perimeter fence went up,' Chrissie said, interrupting his thoughts. 'Over a thousand acres had to be enclosed. Apparently, the workmen started at one end and fenced their way round. Trouble was, they hadn't realised a small herd of deer had wandered onto the airbase land. By the time the workmen joined up the end with the start of the fence, the deer were trapped. I mean it's a secure fence and there is no way those deer were going to escape over it. And remember it's an airbase. They couldn't leave the deer there. You can picture it - carnage on the runways.'

'So what happened?' Nick asked.

'Well they couldn't leave the deer on the airbase and they couldn't release them onto the local farmland. They're pests so…,' Chrissie let her voice trail away.

'I didn't read anythin' about deer on the History of Wattisham website.'

'You wouldn't, Matt. It doesn't really fit the army's image of planning and efficiency, and of course they don't shoot civilians. Bad publicity however it's reported,' Chrissie paused and then added, 'but I bet someone had venison for tea. My round, I think. Everyone their usual?' She gathered up their empty glasses and headed for the bar.

Matt watched her receding back. 'Don't think I've ever had venison. Mind, I've seen venison sausages on the bar menu at Christmas. Never tried them though. Me mum, she only buys economy bangers.'

'You haven't missed much.' Nick said it as if he ate venison all the time, but in fact he'd only tasted it once, in a restaurant; a special celebration meal with his parents when his father got a promotion at work. That seemed light years away from now. Nick was about to say something more when his phone shrilled out its ringtone from his pocket.

'Better see who…,' he said as he pulled it from the depths of his jeans and read the caller's ID. 'No, it's OK mate.' He switched off his mobile. 'I'll call Mel later.'

'Hey, don't mind me. Speak to Melody now if you want.'

'No, and it's not Melody. It's Melanie. Best not call from the pub.' And the thought he needed to put the brakes on, went through his mind. He needed to sort this out but it would have to wait till later. 'Look, we really ought to give Chrissie a hand with this totem pole project. I mean it's a hell of a task. We didn't really cover carving on the course and there's going to be loads. If Chrissie agrees, I'm going to ask Blumfield if I can help. We're over at Utterly on Monday. Let's see what Chrissie says when she comes back with the drinks.'

'I was thinkin' that too.'

'Oh yes?' Nick wasn't convinced.

He must have shown his cynicism because Matt had more to say. 'Maybe not so much use with the carvin', but I could look stuff up - try an' find things to carve. Anythin' you want really.'

By the time Chrissie returned with the drinks they had hatched their plan. She set the glasses down on the small table, and this time there was no spilling of beer onto the now orderly pile of A4 paper. She sipped her ginger beer as Nick and Matt excitedly outlined their proposal. Nick was secretly relieved to see Chrissie's face relax as they offered assistance with the totem pole. He was never completely sure how she'd respond to an offer of help. She was always so fiercely independent.

'I shouldn't think Ron would mind you two coming over to his workshop. What about Monday afternoon when the apprentice day-release teaching's ended? He usually works late into the evening. More than likely he'd enjoy the company. And he likes teaching.' Chrissie was definitely smiling now.

'You said you hadn't done anything about it yet.'

'No, but I've done lots of thinking. Ron reckons that Blumfield ordered the tree ten years ago and it's in storage somewhere. It should be some sort of birch or red cedar. According to Ron the white birch is soft and the red cedar has straight grain and no knots. They're both native to Canada but God knows which was ordered. I was planning on asking Blumfield about it on Monday.'

'If the wood's been stored for ten years then it'll be well seasoned, really dried out by now - may not be quite so easy to carve,' Nick said and then grinned.

'Great! I'll be looking for a twenty-five, maybe thirty foot tree trunk hidden away in some wood yard and as hard as iron.' Chrissie pulled a long face.

'So what you goin' to carve on it?' Matt asked.

'The only things I've thought of so far to represent East Anglia over the last millennium are a Second World War plane that could look a bit like an American eagle, you know with outstretched wings but no feathers; and Oliver Cromwell, who came from Norfolk with a big wart on his chin and forehead,' Chrissie answered.

'What about Nelson? He was born on the North Norfolk coast. You could, sorry *we* could carve his head with his admiral's hat sticking out sideways. It would balance the aircraft wings - might even look artistic.' Nick was enjoying himself. 'By the way,' he added, 'I thought it was called a bald headed eagle, so there wouldn't have been many feathers to carve on the head at least.'

'Nah, it's got white head feathers. What about Boadicea, you know, queen of the Iceni? I could carve a chariot.'

Both Chrissie and Nick looked at Matt. 'Wrong millennium,' they said in unison.

It was only later that evening, as Nick drove home, that he realised he hadn't noticed anyone following or watching Matt in the pub. The man in the green sweatshirt with short sandy hair and a broken nose hadn't been there. Maybe he'd lost interest in Matt. Or was whoever was watching doing it better?

CHAPTER 7

On the whole it had been a great Friday evening, Matt thought, as he made his way up the main Utterly staircase. No birds, just spending time with great mates or, as his mother would have called them in her broad Suffolk accent, grut mets. Nick had even switched his mobile off when Melody rang. How cool was that? Matt wondered if he'd ever dare turn his mobile off if a bird phoned him - as if he'd be so lucky. He glanced at the sheet of crumpled paper he held close to the stretched fabric of his pink sweatshirt. Tom said blokes had to be manly to wear pink and this expanse of pink had the added benefit of *Bruce Springsteen* and *Made in the USA* emblazoned across the front. You couldn't get manlier than Bruce, now could you?

He glanced past the gentle bulge of his stomach. He could see the newspaper article he'd photocopied reporting the discovery of a body in the Willows workshop, the printer ink now smudged by beer spilt at the Nags Head on Friday evening. Nick had scrawled across the paper in bold handwriting *Jan Kowalski* and *Valko Asenov*. But he'd said he wasn't sure how to spell the names, and Matt certainly hadn't a clue so there might be problems with that. Matt sighed. His own spidery lettering covered the rest of the paper: *John Willows junior*, *Phillip Farrow* and his older brothers *Peter* and *Paul*. He had also scribbled down: *Damson Valley Farm*, *fruit picking*, *cars for sale*, *totem poles* and *famous people / places from East Anglia*. He turned the paper over, following his handwriting as it spread to the reverse side like a slug's trail wandering across a rhubarb leaf. And then he held it close to his sweatshirt again.

He was pretty pleased with himself. For once he'd been organised and structured. Even old Blumfield would be impressed, he thought, as he tightened his grasp on the crushed sheet of paper. A few more steps and the library door would be in sight. With any luck Rosie would notice the manly pink. He was looking forward to his day. There would be plenty of time on the computer in the morning, and then lunch with Chrissie and Nick in the newly redecorated Academy canteen. Yes, it held the promise of a thoroughly good Monday. The only blot on the horizon was the meeting with Blumfield. Wonder what he'd think of pink? But then the meeting hadn't been arranged yet.

As Matt sauntered through the library door, the smell of books and magazines conjured up Rosie's image and he glanced around to see if he could spot her. A pang of disappointment surprised him when she wasn't at the librarian's station. So he played it cool and headed for a computer in a secluded corner, making sure he could still keep an eye on both the entrance door and the librarian's desk. He reckoned he was bound to catch a glimpse of her eventually. He preferred to stay out of the way though; didn't want any prying eyes looking at his computer screen. After all, he was in super sleuth mode.

It only took him a few moments to log on to Google and key in the first names on his list. He followed with Facebook, Twitter and MySpace but there were immediate problems.

'Shite, I hadn't thought of that.' Matt frowned and bit his lower lip. He should have guessed - some hits relating to Jan Kowalski were in Polish and most relating to Valko Asenov were in Bulgarian. And there was also the spelling issue. Matt could see he would need to cross reference and stretch his brain with some uncharacteristic lateral thinking, if he was going to find anything useful and in English. He preferred to follow straight lines. Cryptic clues gave him a headache, he didn't know why. He had always been like that.

After thirty minutes of frantic typing and searching, he had his first break. He found the Damson Valley Farm webpage advertising fruit picking jobs. The contact details for hopeful applicants were: *Jan Kowalski, Fruit Picking Personnel Manager*, followed by an email address and contact mobile phone number. So at least he now had the correct spelling. But his next break was bigger. He had been looking on sites advertising sports cars for sale in East Anglia and there, leaping off the screen at him was a sequence of familiar numbers. He was sure he couldn't be mistaken - the mobile phone number matched the number for Jan Kowalski on the fruit picking site.

'Yeah!' he hissed, punching the air.

Matt was good at remembering sequences of numbers. It was probably the only gift he had been born with, and on more than one occasion in the past it had got him out of real trouble. He thought back to the time when he was seven years old and got frighteningly lost. He had been so excited when his mother took him on a rare trip in December to the Ipswich Christmas Market. Matt was overwhelmed by the sight and smell of Christmas food, sweets and exotic spices and didn't notice his mother and brother Tom leaving for the bus station.

At first he thought they were still enjoying the delight and buzz of the market, but then suddenly he couldn't see them anywhere. It was getting dark and he felt scared and alone. He must have cried or something because a stall holder asked, 'Are you all right, luv?'

At that age Matt wasn't very good at reading and didn't know his address, but he knew his home telephone number and amazingly, Tom's new mobile number. Someone phoned and Tom answered, surprised. He was only half a street away. His mum assumed Matt was lagging behind somewhere and hadn't had time to miss him. No doubt she would have noticed eventually.

She didn't smile when she walked back to the stall to collect him, and instead of a big warm hug, she just patted his head and proffered a Jaffa Cake - which she considered was pretty seasonal at the time. Matt, cold and tearful, had been grateful for the little orange, chocolate and sponge offering and had remained rather partial to Jaffa Cakes since that time. But the strange thing was he still associated them with Tom's mobile phone number.

Matt gave himself a little shake and dragged his mind back from Jaffa Cakes to the present and the task in hand - Phillip Farrow, another name on his list. Now that should be easy, he thought. At least the spelling was straightforward and all the hits should be in English. But when he found several hundred Phillip Farrows on Google, and Facebook had at least 182, he started to lose momentum. Where to begin? He took a deep breath and began looking at each one systematically, but it was mind-blowingly tedious and he wasn't getting anywhere. He needed more information to narrow his search.

Inspiration or good old fashioned luck was what he required. Matt rubbed his eyes and glanced over to the librarian's station. Of course Rosie - and the newspaper sites. As quick as a flash he had the Eastern Anglia Daily Tribune up and keyed in the Utterly Academy membership code.

My speciality again - number sequences, he thought, as he paused before typing *reports of court proceedings* and *local man convicted*, in the search box. Ten years should cover it, he thought, as he keyed in the years 2000 to the current date in 2010. And then he sat back and waited, his face flushed pink above his manly sweatshirt. It was getting hot in his rather airless corner of the library, and there had been no sighting of Rosie yet. If it got any warmer he'd have to take off the Springsteen pink, and that would be a pity because he'd dressed with an eye to his outermost layers only. The tee-shirt underneath had been one of Tom's tatty cast-offs, originally found in a charity shop and with a nineties rock band emblazoned across the chest. But *Rage Against the Machine* had seen better days. The Gs had flaked off and some of the other letters had perished, so the words now read, *Rape aint the Maxime*. Not quite the cool look he'd hoped might impress Rosie, unless one counted the hole where a side seam had split.

'I'm in a bloody crime pit,' Matt muttered under his breath, his attention drawn back to the computer screen. His search had thrown up literally thousands of articles: arson, burglary, breaking and entry, assault and battery, antisocial behaviour – and that came in some surprisingly varied forms. The list was endless, and that was before you added drugs, both possession and dealing. He wondered why the paper bothered to report crimes so common they were hardly newsworthy, but he was soon engrossed in some of the more bizarre accounts. Did people really steal underwear from washing lines?

'Stalkin'? Now I hadn't thought of that.' A particularly unpleasant case of stalking had caught his attention. Did the man with short sandy hair and a broken nose, who watched him in the pub, count as a stalker? Where did surveillance end and stalking begin? Matt shook his head. He'd got as far as August 9th 2009 when suddenly an article leapt off the screen at him.

Local Man Found Guilty of Car Theft.

Phillip Farrow, aged 22, of Damson Valley Farm was found guilty to a charge of theft and dealing in stolen cars. Phillip, known locally as "Aphid" appeared in Norwich Crown Court on Tuesday. The judge, in sentencing, said he had taken into consideration the lack of any previous convictions and the defendant's decision to plead guilty. Phillip Farrow was sentenced to a 12 month custodial sentence and is expected to serve at least 6 months of this at H. M. Prison Norwich.

Matt's sleuthing nose was positively twitching with the strong scent of coincidence. Hadn't Nick mentioned something about Jan and Valko's obsession with cars? And then there had been that advertisement for a sports car, and now he'd learnt Phillip had been banged up for car theft. But there was one more thing he wanted to check on – a possible army connection with Jan. It was enough to give him a headache but there had to be a way. It was those cryptic clues again.

It only took him a short while to discover that Poland had compulsory national service until the end of 2008. So, Matt reasoned, if Jan was old enough, then he might well have done his national service before coming to Suffolk and that might explain his military bearing. But there was nothing more he could find out. Kowalski was a very common name in Poland.

'Dinner,' Matt announced under his breath. 'I'm done here now.' He logged off the computer and looked over to the librarian's station. Maybe…. He had an idea.

Matt sauntered over towards the entrance door and book-return table. On the way, he picked a book randomly from a shelf at about shoulder height. That should do it, he thought. Unfortunately it was heavier than he'd expected and it started to slip from his grasp. He tried to grip the book more tightly but the plaster cast got in the way and his other hand was useless, still holding his discarded pink sweatshirt. Either he'd have to dash to the returns desk and toss the tome down before he dropped it, or let it fall to the floor where he stood, with pages splayed and spine split open. He opted for a sprint and launched himself towards the return station at break-neck speed. He had the polished table top in sight. The book was slipping from his hand, so he flung it and hoped for the best. It skidded along the wooden surface, finally coming to rest with a crash as its back cover bent double.

'Can I help?' Rosie appeared as if from nowhere, and silently walked towards the desk.

'I-I….' Matt couldn't find the right words. He had hoped that returning a book might be an excuse to speak to her, but this hadn't been quite the casual approach he'd had in mind.

'Wanted to return a book?' And then after a pause she continued, 'A bowling enthusiast? Or perhaps hurling?'

'Yeah well I….' He caught sight of the title of the book he'd flung on the table.

'*Cross-Dressing. The Art of Drag in The Theatre Through The Ages*,' Rosie read out slowly.

'Ah,' Matt said as he realised with blinding clarity that he'd picked a book from the theatre studies section. Of all the books to choose. Christ, she must think…. He tried to look cool but his face had already started to flush.

'In a hurry were you?' she asked, clipping her words.

'Yeah well I….' But she'd given him an excuse, a let out. All he had to do was nod and hurry away. He looked down at his tee-shirt. *Rape aint the Maxime* was spelled out in red across his chest. Cripes! Why had he put on one of Tom's collection of rock band tee-shirts from the 90s? He should have kept his pink sweatshirt on. And as if that wasn't bad enough, Tom, although almost eight years older, was only half his girth and the sad ancient tee-shirt had ridden up despite the split in the side seam.

'I….' Matt raised his pink sweatshirt to block out the lettering on his chest and the bare flesh around his midriff.

'So I see,' she said, glancing at his chest before turning to gather up the book and carefully straightening out its pages and cover.

Matt looked down at his trainers. How could euphoria so quickly turn to embarrassment and despair? It was time to go before things got worse. He glanced up to give her a smile, but she had already turned away. Looked like he'd blown it. There was nothing for it - time to head for dinner. He knew he could always rely on food. That was probably the only thing his mother had taught him.

The canteen was on the same floor as the library, so it was only a short walk from one to the other. Redecoration had finally been completed. The explosion had only been three weeks earlier, but that three weeks seemed more like

101

three months to a hungry student, and Matt was one hungry student. He made his way along the corridors with the accuracy, but not the speed, of a heat seeking missile, his nose drawn by the irresistible smell of fish and chips. He was duly rewarded with the magnificent sight of the freshly decorated canteen. The Academy authorities had surpassed themselves. Faced with a tight schedule, unexpected expense and no budget, they had settled for the cheapest paint on offer - midnight blue. There had been a lot of wall to cover and the dark paint had hidden the smoke stained surfaces with just one coat.

'Shite...' Matt screwed up his eyes as he entered the canteen. It appeared to be almost completely dark. The meagre light from the low energy light bulbs was largely absorbed by the midnight blue walls. It felt like a cave or grotto. Even the stainless steel service counters, which should have been bright and shiny, looked dull. Matt's eyes took a moment to acclimatise to the dim light before he spotted Chrissie and Nick already sitting at a table where light streamed in through a window.

'Hi! Restful colour, don't you think? Have you been working in the library?' Chrissie asked by way of a greeting as she pushed a plate of almost untouched chips towards him.

Matt could never pass an offer like that and throwing himself down on a new plastic chair, helped himself. It was difficult to speak with his mouth stuffed with chips lavishly covered in ketchup, but he did his best as he excitedly told them everything he had discovered that morning.

'What you laughin' at?' Matt asked, interrupting his account mid-sentence, mouth still full of half-chewed potato and sweet vinegary tomato sauce.

'Just you.' Chrissie cleared her throat, 'It's taken me a while to work out what's written on your tee-shirt. Amazing.'

'Christ, Chrissie; aint you been listenin'? What you think about what I've been sayin'?' Matt tried not to colour up and looked down at the floor where he'd thrown his pink sweatshirt.

'As I said, amazing. On both counts.'

Matt shot a sideways glance at Nick, daring him to laugh. At least he's taking me seriously, Matt thought, as he watched him frown.

It took a few moments before Nick finally spoke. 'So what type of car was being advertised for sale, you know, with Jan's mobile phone number as contact?'

Matt closed his eyes as he recalled the computer screen. 'A 2008 Porsche Boxter RS60 Spyder. I'm sure it said low mileage and they were wantin' £34,000. Yeah, that was it.'

Nick made a low whistle as he sucked some air through his teeth. 'That's a pretty flash car for the Fruit Picking Personnel Manager to own or be selling. I suppose you could phone the number and see if it's Jan's. You know, pretend you're interested in buying the Porsche.'

'What me? I'm not goin' to bloody phone.'

'And, before you ask, neither am I,' Chrissie chipped in. 'But what about Phillip? Phillip Farrow the Aphid boy? He should have served his sentence, be out of Norwich by now. He only had to do six of the twelve months in there. Do we know where he is or what he's doing?'

'Yes, that's a point. I could ask when I go back to the farm later this week. There's a replacement wooden sill to fit - one of the windows in the accommodation huts. To be honest, I'd been dreading going back there, but maybe....'

'Yeah, just mention the Porsche. Drop an RS60 Spyder into the conversation. You can do it casual like.'

'Oh for God's sake, Matt. Not the Porsche. I meant ask about Phillip. What've you got written on the front of that tee-shirt, by the way?'

Matt picked up his pink sweatshirt and pulled it roughly over his head. 'So what time's this meetin' with Blumfield?' he said, ignoring Nick's question.

'I've managed to organise it for 3:30 this afternoon,' Chrissie answered. Matt couldn't see why she was grinning. What was so funny about that?

•••

The afternoon meeting with Mr Blumfield was going surprisingly well for everyone. Matt had been dreading going up to his small office on the administration corridor. He knew that Nick would be all right – he was the favourite. But Matt could never read Blumfield's mood. Sometimes he seemed quite smiley, but more often than not he would be a bit short, snappy even, and Matt could never understand why. Perhaps it was time to try and impress. Yes that was it - impress. They had been in his office for about five minutes and Chrissie had done most of the talking so far.

'Chrissie Jax, Nick Cowley and Matt Finch,' Mr Blumfield said, nodding in approval as he looked at the three apprentices, letting their names hang in the air as his eyes rested on Matt's sweatshirt.

So why my name last, Matt wondered. He caught Chrissie's eye. She was sitting on the Mackintosh chair, the one with the tall straight back and small seat. She shifted her position and straightened one leg. Yes, he remembered the last time he'd sat on that chair when Blumfield told him how he'd be filling his time while his wrist healed. The hard edge of the seat had cut into the back of his thighs, and both his legs went numb. He thought he'd been struck down with something or that Blumfield had special powers. Thank God today he and Nick were standing. He shifted his weight from one leg to the other, respectfully waiting for Blumfield to say more.

'Chrissie Jax, Nick Cowley and Matt Finch,' Blumfield repeated and then smiled.

We know our names. We all know who we are, Matt thought.

'This is wonderful. We have a problem and you three come up with a solution – wonderful. Pulling together. Now Nick, I feel reassured that you'll be involved with this. The carving, well that will be good experience for you.' Blumfield glanced down at Chrissie's foot. He appeared to focus for a moment on her light summer pump. 'Of course, Chrissie, I'm sure you could have completed the totem pole alone, but this way there shouldn't be any further delay.'

Matt could hardly believe it when Blumfield put up his hand as Chrissie started to answer. Even he, a friend, wouldn't dare to cut her off as she started to open her mouth.

'And you Matt, what will you contribute?' he asked.

'I-I've been,' Matt paused as he tried to remember what Chrissie had said. Slowly, that was it, speak slowly.

'Been using me plannin' skills, you know, the Plannin' an' Communication module, Mr Blumfield.' Matt waited for Blumfield to say something.

'And?'

'I've looked some stuff up an'… an' well, one of the carvings could be… a seat of learnin', you know, for the universities in the region.' Matt watched Chrissie shift again on the Mackintosh chair, 'And then… water, you know the fens and broads.' He drew a wavy line in the air and stopped for a moment when he realised Nick was staring at him. But impress, that's what he must do – impress.

He soldiered on, 'An' heads… we're spoilt for choice. I, no *we* thought maybe Oliver Cromwell with 'is warts… or Nelson with 'is admiral's hat.' Matt stared down at his feet, embarrassment grabbing his tongue.

'Go on, Matt.' Chrissie's voice cut through his self-consciousness, 'Go on.'

'Then… an animal or bird could be… well a World War II plane. You know, to represent airfields in the region. I, no *we* thought….' Matt ran out of steam.

'Well Matt, I don't usually give much praise but today I will say well done, Matt Finch.'

Matt felt his round face glow. He put his hand up to touch his cheek and hide his warm flush, but agh! Tiny flecks of tomato ketchup were spattered on his chin. Those friggin' chips, he thought.

'Of course the Academy may not be able to reimburse your travel expenses. We're on a very tight budget. I'll contact Ron Clegg this afternoon and also make arrangements to get that timber transported over to his workshop. And,' he added as an afterthought, 'no injuries please.' And with that, Mr Blumfield ended the meeting.

'I can't think why he looked at you Matt, when he said *no injuries*.' Nick was in a cheerful mood. 'Shall we go home via Ron Clegg's workshop? I can take Matt in my car and follow you in your MG if you like.'

'Sounds good to me. There's no hurry though. If we get there too soon, Blumfield won't have had a chance to phone Ron. And well done, Matt – amazing,' Chrissie said as they made their way out to the student car park and the late afternoon sun.

Nick drove a beat up old blue-coloured Ford Fiesta. It had been the family's second car for years, mainly driven by his mother. Matt remembered Nick telling him that when he was seventeen and learning to drive, he had problems judging the width of the car. His long-suffering mother used to sit in the passenger seat and risk life and limb as she tried to teach him. Over those first few months there were regular brushes with hedgerows as Nick got out of the way to let oncoming cars pass on the narrow lanes. The evidence was still there for all to see - a network of fine scratches down the entire length of the passenger side of the car.

'Looks like you've tried to customise this car with a Brillo pad,' Matt said as he opened the passenger door. 'That Kowalski bloke would believe you'd want to change your car if he saw you drivin' this old banger.'

'It's an unlikely upgrade from twelve year old Ford Fiesta to two year old Porsche Boxter RS60 Spyder. It stretches credibility.' Nick's tone discouraged any further discussion and Matt settled into the passenger seat.

They followed the red MGB, all the while driving at a restrained pace. The afternoon sun caught the polished chrome of its rear bumper, flashing and glinting as the small red car wove its way along the twisting lanes. Matt almost nodded off as the Fiesta gently swayed along, but as they neared the airfield he was all attention. Chrissie turned off the Wattisham Airfield perimeter lane, and they trailed behind as she drove down a track leading to the workshops. They soon found themselves completely hidden, invisible from the road. The rough surface of rubble and gravel made it impossible to drive silently; the sound from the four pairs of tyres loudly announcing their arrival well before they could be seen. Matt wondered how Ron Clegg's customers ever found his workshops.

'Maybe he doesn't want to be found down here,' Nick said, answering Matt's unspoken question.

Matt sat in the car and looked at the deserted court-yard. Dead, perhaps that was the word he was looking for, apart from Chrissie's MGB parked up at one end.

'Peaceful, isn't it?' Nick seemed delighted with the place.

A thundering rumble started to fill the air, getting louder until almost deafeningly overhead. The old Fiesta seemed to vibrate. Time to get out, Matt thought. He swung the car door open, but his ears were assaulted with the in-creasing volume, and now a feeling of pressure added to it all. He looked upwards into the sky. 'Apache,' he said, his voice lost against the background rumble.

'Come on. Chrissie must have already gone in,' Nick shouted.

Matt imagined himself in some Vietnam skirmish as he put his hands to his ears, ducked and ran after Nick. He almost jumped through the barn workshop doorway as the old door creaked closed, then came to a dead halt, his face colliding with the centre of Nick's back.

'What you stop there for?' But then it was obvious. There was no mistaking the smells that met his stubby nose and the sights surrounding him. He gazed, jaw limp and with hands still held to his ears, at the jumble of furniture and piles of wood. There were racks with carefully stored veneers and an enormous tool cabinet. Its door was open displaying an exhaustive range of handsaws, chisels, planes, cramps and old tools that he had never seen before. His nose was almost twitching with the scents from beeswax and methylated spirit. He could see the array of modern tools as well. There was a large electric motored planer, band saw, scroll saw, pillar drill and a large router on its dedicated table. There were band and drum sanders and of course a lathe for turning. It was an Aladdin's cave; completely different from the Utterly workroom. For a start he couldn't see a nail or staple gun.

'Wow, it's huge. I'm well dosselled.'

Ron carefully put down his tools. He had been cutting some dovetail joints by hand before their arrival. He looked calm and slightly dusty, in keeping with the workshop.

'You must be Matt. Mr Blumfield phoned.'

Matt nodded and let his arms drop back down by his sides.

'Nick Cowley,' Nick said as he walked towards Ron and extended his hand smiling.

'Sorry, Mr Clegg, I should have introduced you all,' Chrissie said as she moved towards the kettle. 'Tea, coffee, anyone?'

'Did you see that? An Apache flew right overhead. That were amazin'!' Matt looked down at his plaster cast, 'Sorry, can't really shake....'

'That's OK.' And Ron looked down at his own arthritic hands. 'But yes, they seem to fly right over my workshop as they leave the airfield. There isn't really much of a flight path with helicopters, but it's the next best thing. Chrissie, I think it's definitely time for a large pot of tea.'

Over mugs of strongly brewed afternoon tea, the conversation naturally turned to the totem pole. Matt would have described the tea as stewed rather than brewed, more of a stain than a beverage. It was only drinkable when disguised with lashings of milk and sugar. If the truth were known, he preferred cold drinks, apart from hot chocolate, of course. Now a nice cold pint of Carlsberg would slip down a treat. That might aid everyone's concentration.

'Have you got that, Chrissie? We need to draw the carvings to scale first, that's what you said isn't it Mr Clegg?' Nick asked turning to Ron.

'Yes, you need to lay the drawings along the trunk to plan the length and how the carvings will look when combined, one on top of another. Remember the totem pole carvings shouldn't only look good together in sequence; they're meant to be telling a story. It's also vitally important to leave enough length at the bottom of the pole before the start of the carvings. Remember the totem pole has to be fixed securely upright in prepared ground or concrete.'

Matt chuckled as he imagined burying Oliver Cromwell's head so that just his wart showed above the earth.

'Normally you don't want to bury your carvings in the fixing, but of course you lot may feel differently....' Ron paused to take a sip of tea. There hadn't been enough mugs and he was drinking from a make-do old jam jar. 'So leave plenty at the base beneath the carvings, we can always trim that back at the end if there's too much.'

There was a much longer pause before Ron continued again, 'Of course we don't want the totem pole blowing down. Mr Blumfield said something about putting some steel rods in along the length of the back of the pole to help with the upright fixings. Health & Safety, no doubt. We need to plan for that in the carving.'

'But how do we actually do the carvings?' Nick asked, his round face serious.

'It may seem obvious but it still needs to be said. You start at the bottom of the trunk and work your way up to the top.' Ron smiled at Chrissie and added, 'Of course it will be flat on the ground when you're carving it, not upright in the air. Not got a head for heights then Chrissie?'

They all laughed and Ron continued, 'The bark has to be taken off first. Then I advise you practise each carving first, as you haven't done much before. Better not to make your mistakes on the real thing. You'll be using chisels and gouges and also, maybe for the first time, veiners, parting tools and small axes. There's plenty of spare wood here to practise on,' he said looking around the barn workshop.

'Do we paint it?' Nick asked.

'Yes, that'll help to preserve the wood and also it was traditional to paint the carvings. Now tell me, Matt, how much longer before that wrist cast comes off and you're able to use both hands?'

'The hospital said if all went well I'd be out the cast in six weeks, and it's been at least three so far. I reckon I'm half way.' For the first time that day Matt felt slightly sad. It suddenly struck him that he wasn't looking forward to starting his own apprenticeship at Hepplewhites.

'So I'll be seeing you all on a Monday late afternoon and any other time you want to come. My only stipulation is to bring some more mugs.' As an afterthought Ron added, 'Maybe some biscuits as well.'

CHAPTER 8

Nick gripped the edge of the passenger seat in the white Willows & Son van with the fancy green writing along its side. He knew he should relax. It would make the journey easier. He sighed. It had been relatively simple, cutting the windowsill to the correct size and shape in the workshop. At least he hoped it was correct. He hadn't taken the measurements himself; Dave had done that. He looked across at Dave who was driving the van, a crazed expression distorting his naturally mild face.

They were heading for Damson Valley Farm and Nick was dreading the visit. He closed his eyes and tried harder to relax, but this was proving difficult. How could Dave chat away so happily, one moment braking and the next, accelerating hard? The jolting was bearable but the corners were horrible. Je-e-e-z – if only the safety belt kept me from hitting the side door, Nick thought, as he swallowed hard on some breakfast that threatened to rise in his throat.

He struggled to concentrate on rehearsing the plan in his head. He had his mobile phone ready in his pocket and he'd already keyed in the number on the advertisement for the Porsche. He intended to secretly press the call key when Jan came to meet them. If Jan's mobile phone rang, well that would confirm it was Jan who was selling the expensive sports car. Nick could then just cancel the call. There would be no need to speak. It was foolproof.

Dave swung the van into the Damson Valley Farm entrance at thirty miles an hour. Nick guessed he'd planned to end the journey with a spectacular demonstration of the brakes, but as it turned out the emergency stop was for real.

They came face to face with a huge lorry as it backed up to one of the warehouse units to load fruit. Jan stood in the yard waving his arms, supervising just as Dave swerved sideways. Nick jerked forwards against his safety belt as the tyres locked onto the concrete. The so-called Green Widows had arrived.

Jan walked over to meet them. He held himself stiffly, with his shoulders pulled back as if on a parade ground.

'Good morning Mr Widows. As you see, we load fruits now. You know where to go?'

'Morning. I'm not Mr Willows. I'm Dave and this is Nick and we work for Mr WiLLows. Yes, we know where to go, thanks. Shouldn't take us long.'

Nick jumped out of the van and began unloading the tools and windowsill. Now's the moment, he thought and pressed the call button while Dave spoke to Jan.

Nothing happened for a few seconds and then the satellite connections beamed down his call and Jan's phone rang loud and clear. Yes, result, Nick thought triumphantly, as Jan reached to answer his phone and then frowned when the line went dead.

Nick turned away smiling and started walking with Dave in the direction of the accommodation huts. Yes, that was a simple trick, neatly executed. But he'd hardly taken more than a few paces when his own phone suddenly rang its strident jingle from his pocket.

He tried to smother it with his hand as his finger sought the off button. Damn, he'd forgotten to put withhold number or silent mode on his mobile and of course Jan had merely used callback. Now he had Nick's number and maybe he thought... but what did he think? That Nick was playing silly buggers with him?

He glanced back, his cheeks burning and caught sight of Jan, who stood still and stared at him, obviously puzzled. If he hadn't blushed perhaps Jan might have thought it was Dave's phone, but when Dave asked loudly, 'Aren't you going to answer that, Nick?' his guilt was obvious. He felt both stupid and frightened.

'It'll only be Mel. I'll get back to her later,' he lied, unable to stop himself from turning to check Jan heard. And that just made it worse. Now Jan would be really curious. He probably thinks I want him to call me back when no one's around, Nick thought. Christ! Now I'm really in deep. I get the feeling nobody messes with Jan, or for that matter Valko, and that's exactly what I've done. What do I do now? He surreptitiously checked his mobile was turned off and resisted the urge to fling it away into a pile of rotting fruit.

Nick tried to distract himself by thinking about the windowsill. If he'd cut the wood correctly, then it should be a quick job and they could be out of there and away before Jan could get to him. All they had to do was chisel out the old split and water damaged sill and prepare the area.

'Hopefully we'll be left in peace to get on with our work this time. Looks like they're too taken up with loading fruit to bother with us, thank God,' Dave remarked smiling.

Nick smiled back, nodding. Dave had guessed correctly and there was no sign of Valko as they stepped carefully into the accommodation hut. Nick was surprised to hear a pleasant female voice call a greeting.

'Hello I'm Denisa.'

Nick glanced around to locate the source of the voice.

'I'm not well so I stay back here, today. Everyone busy picking and packing fruit. I eat too many strawberries and now sick. But good, I'm glad you're here. I can talk and practise English. You know, while you work. I soon get lonely if no one here.' Denisa finally paused to take a breath.

She stood near the window and Nick gazed at her short red hair. The sunlight caught her from behind, and it made her look as if she had smouldering embers above her round pleasant face. He was struck by a wicked thought. He might have finally met someone who could out-talk Dave. No doubt she was a hot contender for the greatest-number-of-words-spoken-on-a single-breath record.

'So, Denisa, how long have you been a fruit picker at Damson Valley Farm?' Nick felt he needed to say something as she gazed at him expectantly. If the truth were known, she was rather pretty and starting to make him feel slightly self-conscious.

She flashed a smile at tubby, middle-aged Dave and Nick surprised himself with the urge to get those hazel eyes to turn the spotlight back on him.

All he had to do was say, 'Hi, I'm Nick, by the way,' and he had her full attention again.

'I come on work permit. I think grand name, Seasonal Agricultural Workers Scheme.' She stood up straight as she declared the official name and then giggled. 'I work six months as agricultural student and also learn English. Then I go home - Romania.'

'Do they treat you OK here?' Dave asked, getting a word in while Denisa drew another breath.

'You speak very good English already,' Nick added. He couldn't help it; he wanted to draw the girl's attention back to him and he was rewarded with a bright smile. Whoops, if he wasn't more subtle, Dave would soon be telling him to concentrate on his work and that wouldn't look very sexy – a ticking off in front of this hot Romanian.

'They are OK here. The rooms are clean. They pay us and we get plenty work. Better than many places. The Farrows are nice peoples, well not the strange one. The others are OK.'

'What about Valko and Jan?' Nick asked. It was hardly a chat-up line but he wanted to find out more. Now that he had her attention, he'd play it cool.

'Jan is manager. He very fair, always pays - no trouble. Valko not here much; goes away, comes back, never says much. If I had, what you say - fibreglass curves?' She smiled as she searched for her next word, 'Metallic body – he like me.' She illustrated her meaning by moving her hands down her sides, outlining some ridiculously curved figure, not her own. Then she shrieked with laughter and added, 'He has eye for cars only. The youngest one; now he the strange one.'

'You mean Phillip Farrow?'

'Maybe. The one with funny hair.' She touched her face. 'What you say?'

'A beard?' Nick asked.

'Yes, beard. Name is Mohammed or Mahmoud or something. Very quiet, doesn't speak. Goes to college. I think Jan say car studies or something.'

'You probably mean Car Maintenance; there's a course at Utterly Academy. I don't remember seeing anyone quite like that though.' Nick smiled at her and was rewarded with another flash of her small, pearly white teeth.

'So where does all the fruit go?' Dave asked.

'Well, many places; depends on fruit. Today strawberries and for local shops, but sometimes there is big truck, I think is called a container. Valko drives to Harwich then Europe. I like farmers markets best. We go if we like. Less pay but meet English people and speak English. Is fun. Maybe you come to farmers market Saturday? Needham Market. I meet you there?' She looked at Nick, tilting her chin so that she looked up at him through her eyelashes, Diana style.

'Why would you want to take strawberries to Europe? They grow plenty of their own surely?' Nick asked, side-stepping Denisa's invitation while he decided how to respond.

'Not just strawberries, all fruits: apples, pears. There are many markets in Europe. Valko organises Bulgarian friends. He drives; is big money I think. Everyone very happy. Is Saturday good?'

'You think you'll be feeling OK by then?' Nick asked. He was starting to find her directness amusing.

'C'mon, Nick. Time to get to work.' Dave had reached tolerance level with Nick's flirting, so Nick left Dave chatting to Denisa while he concentrated on the windowsill. It was time to get the job done and get away before Jan came to look for him. But she had been surprisingly fun and where was the risk in seeing her on Saturday? She'd said she was only around for six months.

'Why's she got a boy's name?' Dave asked forty minutes later as they walked back to the van. The new sill had fitted perfectly and Nick was feeling proud of his handiwork.

'What d'you mean, a boy's name?'

'Well she's called Dennis. That's a boy's name isn't it?'

'No, it's Denisa. You know - its Eastern European, a girl's name.'

'Denisa; Dennis... isn't that the name on the front of fire engines, Nick?'

They both laughed and a mental image of a huge red fire appliance with Denisa's smiling mouth replacing the radiator grill, and her flashing hazel eyes where the lamps should be, leapt into his mind.

'Well whatever. An attractive girl though.' Dave looked sideways at Nick fleetingly before continuing, 'Let's get going before that creepy Jan appears. You know I've always fancied having a go at driving one of those fire engines: bell ringing; jumping red lights; wrong side of the road; real emergencies - and the uniform.'

'You might have to maintain radio silence. Had you thought of that?' Nick said as he climbed up into the van. All this talk was starting to make him feel nervous for the homeward journey. 'We've got an unmanned level crossing on our way back, so remember we're not in a Dennis, Dave.'

The journey back to the Willows workshop seemed to pass even more rapidly than the outward ride to the fruit farm. In fact each journey in the van with Dave seemed to become faster and faster. Nick wondered if Dave really was driving more recklessly or if he had just become increasingly sensitised to the white-knuckle roller coaster rides. He was starting to feel a little sick.

'You look a bit pale lad,' Dave observed, as he parked up at Willows & Son. 'Better get yourself off home.'

Nick ignored Dave's advice and went into the workshop to sit down quietly and recover. He rested his head in his hands. He felt on edge. Jan had freaked him out, and

Denisa had given him a bit too much to think about. He needed to compose his thoughts, maybe talk to Chrissie. She would knock some sense into him, tell him that Jan wasn't a sinister gang leader and Valko wasn't his murderous "enforcer" transporting God knows what to Europe. Cars definitely had something to do with it and whatever it was, he felt sure it wasn't legal. He just hoped to God that Jan wouldn't follow up on the phone call or come looking for him.

There was no point in going home until he'd sorted out the chaos in his mind. If he went now his parents would want to know too much about his day and he wasn't ready to tell. It was fine to be still living at home when you're on a pittance, but the convenience had a downside and sometimes it got on his nerves.

He made a decision. He phoned Chrissie and asked her to call by on her way home. He knew she wouldn't mind, after all she had said she wanted to see the Willows workshop. It was modern and well equipped; the opposite to the Clegg workshops.

Nick busied himself with sweeping up and tidying away while he waited for Chrissie. It was unusual for him to phone her during the day and predictably she had not asked any questions; but that of course was why he had phoned her. If he had wanted to be questioned he could simply have gone straight home. By the time she arrived he had swept up every last speck of wood shavings from the workshop floor and the activity had calmed him. He'd also switched off his mobile phone in case Jan tried to call. Making decisions helped him feel back in control.

'Why'd you switch off you mobile? You knew I've not been out here before and I get bloody lost.'

It wasn't quite the greeting he'd expected from Chrissie, but then he hadn't been thinking about anyone but himself after he'd phoned her. She looked flustered, with her short blonde hair in a riot.

'Sorry.' There really wasn't much else he could say.

'So the grand tour please,' Chrissie said as she slammed her car door shut on the seat belt buckle.

'Sorry. I'll explain about my phone later, but come on inside the workshop. Just about everyone's gone home now so you can have a good look around. Come on, I'll make a cup of tea.' Nick led Chrissie through the large warehouse-like building.

'Wow!'

'Yes, it's a bit different to the Clegg workshops. For a start, there's loads of light and space.'

Nick pointed out the dust extractors, hooked up to the planers and large bench saws. He'd always thought they looked like prehistoric creatures with huge trunks. He took her past every piece of motorised carpentry equipment that one could dream of.

'But just look at this, Chrissie,' he said, stopping to touch something that looked like a huge press. It was a brand new computerised unit that could cut just about anything to any shape or size. That is if one could key in the correct instructions, and only a few had mastered that particular skill. Nick laughed when Chrissie was lost for words.

'Come on, the kettle is in the office through this way.'

'Thank God, something low tech at last. A kettle.'

The office was partly a working office with a computer, fax, scanner and printer but also doubled up as an area to relax in.

'Sit down if you like,' he said waving his hand vaguely in the direction of some comfortable but rather worn chairs that partly blocked a view of the sink, kettle and large fridge.

'No thanks.'

It was all clean and tidy but had a well-used feel to it. There was a row of large filing cabinets against one wall. Nick sensed that Chrissie was more at home in the lived-in, tired office than the high-tech workshop. While he busied himself making a couple of mugs of tea she wandered over to the filing cabinets.

'Are these locked?'

'No, I don't think so. After all, when we go out on a job we may have to refer to the previous plans. The customers are always given a copy but they never seem to keep them. Old man Willows says it's best to keep your own copies. You'd think it would all be on computer, but some of these plans go back many years. Take today for example. The windowsill we replaced at Damson Valley Farm. The exact measurements should be on file with the original plans. We could've looked up the plans instead of measuring up on the job.'

'Bit risky though.'

Nick nodded and walked over to the filing cabinets. As he spoke he pulled at a draw. 'Do you think it would be filed under F for Farrow or D for Damson?' he asked.

'Well D is in this draw and F is in the next cabinet. So let's start here.'

They found what they were looking for under F for Farrow. Nick was surprised by the sheer number of scaled drawings showing different aspects of the fruit pickers' accommodation. There were small scale plans showing details for the timber construction for the floors, walls, roof and room partitions. He pulled out a separate diagram, drawn to large scale, focusing on smaller details such as the floor joist fixings. 'Who draws up all these plans?'

He picked out four scaled drawings that were on different paper, but despite turning the drawings in every direction, he couldn't see how they related to the accommodation huts. What was he looking at? It didn't make sense – a flat, almost square wooden structure, about seven and a half feet wide and eight, no… almost nine feet high.

'What have you got there?' Chrissie asked as she looked over his shoulder at the papers in his hand.

'I don't know. It doesn't make sense,' he repeated out loud.

Chrissie took three of the sheets of paper and looked at them closely. 'What's large, rectangular and flat? And that's not a cracker joke.'

Nick thought for a moment. 'I don't know. A cricket screen, you know to help the batsman see the ball better? A cricket-sight screen?'

'Aren't they usually slatted and on a stand with wheels? Anyway I didn't know there was a Green Widows cricket eleven.'

'There isn't. And there isn't a Farrows Fruit Picking eleven either.'

'Well let's look at what information we've got. There's JWj written here at the bottom of this one. Hmm… JWj. John Willows junior, maybe? And here – there's a VA over here. Almost rubbed out.' She pointed to the left-hand bottom corner. 'I'm sure as hell that VA doesn't stand for the Victoria & Albert Museum. What's the date on these?'

Nick looked closely at the plans. 'May 2009. John Willows junior was still alive then. JWj could be his initials.'

'What were the names of your vampires?'

Nick glanced at Chrissie, but he was relieved to see she was grinning. For a moment he'd thought she was being serious about vampires. 'Valko, Valko Asenov; VA that would fit. But why would JWj draw up separate plans for VA amongst the accommodation plans for Mr Farrow? This big flat rectangular thing was never part of the accommodation huts. Unless it's just some miss-filing.' Nick spoke his thoughts aloud.

'Do vampires play table tennis on outsized tables?' Chrissie was still in jokey mood.

'No and a table tennis table comes in two halves. Let's photocopy these four plans and put the originals back. This is starting to make me feel nervous again. Reminds me of what Denisa said today.'

Nick was secretly pleased when Chrissie shot him a questioning glance but he wasn't ready to elaborate yet. He allowed himself a coy smile as Chrissie maintained her questioning glance and added raised eyebrows to the effect.

'Well, you remember me saying I had to go over to Damson Valley Farm today?'

'You're blushing. I do believe you're blushing. Come on, let's sit down and I can drink my tea while you tell me.'

Nick pulled a face and slumped onto one of the worn chairs. An old cigarette burn had singed through the woven fabric revealing some foam padding beneath. He traced it with his finger. It summed up his feelings. The dark green weave of the material should have felt like a tough outer shell. But that was the problem. It felt slightly grubby and fatigued, tainted even. And there was a hole so it no longer contained and compressed the foam cushioning beneath.

It was as if Jan had burnt that hole when he'd called Nick's mobile that morning. And now Nick was exposed. If he didn't take care, he'd be as visible as if he was trying to hide inside a string vest.

He spoke slowly at first, but bit by bit he recounted his day at the fruit farm and tried to explain his growing suspicions. Finally he stopped speaking and waited for Chrissie to laugh and make some wisecrack about vampires again. But Chrissie had listened without interruption and there was a long silence while they both digested their own thoughts.

'Let me have a look at those scale drawings again, Nick,' she said, finally breaking the stillness. There was a long pause while she studied the plans.

'You said a huge lorry was loading fruit when you arrived. What are the dimensions of a container, you know the ones that go from Felixstowe and Harwich?'

Nick shrugged. He had no idea.

'It's possible isn't it? It could represent the drawings for a false partition in a container. You know a 40 foot container with a false end - say 20 feet down its length. Enough space for a sports car hidden behind. If the container is refrigerated, no one's going to poke around in there for long. It's too cold and uncomfortable. You could stack the fruit crates in front of the false end and conceal whatever you wanted behind.' She sat back in her chair and closed her eyes.

'You may be right Chrissie. This is really spooky. I thought you'd say I was being ridiculous about Damson Valley Farm. But now you're really frightening me. You're, well you're suggesting something really could be going on.

This may be evidence. For all we know this may have been why John Willows junior died.'

'I know, but it's not proof of anything, just highly suggestive. And that reminds me, you haven't shown me the nail gun yet. A visit to this workshop wouldn't be complete without having a look. You don't suppose it was used on the construction of a so-called false partition? I wonder... do you think nails are marked uniquely when they're fired? You know, like bullets from the barrel of a gun?'

'Now that really is a bit too fanciful, even for me.' Nick started to laugh.

'It's just a theory. We need to use our brains and decide whether to stay out of this or probe a bit. Would it be worthwhile meeting Denisa on Saturday at the Needham Market Farmers Market? Find out a bit more? You could even make some enquiries; pretend you're interested in buying a car. The problem is we have so few facts, just a very bad feeling and lots of suspicion. We've nothing we could take to the police. I mean no one nailed the plans to JWj's neck. It's all circumstantial; no proof.' Chrissie paused before continuing, 'We could always use Matt as a decoy if you're reluctant to get too involved with this Denisa character. I doubt he'd mind.'

Despite himself, Nick started to laugh at the thought. He wasn't going to say anything, but he rather relished the idea of renewing Denisa's acquaintance on any pretext.

'We're not detectives, surely there's a line we shouldn't cross?'

'Quite right, now lead on. Show me the nail gun.'

'There isn't much to see. Remember the police took it away after the accident - but come on, it's out in the workshop. This way, follow me.'

CHAPTER 9

Chrissie stood on the edge of the Doggett Brothers' timber yard, on the outskirts of Ipswich. Armed with a fading receipted order form, she surveyed the piles of wood that confronted her. It felt like a small city, with heaps of logs and neatly-planked wood in orderly stacks casting shadows like real buildings. She was looking for a twenty-five-foot-long section of tree trunk; western red cedar, to be precise. She wondered what colour the bark would be after all this time. Ten years, in fact – if the date on the receipt was to be believed. Blumfield had produced the documents for her, the paper trail that with luck should lead to the trunk's location.

She could have been forgiven for thinking it would be easy to find something so large. But the trunk had been forgotten for ten years and she doubted she'd be able to walk into the timber yard, simply gaze across a vista of dead wood and say, 'That's the one, over there.' And, ever the pessimist, she was right, of course.

'We only got the call from Utterly late Monday. It's been a bloody nightmare after all this time.' The foreman's gruff tones seemed to match the rough wood.

'You did find it though? It's still here, isn't it?'

'Yeah, yeah, yeah. Definitely here somewhere. We're working on it.'

'But you said on the phone you'd got it. The transport's arranged… everything.'

She'd arrived early. It was in her nature to be involved from the start. And as she watched, she worried. Without her presence the timber yard might call time on the search and give up too soon. As it turned out, even Time Team would have been proud of the hunt that eventually identified it behind piles of logs and timber. It reminded her of the daily hunt for her car keys - all the frustration and irritation of knowing she had thrown them down somewhere obvious; so obvious in fact that she could never find them. Likewise with the tree trunk - no doubt it had been obvious to the timber yard workers ten years ago. And as she watched, she resisted the compulsion to check she'd put her car keys, along with her camera, in the handbag now held close to her side.

She listened to the forklift's engine as it moved, somewhere out of view. Clunking sounds and hollow thuds carried through the air. She guessed pallets piled with wood were being shifted in the search. She heard shouting but couldn't make out the words, so she walked, following the direction of the noise. Passing behind an open structured barn, she peered at the saw milling line, headed with the cutting mechanism hidden in its protective metal casing. Stepping over sawdust and bark, she ventured beyond and into the suburbs of the sprawling wood city.

'Found it! Its back here,' someone yelled.

She could sense the surprise as well as the triumph as she hurried in the direction of the disembodied voice.

'Why's it under all that wood?' she asked, catching her breath as Sam, a young wiry woodyard worker, pointed out one end of the trunk.

'God knows, don't ask me. I've only been here a couple of years.'

She should have known better. Anxious questions always sounded accusatory and now wasn't the moment to antagonise anyone. Time to backtrack a little. 'Well done,' she said and beamed a smile, 'for finding it, I mean.'

Sam grinned back. 'It won't take long now.'

Chrissie watched as some neighbouring logs were cleared to allow a large-wheeled loader to manoeuvre with forks and a grapple. Taking the camera out of her handbag, she lined up some shots as the trunk started to move. And just at that moment an image of Matt leapt into her mind - struggling to scoop up a particularly fat chip with a blunt canteen fork. The difference being that Matt would have covered the plate in tomato sauce. Thank God, no red stuff here yet. But why should she suddenly think of Matt, and blood and accidents? Maybe it was all that talk of nail guns and necks? She shivered involuntarily. It was horrible to watch as some bark fell away like dead flesh. She had been right. After ten years in the timber yard, there was little evidence of the red colour that gave the tree its name.

'Watch that end!'

'You're ok now.'

'Shit – slowly now.'

Chrissie listened and watched as the foreman and Sam shouted across the trunk and above the engine noise. Eventually the lifting mechanism engaged, and for a moment Chrissie held her breath as the trunk settled and balanced. It looked huge. How was she going to transform this into a totem pole? Anxiety, then mild panic, churned in her stomach. Ten years. She could see why brandy left for that length of time was described as mature, but wood as seasoned. Perhaps weathered would have been more apt.

Chrissie instinctively stepped back and took more pictures. Mr Blumfield was the one who had suggested it might be fun to photograph the process of constructing the totem pole and make a poster illustrating the whole project, from start to finish. Chrissie wasn't too sure about the finish so she was concentrating her visual record on the "birth" of the totem pole, as it were. And so far there had been plenty of shots, though what old Blumfield would think of them, well best not worry about him.

Chrissie moved to get the transporter into her photo. It was articulated with a small hydraulic crane mechanism at the driver's cab end for loading and unloading. She couldn't imagine how Donald, the middle-aged driver, would get the transporter into the Clegg courtyard, or how they were going to get the trunk under cover, once there. Her thoughts were interrupted by Donald as he asked if she would be leading the way to the Clegg workshops.

'You must be joking; not unless you want to get totally lost.' And then she coloured up as she realised she must sound a complete fool. No bloke would have admitted to being so useless at finding the way, even if rendered completely blind. 'I was hoping to follow you back onto the A14 from here.' At least that made it sound as if she knew the way once she was on the A14. Her husband Bill had always said she had a good sense of misdirection, and he was trying to be kind.

'I expect you'd take us under that low railway bridge at Needham Market.'

Chrissie grinned and nodded. 'Smile boys!' she said as she hid behind her camera and took another photo. She had never considered low bridges before. When you are small and drive a low slung MG, you don't need to worry about height weight or width restrictions; at least not while driving. A transporter with a small crane was an altogether different proposition.

'Best avoid that bridge. We'll leave the A14 at the junction before and go through Great Blakenham,' Donald said over his shoulder as he stepped up into the cab.

'The satnav'll tell us.' Sam looked at Chrissie and grinned before adding, 'You follow us then, ok?'

Chrissie got into her red MGB. It started first turn of the ignition key and she revved the engine hard for effect. It was time to save face with Sam and Donald. She expected the transporter to move slowly, maybe at a sedate 30 miles per hour. But if she'd thought about it for a moment, then she'd have remembered it was empty - apart from the twenty-five-foot tree trunk. She heard the hiss as Donald released the air brakes and then the transporter literally took off, the powerful diesel engine hardly noticing the load. They just went, waiting for no one, taking no prisoners. Chrissie had to drive hard to keep up on the A14, but when they turned off the dual carriageway onto the smaller roads, she started to relax. All ideas of taking photos on route went clean out the window.

She switched on the radio. It was still tuned to Heart FM, a local station. She liked to alternate between that and Radio Suffolk. *Long delays on the A14 between junctions 49 and 50*, the melodic voice announced. Where's junction 49, she wondered and as if on cue the traffic update continued, *an accident has blocked the southbound carriageway beyond the Haughley / Stowmarket turning. There are reports of traffic building up and heavy congestion in Stowmarket and the surrounding area as drivers try to find a way past the jam. Longstanding road works on the junction 50 slip road and roundabout have also added to the problem.* Thank God I'm off the motorway, she thought. And as she drove on, she remembered she had in fact travelled northwards on the A14 from Ipswich and was now moving in the opposite direction to the re-routing traffic.

Chrissie turned off the radio and tried to concentrate on following Sam and Donald. Hedgerows and farm buildings sped past as the engine hummed and the old suspension swayed. It started to make her feel lethargic. She didn't remember having problems keeping focused when Bill was alive, but since his death, despite her best efforts, she had trouble corralling her thoughts and emotions. And now, she told herself, was not the time to think about the plans she'd seen in the Willows office. She was supposed to be concentrating on the road ahead. Dropping down a gear to take a sharp blind bend, she decided now was definitely not the time. But what had John junior got mixed up in? Chrissie shook her head and then smiled – there, her mind was wandering off again. If she had been leading the way with the transporter following her, then she couldn't have allowed her mind to ramble along its own path.

Chrissie braked gently. She watched in a dreamy state as the transporter carrying the trunk paused at a T-junction ahead, before turning slowly onto the Wattisham perimeter lane. Not far now, she thought as the tail of the transporter followed the driver's cab out of the junction. Suddenly a metallic squeal ripped through the air. Instinctively, she slammed her foot down hard on the brake pedal, lurching to a halt well short of the junction.

'Oh my God!' she shrieked as a container lorry hurtled into view along the perimeter lane, appearing as if from nowhere and closing on the tail of the transporter ahead. She was safe in her stationery position at the T-junction, but what about Donald, what could he do? She watched, transfixed as Donald continued to accelerate. He was already committed to turning onto the lane and into the path of the speeding lorry. She cringed, tensing for the inevitable explosive thud. And when it came it was sickening. Metal scrapped against metal as the container lorry struck the rear side of the transporter, carrying it forwards in its path. The driver braked hard, but it took a greater distance than the lorry's own length before it skidded, wheels locked, to a standstill. There was an ominous groaning of metal as the container slowly tipped sideways into the ditch. Finally there was silence.

It took a moment for Chrissie to take it all in. She could hardly believe what she'd just seen and heard. This was real; this had actually happened right in front of her and it was horrible. She switched off the engine and got out of the MG. Years of habit meant that she automatically reached for her handbag before running along the lane to where the wreckage had finally slewed to a halt, half on the road and part in the ditch. Nothing could have prepared her for the carnage that met her eyes. The lane was littered with debris. She picked her way carefully over the broken glass. Radiator fluid and tyre marks covered the tarmac. It looked as if the two lorries were locked in the death throes of some awful mortal combat.

'Oh my God! What do I do?' she wailed. Should she rush to the closest lorry cab, or phone 999? A sickening realisation struck; she was the first and only person at the scene of a horrific accident - well, the only person who might still be uninjured. She tried to block out her emotions, just to see but not feel, to think and be coldly logical.

'Christ Almighty,' Donald groaned as he stepped out of the transporter cab and surveyed the scene.

'Oh thank God you're alive.' Chrissie's relief was almost palpable and her fingers sprang into action. She rummaged through her handbag for her mobile phone.

'There's been an accident on the Wattisham Airfield perimeter road.... My name? Chrissie Jax.... Yes, I'm phoning from my mobile. I was driving behind.... Just two lorries involved.... Yes, a collision. One lorry is in the ditch.... Yes, there are people injured.... I don't know how many but I can see blood on the windscreen of one of the lorries.'

'Do women ever stop talking?' Donald muttered as he limped to the container lorry and stared at the driver's cab, half on its side.

Chrissie forced herself to look away from the blood covering the inside of the windscreen. Thank God I can't see into the cab from here, she thought. It's a warning. No one can have bled like that and survived. She stood for a moment, rooted to the spot, not daring to hope. Suddenly the passenger door sprang open and a stocky man with swarthy skin and dark features leapt out onto the tarmac. He wore a leather jacket despite the summer sunshine.

'Aah!' Chrissie screamed, almost choking with shock and emotion.

'Hey!' Donald shouted, 'Are you ok?'

The man ignored Donald. In fact he kept his back towards Donald and gazed at the container lying on its side, half in the ditch. As he stared, the cab door swung closed with a solid clunk and the noise seemed to startle him. He turned and Chrissie caught a better view of his face. His eyes were cold, his face expressionless. She watched as he appraised the situation, but then when he looked directly at her, she recoiled. His dark brown eyes seemed to bore deep in a calculating way. For a fleeting second, she felt chilled as she sensed his unspoken threat. Chrissie gripped her handbag close, for the moment speechless.

Donald started to limp towards him. 'Hey….'

Chrissie watched, transfixed, as the man started to reach for something inside his leather jacket, but then he hesitated. He seemed to make a decision and let his arm drop back by his side. He started to run. Chrissie couldn't believe what was happening. It was surreal. She turned and watched as he sprinted back up the lane.

'What the hell? Hey stop, you don't need to run away. Hey stop!' Donald shouted at the running figure.

'What was all that about?' Chrissie asked, finally finding her voice as he darted out of sight.

'I don't know, but if he can run like that he must be OK. Scared as hell, most like.'

A sudden sound cut through the air. A throaty engine misfired, stalled and died.

'That's my car,' she shrieked. 'He's trying to start my car.'

The starter motor rang out again and she knew she had to move fast. Ignoring the glass and radiator fluid on the tarmac, she ran up the lane, cursing herself for having left her car keys in the ignition. She reached the turning at the T-junction just as the engine finally caught and leapt into life. Chrissie stood panting and faced her MG as she shouted, 'Hey stop! That's my car.'

The man smiled and with a grinding crunch engaged first gear. The car started to advance slowly towards her.

'What the hell…?' She had no choice but to step aside. White rage coursed through her as the wing mirror clipped her handbag, knocking it out of her sweaty grasp and onto the ground. Instinctively she ducked, gasping as she tried to retrieve it, the contents spilling out under the tyres. She managed to pluck the camera from the path of the Pirelli tread and stood back. The MG kept moving as the driver turned onto the perimeter lane and steered the car away, in the opposite direction from the crash. She held up her hand and still gripping the camera yelled, 'Hey - stop!'

The man glanced over his shoulder and showed his teeth. Chrissie couldn't tell whether it was a snarl or a smile, but by then her camera was switched on. Snap! She'd got him. It had taken him less than thirty seconds to steal her car.

'Did you see that Donald?' she shouted as she made her way back to the wreckage. 'He stole my car!'

'He won't get far.'

Chrissie was about to say more, but Donald cut in, 'There's something very bad in here.' He had turned his attention back to the driver's cab. 'This door's jammed.'

'But where's Sam? Is Sam OK?' Chrissie asked. In all the commotion she hadn't seen him. But then, just like in the movies, he appeared, dazed - walking from the wreckage.

'I... I needed to.... I needed to... sit and... calm down,' Sam whispered. 'Is anyone...? Are you OK?'

No one answered because Donald had finally wrenched the driver's cab door open. Sometimes listening to silence is more frightening than hearing words, and when Donald said nothing but just kept looking, Chrissie's stomach flipped. She didn't want to know what a crushed body looked like. She expected Donald to cry out in horror or speak to the driver, but when he was tongue-tied, bilious nausea rose in her throat.

'The driver... is he... alive?' Sam asked, paler than limewash as he climbed up to look in through the door.

Chrissie wasn't far behind, although her short legs made it difficult to climb up and peer into the cab.

'What the hell?' Donald finally hissed through his teeth.

'Sh-i-t. There's blood... covering the windscreen.' Any remaining colour drained from Sam's face.

'I don't....' Chrissie elbowed her way past Sam for a better view. 'Good God, I can smell strawberries. That's not blood it's strawberries. Look - a punnet of strawberries must have... been flung. The force of the collision must have done that.' Chrissie wrinkled her nose before adding, 'Christ, it smells like the Body Shop in here.'

'There's no... body. It's empty.'

'So the driver...?' Sam asked.

'He must've been the chap who jumped out the passenger door and then ran up the lane.' Donald climbed down from the cab. 'I thought I'd killed someone. I really thought... someone's dead in this cab. Thank God he's OK.' And he sat down and cradled his head in his hands.

'But he stole my car.'

In the distance Chrissie heard the sirens as the emergency vehicles approached. A police car with flashing lights screeched to a halt at the junction of the perimeter lane and the road where Chrissie had left the MGB. She watched, feeling strangely light headed as a young policeman got out of the car and walked towards them, putting on his cap as he stepped over some broken glass. She waited for him to speak, but his voice was drowned by an ambulance as it arrived - the driver ignoring the police car with

136

its flashing hazard lights, and squeezing past to get closer to its quarry.

For a moment Chrissie felt as if she was welcoming aid workers to the site of some natural disaster; her natural disaster. She almost felt like the hostess at a macabre social function showing the visitors the accident scene, explaining where everything was, how it had happened. Drinks anyone? Sorry, radiator fluid over here, and canapés? Sorry, broken glass over there.

Chrissie felt strangely dissociated, as if she was somewhere outside her body and observing from a distance. Donald had gone very quiet; perhaps it was the shock. Sam seemed to slowly find his voice and eventually answered some questions while the ambulance crew swarmed over the two trucks. She supposed they were looking for an injured body and, when they found nothing, she watched them search for a dead one in the ditch.

'I don't believe it; they're looking for a body. They probably think we've hidden the driver and we're lying. For trained ambulance crew, you'd think they'd know the difference between blood and strawberries.' Chrissie was starting to get irritated.

'Disappointed there's no one to cart off in that ambulance of theirs,' Donald replied.

'Oh my God, I've just remembered the cedar. Is it OK?'

'Well let's have a look,' Donald suggested and limped to the transporter. They both peered over its damaged metal rail. Chrissie couldn't believe her eyes. The trunk was still snuggly tethered and secure on one side of the transporter, the side furthest from the full impact of the container lorry.

'That's amazing But are you sure you're OK, Donald? You still seem to be limping.' They turned as a policeman came to speak to Chrissie again.

'You say you got a good view of the driver, Mrs Jax. Could you describe him for us?'

'Well I assume he was the driver. There didn't seem to be anyone else in the cab. But I can do better than that. I took a photo as he stole my MGB. Here, have a look.'

She proceeded to scroll back through the pictures on her digital camera. To be honest, she was rather disappointed when she found the shot. It was very blurry and there was a lot of movement artefact – the car had been accelerating away at the time. She had snapped, one finger partially across the lens, just as the man threw his snarling smile at her and then turned away. Only half a face had been captured and only one eye. Even that was half obscured by a hooded lid, blinking against the sunlight.

'What was he doing driving a great container lorry like that down this narrow lane anyway?' she asked as she handed over the camera. 'He was going really fast. He must have been speeding.'

'Probably came off the A14 to get round that traffic jam.' The policeman frowned as he peered at the camera's small screen. 'So no one else saw his face? I'm not sure how useful this is going to be, but thank you, Mrs Jax. We may need to keep this as evidence.' Still holding the camera he added, 'He shouldn't have run from the scene of an accident.'

'No, and he shouldn't have stolen my car. Do you need the whole camera for just one photo? Can't I just print it off for you or download it onto a memory stick?'

'Well to be honest, I can't really make his face out on this. Your description of the man will probably be sufficient.' He handed back the camera. 'I'm sorry, Mrs Jax, it's a lousy picture. But don't delete it, we may still want it.'

She didn't know how to react. The implied put-down of her photographic skills was quite frankly insulting, but at least she still had her camera. Why couldn't he have said something like, *how resourceful you are, Mrs Jax; shame your finger was across the lens.*

'So, how did he get the car keys?' The policeman's question jolted Chrissie back to the present.

'I left them in the ignition.' She turned away as she made the humiliating confession. She didn't want the policeman to see her misery and for a moment she watched, moist eyed as an ambulance reversed back up the lane. At least it's got a prize, she thought; now it can leave the party, still festive with its flashing lights. The paramedics had finally persuaded Donald to accept a lift to the A & E department.

'What make of car did you say, Mrs Jax?' The policeman got out his notebook and sighed. She blew her nose while he took down the details. 'You think you left the keys in the ignition,' he repeated slowly, shaking his head. 'It shouldn't be difficult to spot a red MGB – can't be too many around. We can put out an alert straight away.'

'But why would he take it?' Chrissie moaned.

'Wanted to get away, I reckon. He really didn't want to be identified did he? I wonder what else he's done. We'll give you a lift back to the station when we've finished up here.'

It took another few hours before the perimeter lane was cleared. All the while helicopters from the airbase hovered in the sky above, keeping a noisy watch on the proceedings. Chrissie took more photos and a huge tractor with some heavy lifting gear arrived to haul the container out of the ditch. The towing vehicles were as massive as the wreckage they pulled away, and by the end, the lane looked as if a small bomb had exploded. Earth and tyre marks were everywhere; the grass verge was torn and scared.

'C'mon, we can go now. Maybe a cup of tea back at the station'll make you feel better?'

Chrissie sat in the back of the police car and thought, *as if.*

CHAPTER 10

Matt stared down at his tee-shirt. When he'd glanced at his reflection in the mirror earlier that morning, he'd thought he looked pretty much OK. Well more than OK - cool, certainly for Stowmarket. He'd found the tee-shirt in a charity shop, and the one positive thing he could say about Stowmarket was it had plenty of charity shops. The fit was snug and when he'd held it up to check the size, the girl in the shop said it would make him look slimmer. But slimmer than what? Hmm.... He'd been immediately attracted to the design on the front. The symmetry pleased him. It said *FaLL* but the *L*s had been reversed and stacked so they looked like an upside down F, at least at first glance. Whichever way he read it, from above or straight on, it appeared the same. Clever. He liked that. But there was a downside. He'd discovered the Fall was a late 70s band and Tom hadn't liked them. So, maybe not so cool. At least Rosie couldn't mistake the design as saying *F*ck*.

There was a limit to how long Matt could admire his tee-shirt before his thoughts returned to Nick's phone call. It had woken him only a few hours earlier. He had been at home in bed at the time, cocooned in his duvet and somewhere half between sleep and hunger, the pangs not yet sharp enough to force him up and into the day.

'Wotcha, mate!' Nick had said, and when Matt merely groaned, he had continued, 'Aren't you up yet, you lazy git?'

Matt had grunted and nearly dropped his mobile as he turned to lie on his back. 'Bloody apprentice,' he finally managed to mutter.

'Look, you lazy bastard, some of us are already at work. Now get off your bloody backside and find something out for me.'

And so Nick had burst into Matt's day and Matt had been secretly thrilled. Someone needed him, or perhaps just his computer skills, but either way he was the contact, the mole at the Academy who could check out the Car Maintenance course and track down a Mohamed – or maybe a Mahmoud. If Phillip Farrow had a doppelganger, well now Matt had something to work on. Nick had given him a name, in fact two possible names. And while Nick described Chrissie's search of the Willows office, his mind started to buzz with excitement. This was starting to turn into something meaty. Thank God, Chrissie didn't ask me to come to the timber yard when she collected the tree trunk this morning, he thought. She'd probably be there for hours and he had more important things to attend to; a morning spent in the library warranted dressing with care, and the right tee-shirt might finally persuade Rosie that he was a thinking girl's bit-of-all-right.

Nick had said something about a Denisa and the farmers market on Saturday. So, if things with Rosie didn't turn out too well, there was always the possibility that Denisa, who Nick had described as a red-headed fruit picker from Romania, might be a backup bird to consider. Yes, things were looking up. Life was OK and he had tomorrow to look forward to when he'd meet up with Nick and Chrissie at the Nags Head.

Where to begin? He settled into his customary place in the corner of the library, well away from prying eyes, and scanned the room for Rosie. But as usual, she was nowhere to be seen. He hoped she'd appear from behind some bookcase, and disappointed, he logged onto the Academy site. The Car Maintenance course seemed the obvious place to start, but there wasn't a list of the students on the course, so he tried Pastoral Care and Student Activities - the clubs and societies. He thought it was unlikely that Mahmoud or Mohamed would have joined the Utterly Free Church or Anglicans in East Anglia, but the Utterly Young Muslim Association, now that was a stronger possibility. He waited for the page to load. And there it was, as clear as day:

The Utterly Young Muslim Association
President: Mohamed Zahir. Department: Business Studies (2nd year).
Membership Secretary: Mahmoud Aseed. Department: Car Maintenance.
Contact: Meeting Room: 259B, main block.

'But that don't mean this Mahmoud is the Phillip aka Aphid aka Mahmoud, Mahmoud,' Matt sighed and then smiled, despite himself. Too many Mahmouds. If this was Phillip, then the address would be Damson Valley Farm, but how to find out where he lived? Matt couldn't remember ever writing an address in his life. The application for Utterly came with a ready printed envelope. No, Matt had lived his life so far without ever sending a card or message via the postal service. He had no need for addresses. He was an extra-mail-estrial. Perhaps it was time to type *how to find an address from a name,* into Google.

He chose 192.com and clicked on the people finder option. But what's this, he thought as a warning popped up on his screen. 'A fee? You must be bloody jokin'?' he hissed under his breath. Since when had he been searching for *premium* information? He read on. The terms and conditions said plainly that there would be a fee for names found using the current electoral role. Bugger, he thought, I'm not paying good money for that.

It was time to use his brain. If Phillip had only recently changed his name, then it followed that his new name was unlikely to be on the current electoral role. And anyway, who would have registered his new name while detained at Her Majesty's pleasure in Norwich prison? He'd been there, after all, till a few months ago. Matt shook his head. Whichever search site he used he'd meet a dead end.

But why had he changed his name in the first place? Matt couldn't imagine. If he went into prison as Phillip Farrow and came out as a Mahmoud… well, either he'd been given a new identity, or he'd discovered religion. And his choice of name suggested it was unlikely to be the Roman Catholic Church. Matt typed *radicalisation & Muslim* in Google search, and waited.

'How's your wrist?' The voice came from nowhere.

'Ahha…. Ah! Hi!' Matt swallowed his surprise and gasped a greeting.

'Sorry, didn't mean to startle you.'

'No, no you… I mean I was….' Matt felt his cheeks burn as he tried to cover his confusion. Where had she popped up from? It was that librarian's old trick of appearing out of nowhere; the one where they had a licence to apparate, Harry Potter style. He dropped his gaze to check out how she moved so silently. Was she hovering, or on rollers like a Dalek? 'Hi… hi, Rosie.'

'So how's your wrist?' And not waiting for a reply she looked past him to the computer screen.

'OK, I'm OK.' It was obvious she wasn't listening. He turned to see what she found so absorbing.

'Richard Read,' she said looking at the screen. 'Wasn't he the shoe bomber? Oh yes…. It says something about petty crime… converted to an extreme form of Islam while serving a sentence.'

'Yeah, well… I was just lookin' up–'

'Radicalisation & Muslim,' she interrupted, 'That's what it says in the top search box.' She paused, letting her eyes rest for the first time on his tee-shirt.

'Yeah, they were big in the 70s,' he said, looking down at the logo on his chest. Great, he'd known the tee-shirt would be a winner. He was still in with a chance. Now, if he could just pull off one of his cool half smiles then maybe Rosie….

'What? People like Richard Read in the 70s? Too long ago. It's a more modern problem. Well, feeling isolated, disconnected… that's not modern.'

'Punk, it were called punk in the 70s.' He tried a cheeky half leer, part grin.

'Are you all right? Have you got something in your eye?

'No, no. I was just smilin'.'

'Oh,' and she turned away.

He watched confused, as she walked away, back to the librarian's station. Bugger, now why had she gone off like that, he wondered. He'd demonstrated his deep understanding of music, so what could possibly be wrong with that? He'd shown he was a thinking man – but those legs, they were definitely top crumpet category. Maybe she was playing hard to get? He practised his sexy smile again, before turning his attention back to the computer. What had Rosie said? Isolated, disconnected. He read on.

By the time Matt finished reading, he had a much better understanding of what might have happened to Phillip. Firstly, he asked himself, had Phillip felt isolated, maybe depressed? More than likely was the answer; he was in prison after all, not a place renowned for high self-esteem and laughter. And he was a captive audience - that went without saying. But had he been a vulnerable target? Well probably, Matt guessed. He had more than likely been bored out of his mind, so the Friday prayer meetings might have seemed like a good place to pass the time. Discovering a religion could have given a new meaning and purpose to his life. Trouble is, what had they been preaching at the prayer meetings? Extreme and violent ideas wouldn't have seemed out of place to Phillip, he was, after all, in a prison setting. Matt reckoned that all he needed was to have come up against one Islamist with extreme views intent on creating a jihadist fanatic, and bingo – radicalisation and an amateur home-grown terrorist ready for release back into the community. Shite, Matt thought, the community could be Utterly Academy. 'Shite,' Matt muttered, looking at the plaster cast on his wrist.

He closed his eyes. But I've felt alone, disillusioned and isolated, and nobody targeted me, he thought. Well, not unless he counted the Jehovah's Witnesses. Mind you, they only came knocking on the front door on the off-chance someone might listen. They didn't know he was there and vulnerable. But then Tumble Weed Drive was a tough area for canvasing, and true to form his mother had sent them packing. Would prison be less hostile? He doubted it. But what about Phillip? He had two older brothers and a huge, family fruit-growing business waiting for him, plus of course a father.

Matt groaned. The lucky bastard still had a father. Matt liked the idea of a dad. His walked out when he was only five years old. At first he hadn't noticed he'd gone because his dad never spent much time at home. But as Matt got older, well there was a gap and his mum filled it with coldness. Sometimes Matt thought she actually tried to be as emotionally remote as his absent father, to punish him. But for what? His dad walking out? He shook his head. Matt didn't even know what his father had done or where he was now, and it certainly wasn't worth risking more of his mother's resentment to find out. No, on the face of it, Phillip had been no more alone and isolated than he had been, and he hadn't been targeted. If Phillip had indeed found religion while in prison, then it didn't automatically follow that he held extreme views. No, Matt thought, if Phillip was fanatical about anything, then it would be more likely to be cars than religion.

'Car Maintenance, that's where I'll find him,' Matt said under his breath, and then smiled slowly. If he timed it right, he might just manage a pit stop in the canteen. His personal preference in combustible fuels was vegetable oil, and the delivery system - chips. He was running close on empty and it was time to make a move. God, he thought, all this talk of cars. He logged off and stood up.

It didn't take Matt long to find the car workshop. He guessed it would be somewhere on the ground floor. It was just a question of asking the right student, the one he spotted near the main staircase with a design of interlocking tyre treads on his sweatshirt. And Matt was in luck; the morning session was just ending as he arrived. The students were packing away their tools. Perfect timing.

'Hi, d'you know where Mahmoud Aseed is?' Matt asked an open-faced, friendly, young student who was taking off his overalls. He waited while the lad glanced around the workshop. It felt more like a warehouse than a teaching space, with a concrete floor and large sliding garage doors at the far end.

'He must've gone. You've just missed him.'

'It's important. You sure?' Matt watched as the young student scanned the workshop again.

'Nope, not here,' he said shaking his head.

'Shite.'

'Well if you're quick, you might catch him.'

'I don't know....' Matt shook his head. He didn't do quick.

'You can't miss him. He's kind of medium height and got a goatee beard. We're back in here this afternoon. You could try again then. Mind you, he doesn't always turn up.'

'Shit.' Matt was running out of things to say. Shit was all he could think of.

The young student seemed to consider Matt. He looked him directly in the face before studying the concrete floor. 'If he's trying to flog you a car, check it's legal, you know - not stolen.' There was a long pause while he let his words sink in. 'No, I shouldn't 've said that, but check anyway.'

'Sh-i-t.' Matt hoped he'd put a wealth of meaning into the single word.

'Well it's just a feeling but I think he's got history. He let slip once about when he was "inside", so I guess.... And he knows more than old Horlock our tutor, about locks and car alarms. So....' He let his voice die away before adding, 'I'm not saying anything, mind. Can I give him a name?'

'Well yeah - Matt Finch, if 'e asks. And, thanks mate.'

Matt turned away, hiding his grin. God he was good. He'd managed to tease out the information by only saying shit. I'm a genius, he thought; a master of the word.

Automatically he headed for the canteen. What had the student said? A goatee beard? Now that's hideous, Matt thought, not something he'd want; a vile look, worse than dated. So when was the last time he'd seen any student with long sparse hair growth on the face? 'Of course, you grut lummox,' he said, stopping dead on the main stairs, 'The goatee in the student car park.' He shook his head just as someone swore at him from behind and the hard edges of a book dug into his back.

'What d'you stop like that for?'

Matt turned to look into the eyes of an angry young women with blonde hair pulled tightly back into a pony tail.

'Err... sorry,' and he felt his face redden. Why did birds always make him blush?

'Well watch where you're going.' She hurried past him up the stairs.

'Watch where I'm going?' She was the one who needed to do the watching, he thought. Wearily he resumed his climb. The sunlight glinted on the metal strips reinforcing the edge of each step, and he started to count, 'One, two, three....' He stopped again.

'Two hundred and fifty-nine,' he muttered. 'Of course Room 259B.'

Matt resolutely walked on past the canteen and up the narrower flight of stairs to the second floor. It was quieter up there and he made his way along a corridor, counting off the number on each door as he went. It didn't take him long. 259B was right at the end. The door was wide open. He hesitated, wondering if he dared go in.

'Hey, come in if you're coming and then shut the door. We need to get started.' A tall thin man stood facing Matt, a pair of glasses in one hand and a clip board in the other. Excited voices echoed around the room as a group of about ten students chatted and shuffled scripts. Some chairs had been arranged in a rough circle, the rest were stacked against one wall. There wasn't much furniture in the room, but Matt noticed the empty shoe rack near the door.

'Err - is this the Utterly Young Muslim meeting?' he asked.

The man with the clip board put on his glasses. He ignored Matt's question and said, 'We've only got another couple of weeks to go. Now come in, come in. We need to get down to business. So are you in charge of costumes? Stage set?'

Matt felt his cheeks burn. Instinctively he touched his tee-shirt. His plaster cast was starting to look worn and grubby and he wasn't sure if the guy was being serious or complimenting him on the logo on his chest. 'Yeah – thanks. No, I….'

'So, you weren't kidding? You really are looking for the Muslim meeting?'

'Yeah.' Matt nodded.

'You're not here for the Edinburgh Fringe production? The understudy read-through and final planning meeting?'

All eyes in the room were now on Matt. For a moment he felt like the proverbial rabbit caught in the spotlight.

'No,' he said and a hush settled on the troupe. He had the distinct feeling they were looking at him as if he'd suddenly turned into a pumpkin or turnip – just like the nursery tale when the clock chimes midnight. If this was what they meant by dying on stage, then he didn't want any part of it.

'No,' he repeated.

'It'll say in the book on the table in the corridor, but I think they use this room tomorrow lunchtime. Now come on everyone. We need to get started,' and the man with the clip board turned away.

Matt needed to make his exit. He should have known it was a stupid idea to come up to Room 259B without a plan, but then he'd acted on impulse, buoyed up by his earlier success in the car maintenance workshop. He retreated toward the door. As he glanced at the shoe rack, something caught his eye. A tatty brown envelope lay on its top shelf. The neatly typed address was crossed through and bold handwriting covered its face. The name Mahmoud Aseed seemed to leap off the paper. He didn't think; he just reacted. In one swift and uncharacteristically deft movement, he grasped the envelope. There, the deed was done. He tried to control his breathing and immediately flushed again, this time with guilt. He headed through the doorway. No one seemed to notice.

He stood in the relative safety of the corridor and read the crumpled envelope. *Phillip Farrow, Car Maintenance, Utterly Academy, Stowmarket.*

Someone had crossed out *Phillip Farrow* and written *Mahmoud Aseed* above in biro. A different hand had scrawled *not known* against the Car Maintenance address and penned in felt tip: *try Utterly Young Muslim Association, Room 259B*. The paper was tired and dog-eared; it had certainly done the rounds. It might not say Damson Valley Farm, but it was the next best thing in linking the two names. 'Yeah,' he hissed and punched the air.

Matt wanted to open it somewhere quiet and in private, and the middle of the corridor was hardly the place. He stuffed it quickly into his pocket. The excitement was exhilarating.

'I need food,' he said and headed for the canteen.

•••

Hi. Are you through for the day?

Nick's text broke into the boredom of Matt's afternoon. He still hadn't opened the brown envelope hidden in the depths of his pocket. Visiting Room 259B had taken longer than he'd thought and there had barely been time to bolt down some lunch before his tutorial – the planning section of the Communication & Planning module. For the last twenty minutes he'd lost the thread of the teaching and his mind was wandering. The text message pulled him back to the present with a jerk.

5 mins, Matt texted back. He slipped the mobile back into his pocket, but the plaster cast caught on the edge of the denim and his fingers couldn't quite reach the brown envelope. It was tantalisingly close but beyond his grasp and deep in his jeans. Damn; it would have to wait longer. Surely there wasn't any more the tutor could say about preparing an estimate? The session must be ending soon.

It was closer to ten minutes before Matt was free to contact Nick. 'Hi, it's Matt.' He was excited with too much to say to text; it warranted a call.

'Great, you're free. Look, Chrissie just phoned. She's really upset….' Nick let his words hang in the air.

Matt couldn't think what to say so he let the silence stretch out.

'You know the tree trunk was being transported to the Clegg workshops today?' Nick continued, 'Well, there's been an accident.'

'Shit.'

'And somehow Chrissie's car was stolen.'

'Bloody hell. She OK?'

'Didn't sound too good on the phone. She was calling from Bury Police Station.'

'What?'

'The police took her there to make a statement. I don't think she's been injured, thank God... well, other than her pride. I said I'd drive over and give her a lift home. Sounds like she'll need cheering up. Want to come too? There's room in my car. Are you still there?'

'I don't believe... you're kiddin' me, right?'

'No. Chrissie's in trouble - really. Look I'm driving past the Academy on my way to Bury, so if you want to come, I'll be there in ten minutes. See you outside the main entrance.'

'Yeah, OK; see you in ten.'

Matt made his way to the main entrance, all thoughts of envelopes and Mahmoud forgotten for the moment. What had Chrissie been doing, he wondered. He knew she could be absent minded; after all, she mislaid her car regularly in the student car park. But stolen? Was she absolutely sure she hadn't just left it somewhere? He sensed it would be more than his life's worth to suggest it, though.

It didn't take long before he spotted Nick pulling up in the Ford Fiesta, the one with the Brillo pad paint finish all down one side. 'So where're we headin'?' Matt asked as he opened the passenger door.

'Bury St Edmunds Police Station, Raingate Street. It should take about 25 minutes. Come on, get in.' Nick accelerated away before Matt had time to slam the car door shut. Nick drove in silence as he negotiated the exit from the Academy grounds. 'So, find anything out about Phillip Farrow?' he finally asked when he was clear of the Academy.

Matt thought for a moment. He needed to sort the facts into some kind of order. 'Yeah, I think I've nailed it. Phillip Farrow *is* Mahmoud Aseed. Or, you could say Mahmoud Aseed *was* Phillip Farrow.'

Nick negotiated a roundabout and joined the slip road onto the A14. 'Well go on, is there more?'

'Yeah; I found 'is name on the Utterly Young Muslim Association website. Said his contact was Car Maintenance... so I went an' asked.'

'Really? No kidding?'

'Yeah. Spoke to a bloke on the course. Said to watch out if I was buyin' a car from 'im.'

'But you can't drive.'

'Oh piss off. I was under cover weren't I? Anyway 'e described him as havin' a goatee. You know, wispy fuzz on 'is face. Well I saw a bloke like that lookin' at Chrissie's car a few weeks back. Didn't say at the time, but,' Matt paused to think, 'you don't think he could've...?'

'It's possible, I suppose.'

'Yeah, but the bloke said Phillip, sorry, Mahmoud was in the car workshop this mornin'. Said I'd just missed 'im. Difficult to be out thievin' at the same time, don't you think?'

'Hmm. But why did he change his name?'

'I reckon he got religion when he was banged up in Norwich slammer for nickin' cars.'

'Well, he must've known Jan and Valko from the fruit farm. I bet they were the ones who taught him to nick cars in the first place.'

'Yeah... reckon so. But you haven't told me 'bout Chrissie. What happened?'

Nick recounted Chrissie's call, but when he'd finished speaking, they fell into silence. By the time they reached Bury St Edmunds, they'd hit the afternoon rush hour. It was as if a madness had smitten Bury, one in which every driver fought to edge forwards just a few feet despite the crush. The roads were completely snarled up and traffic on the ring road was stationary.

'We'll never get there at this rate,' Matt moaned as they inched over a mini roundabout.

'I've got an idea.' Nick turned down a narrow side road into the centre of the town.

'Where's this take us?

'No idea, but at least it's moving this way.' Nick weaved through the network of old lanes before turning onto a busy road leading past the Abbey Gardens. They drove past the Cathedral and on towards Raingate Street.

Matt craned his neck to look back at the Cathedral's recently completed gothic tower glowing in the afternoon sun, but before he could say anything they were turning into the police station car park and it was time to go in and collect Chrissie. They found her sitting near a window in the waiting room studying her hands. Matt had expected her to be pleased to see them, but when Nick spoke she burst into tears, which didn't make sense to him at all.

'Hi, sorry we're late,' Nick repeated before adding, 'The traffic's been dreadful.'

'You OK?' Matt noticed her smudged mascara. It gave her a kind of wild Alice Cooper look. Tom would have thought it cool.

'Come on, let's get out of here,' she said, swallowing a sob as she wiped her nose on the back of her hand.

'Hmm... Bury's one big traffic jam at the moment. You look as if you could do with a drink. Come on let's find a pub while we're waiting for the roads to clear. I know - the Dog and Bone. They used to have loads of guest beers,' Nick said already heading for the door.

'Bloody should be some good beer round here. There's a brewery in the centre of town,' Matt added.

Within a few moments they were out in the warm, late afternoon air. They walked in silence. Nick didn't say anything and Matt thought it best to follow his lead. He knew it was difficult, this business of saying the right thing when a girl was upset. Least ways, that's what Tom had said once. They headed towards the ancient heart of the town, walking on the old paving stones of Crown Street and Angel Hill and passing the Cathedral.

'If you ever get a chance to go inside, look at the carving and panels in the newly completed tower. They used lasers and computers to work out the exact measurements. Old Alfred, my foreman, would've had a fit. And it's painted reds, greens and blues; oh yes, and gold.' Nick smiled. 'Really, Chrissie, if you ever get a chance....'

Matt waited for Chrissie to say something but she didn't seem to have heard. He was about to ask about the gold but Nick pulled a face and shook his head. Tom was right, birds were tricky. They walked on in silence past the cathedral.

'Come on, let's find that drink,' Chrissie said, and Nick pointed in the direction of the Dog and Bone.

The Dog and Bone had an external Edwardian brick façade, but once inside the bar, they sat beneath the more ancient oak beams from an earlier age. They had naturally headed to some well used chairs in a quiet corner and while Nick went to get some drinks, Matt searched for something to say that wasn't about the gold paint or could be deemed insensitive.

'Sounds like you've 'ad the worst day ever,' Matt said, breaking the silence.

'I've had worse, but on a scale of one to ten, I'd say it's up there with at least an eight.' Chrissie didn't seem inclined to say more and stared down at her small hands as she hugged her handbag close on her lap.

'Nick said what happened. That tree's got bad karma. I think it's beggin' to be floorboards, not a bleedin' totem pole. So how much damage?'

'Amazingly, it was the only thing not shaken up by the impact.'

'But old Blumfield don't need know that. You tell him it's smashed, needs scrappin',' Matt suggested and when Chrissie laughed he started to relax.

'Good, you're laughing,' Nick said as he arrived back with their drinks. 'Yours is a gin & tonic, Chrissie. I think this calls for more than the usual ginger beer. You're not driving, after all. So start at the beginning.'

Matt gulped at his pint while Chrissie related the events of the day, starting with the search for the red cedar trunk in the timber yard. No one interrupted. To be honest, Matt didn't dare.

'Did the police keep your camera?' Nick asked.

'Well no, they were more interested in my description of the thieving bastard who legged it. In fact they were rather rude about my photo. I know it's blurry, but still....'

'Have you got your camera with you?

Chrissie peered into the depths of her handbag and rummaged around with one hand, as if turning over stony soil ready for planting. The camera eventually rose to the surface, riding on the detritus she had collected during the day. 'Here it is.' She plucked out the camera, disentangling it from a shred of tissue. 'They're on here somewhere,' she said, scrolling through the photos. 'Here, have a look.'

Matt leant forward to peer at the camera. 'What's that?' he asked, pointing at something on its screen.

'My finger.'

'Your finger?'

'Can we enlarge this,' Nick asked as he looked at the blurry image.

Chrissie pressed at the dials. 'There, any better?'

'Hey just a minute, I've seen this man before. Christ, it's Valko. There's only half a face on this but he's got the same brown eyes, dark hair and swarthy skin. Yes, it's definitely him. There's no mistaking his... pity he's looking away from the camera. Even that one eye seems to be challenging you.' Nick stared at the screen as Chrissie frowned.

'Can I?' Matt moved the camera, trying to hold it at a better angle as he scrutinised the photo. 'I can't see much but your... you're sayin' that blob is Valko from Damson Valley Farm?'

'He's unmistakable. It's his eyes. And every time I've seen him he he's been wearing a leather jacket just like this,' Nick replied, tapping the screen.

'Are you sure it's Valko Asenov, your fruit farm man? Why would he be driving a container lorry near Wattisham Airfield? I know there was that hold up on the A14 but this is too much of a coincidence. It's almost as believable as… transporting Transylvanian soil for Dracula to sleep on, and then fleeing like a bat out of hell. Now come on, I mean honestly.'

Matt guessed Chrissie was back to her usual self. Why else would she make references to vampires? It was usually a good sign. He watched, fascinated, as she rummaged in her handbag again. Finally she pulled out some kind of leaflet.

'Look,' she said triumphantly, 'if you really think you can identify this man then we'd better get back to the police station. It says on here it closes at eight this evening.'

They left the Dog and Bone, retracing their steps back to the Raingate Police Station. Matt avoided stepping on any of the cracks between the paving stones, this time. The roads were quiet and the warm air was balmy with the scent of flowers as they passed the Abbey gardens. The duty sergeant politely took down Valko's name and the Damson Valley Farm address along with Nick's details. He promised to hand the information on to the investigating team and Detective Inspector Merry, in the morning. DI Merry? Now I've heard it all, Matt thought. After that there was nothing else for it but to either walk back for another drink or head home.

CHAPTER 11

Friday, the day after the crash, was difficult for everyone. Chrissie had gone to sleep soothed by gin & tonic, but woke in a panic. Thoughts whirled round in her head so fast she swore they actually buzzed. Her stomach felt raw and gripey and her radio alarm clock blasted out the seven o'clock news.

'What do I do?' she moaned, sitting up and hugging the duvet. 'I haven't phoned the insurance company yet. Oh God!' To be fair, the documents were in the glove compartment of her car and that was somewhere…. 'A hire car, I must arrange a hire car. But will the insurance cover one? Should I check with the police first and see if there's any news of my car before I phone the insurers? Oh God, what do I do?'

She turned the radio off. It wasn't helping. 'I don't even know where the bloody tree trunk is and I haven't told Blumfield what's happened yet… and Ron… he was expecting the trunk yesterday and nothing…. God, what a mess.' She threw the duvet to one side and shuffled slipperless to the head of the steep narrow, cottage stairs. Maybe a cup of strong tea would help? The timber yard would know where the trunk was, she reasoned, so that would be all right; but she mustn't forget to ask after Donald the driver when she spoke to them. God, that was another phone call.

And then it all came flooding back. She'd tried so hard to block it out - all the pain and misery after Bill died. It crashed down on her like a tidal wave. She stood at the sink, holding the kettle under the tap and sobbed. With Bill's death she'd had so many things to organise, so many people to keep informed and so many phone calls. It was a recurring nightmare. Something had been plucked away and just like the last time, she felt bereft. Her life was changed.

'Now get a grip, Chrissie Jax. It's only a car and a massive plank of wood this time,' she said as the kettle overflowed with water. 'Breathe slowly and think. Now what should I…? Of course.' She gazed through her kitchen window with streaming eyes and sniffed hard. This kitchen must have seen worse dramas than mine, she thought. Now just get a grip and pull yourself together.

'Yes, when in trouble make a list, eat some chocolate and phone a friend,' she muttered to herself. That was the winning formula, in any order but perhaps starting with the list. A cup of strong tea came high on the agenda, probably higher than the chocolate, but the bones of her action plan sounded good. She must cope; she would get through this. She would even multitask. She switched the kettle on.

Making a list made her problems look mundane. Seeing them written in her neat handwriting on the back of an old envelope that just happened to be conveniently on the kitchen table somehow restored her sense of proportion. After all, they were only words on paper. After deliberating between the police and the insurance company, she decided to phone Ron Clegg first. He was on her to-do list and almost counted as a friend. Two birds with one….

'Hello? It's Chrissie here,' she said trying to sound bright and capable.

'Ah Mrs Jax. Are you all right?'

'Y-yes, Mr Clegg. I'm really sorry, I should've phoned yesterday, but….' She'd rehearsed what she wanted to say before she made the call, but the words died in her mouth. She hadn't expected emotion to grip her throat, squeezing her breath into a choking sob. She thought she could hold herself firmly under control. So what had happened to all that resolve?

'It's a bad line, Mrs Jax. I can't quite catch what you're saying. Can you hear me?'

'Y-yes.' She inhaled another sob and then blew her nose.

'The line's breaking up but if you can hear me, there's some good news this end. The fella from Doggetts....'

'Donald? Sam?'

'Ah that's better, I can hear you now. Yes, Sam. It turned out the transporter wasn't too badly damaged. He persuaded the tow-truck, well he knew the driver as it turned out and asked him to tow the transporter past my workshop. The accident was only a few hundred yards from here and... well to cut it short; we have the cedar trunk.'

'Good heavens. That's great news. So they left the transporter with you as well?'

'No, no. They towed that away somewhere. Sam said something about your car disappearing, and the police took you back to the station. Is that right? Are you OK?'

'Yes, yes; I'm OK. But it's a long story Mr Clegg. I'm organising a hire car and I'll tell you all about it when I get over to the workshop. I'm afraid I'll be a bit late. I don't know when....'

'That's all right, Mrs Jax. It'll take as long as it takes.' There was a lengthy pause before he added, 'Sometimes it's best to keep busy.'

Chrissie smiled for the first time that morning as she ended the call.

•••

Nick hadn't slept well. The morning alarm woke him from his troubled dreams and for once he was pleased to get up and escape his imagination. He knew his mother would already be opening the fridge and reaching for the orange juice. Next, she would trim the fat off the bacon. Three slices - that was his ration. She liked to prepare breakfast for her menfolk: Nick, a Full English; his father, muesli and fruit. It was strange how she never ate any of it herself. This morning she seemed to be frying with particular hostility. He could hear the fat sizzling as he came down the open-plan staircase in the centre of the ultra-modern family house. He'd always felt it was a bit out of place in a small village like Barking Tye.

'Morning, Mum.'

'Morning dear,' she tossed over her shoulder as she worked at the frying pan, scooping up the bacon, turning it over, casting it back into the pan before pressing it down hard with the slice. The fat hissed and crackled. He could tell she was angry.

'You were late getting back last night. Woke us up.'

'Sorry, Mum. Remember I told you? I wasn't coming back for my tea. Had to go up to Bury to collect Chrissie from the police station. Remember I told you about her accident when I phoned? By the time I'd dropped her off in Woolpit and Matt back in Stowmarket, well it was late.'

'Hmm.'

'Look I'm sorry. If you want me to move out….' He'd played this winning card many times before.

'No, no. It's just that I worry about you.'

'Well I'm worried about Chrissie. She was really upset yesterday. When I dropped her off it struck me she's alone. I don't know but I think this Valko bloke – I've told you about him before – he might go there. I mean he's got her address and everything from the insurance papers in the car. Probably even the house keys as well. Knowing Chrissie, she'd have left them with her car keys.'

'Hmm.'

'Look its Friday today. Can I ask her to stay here over the weekend, till the police have sorted things out? Then she'll be safe with us.' He watched his mother's back straighten.

'This Chrissie; she's that blonde widow, yes? The middle-aged woman on your course?' Her voice was edgy and the words clipped.

'Err, yes.'

'Hmm. What about Mel? Wouldn't she…?'

'Don't be ridiculous, Mum. Anyway, Chrissie's just a friend, not an old bird looking for a toy boy. Relax.' He couldn't stop himself adding, 'She's a rich widow, mind.'

He ate his breakfast in silence. Perhaps it was best not to mention Denisa as the collateral proof he wasn't interested in Chrissie. The words frying pan and fire, along with out of and into, shot though his mind. He needed to leave for Willows as soon as possible. If he stayed any longer he'd still be in the kitchen when his father came down for his muesli and fruit, and then there would be even more questions. I wonder if Matt gets this kind of grief over breakfast, he thought. And that gave him a wicked idea.

'Actually Mum, I think it's Matt who's after Chrissie.' That should do it, he thought.

•••

Matt's morning started early, if you considered eight o'clock early, and Matt did. His night had been restless, spent sifting through the events of the previous day, or what

164

he now thought of as the day of the crash. He couldn't get the image of Mahmoud out of his mind. Why had he been looking so intently at Chrissie's car that time in the car park? And then it was Valko who stole the car. But why? Whichever way he asked himself the question, there was no satisfactory answer unless you believed in coincidence, and Matt had never understood coincidence. He certainly didn't believe in it. What was it anyway? Tom had once said it was just chance, a fluke, a twist of fate even; but that was all crap. There had to be a logical explanation, surely? The pieces of the jigsaw just wouldn't fit together, however hard he pushed. What was it he kept missing? He scratched his head and tried to formulate a plan.

If the time on his mobile phone was to be believed, he still had two hours before his morning lecture. He sat up and peered at it again. Yes, it definitely said 8:03 and no plan was complete without food. First he needed breakfast. He stepped gingerly out of bed still wearing his slim fit boxer shorts from the day before - the counterfeit Calvin Klein's with Bart Simpson on the bottom. No one stood on ceremony in Tumble Weed drive.

He should have guessed; there was no bread in the breadbin and no milk in the fridge, so he settled for the left-over cold pizza on the countertop near the sink. Luckily for him, his mum never finished the last section of her pizza. It was as if she needed to say to the world, and Matt in partic-ular, look I'm not a greedy fat slob, honest. Matt just wished she'd buy ones without pineapple on the top. God, he loathed pineapple.

And then he had it. The plan took shape as he munched on the cold tomato soaked dough. All he needed to do was pretend he wanted to buy a car; an MGB, any

165

colour but preferably red. He'd have time to visit the car maintenance workroom before his lecture and then he could ask Mahmoud if he knew of one going cheap. Yes that might work, Matt thought. Yes that might just work.

The car maintenance session had been in full swing for about an hour by the time Matt arrived. No one seemed to notice him as he walked into the workshop. It was too noisy and informal for the tutor to spot an extra body, and he tried to stay unobtrusive near the sinks.

'I don't think he's here,' Matt said under his breath as he scanned the work benches. 'Shit!' But he'd said the magic word, and just as one might summon the genie of the lamp, the friendly-faced student looked up, spotted him near the sinks and smiled in recognition. Matt strolled over and said in what he hoped was a casual manner, 'Hi, have you seen…?'

'Sorry, mate. Not today. It's Mahmoud you're looking for, I take it?'

Matt nodded. 'Yeah it's about a car,' and then added, 'Any idea how to get hold of 'im?'

'It's Friday, mate. Probably won't come in now. Try again on Monday. Sorry,' he shrugged, smiled and then turned his attention back to the engine parts on his work-bench.

Bugger, Matt thought and before he'd had time to run through his full repertoire of alternative expletives, inspiration dawned. What had the student said? Of course. It was Friday. How could he have been so stupid? It was the day for prayer meetings - something he'd learnt from his computer searches. He could try room 259B again. What had that bloke with the clip board said? Something about the Utterly Young Muslim Association using the room tomorrow - and that was now today. But he'd have to wait till midday. Hmm... and he drove his hands into his pockets.

The touch of the paper felt like an electric shock. How could he be so stupid, he wondered. How could he have forgotten the letter addressed to Phillip Farrow? The one with his name crossed through and changed to Mahmoud Aseed. It was still in his pocket unopened. Gingerly, he pulled the rather crumpled envelope from its dark hiding place. No one seemed to notice him but... the toilets, that was the place. The gents were just round the corner. He'd find all the privacy he needed in one of the cubicles.

A few moments later, well away from prying eyes, he examined the envelope more closely. It was stamped and postmarked but he couldn't make out the date. So not generated from Utterly Academy, he thought. He opened the envelope carefully and quietly, although he reckoned the sound of rustling paper wasn't suspicious from inside a locked toilet cubicle. His heart raced as he pulled out the sheets of paper and read:

June 25th 2010

Dear Mr Farrow,

Thank you for expressing an interest in joining our gliding club. Firstly I must explain that the club was primarily intended for service personnel to introduce them to gliding. There are however, a limited number of civilian memberships also available and I have enclosed a membership application form. Please note that if you are not a member of the forces you will need to return the completed application form along with two character references, and you may also be subject to a security check.

I have enclosed some further information about our gliding club and club facilities that may be of interest to you.

Yours faithfully,
Lieutenant Colonel C D Sparrow
Anglian Gliding Club, Wattisham Airbase.

Matt sucked some air back between his teeth and made a low whistle before shuffling through the enclosures. As he read the club information page, he noticed the club only flew at weekends, and in summer the weekend gliding started on Friday afternoons. When the gliders flew, the helicopters were largely grounded. Strange, he thought, anyone would have expected the military to work non-stop and in all seasons. He shook his head. On face value the letter seemed pretty innocent, even a little boring and to be honest, Matt was disappointed. But why would Mahmoud want to join a gliding club, and a Wattisham gliding club in particular? Matt scratched his head. Could it be something to do with the proximity of the helicopters and airbase? No, he was letting his imagination run riot. It was time to put away the stolen letter. He had a lecture to attend, or was it a supervision meeting? Either way he didn't need old Blumfield on his back.

A little over an hour later, Matt made his way to room 259B. He couldn't have told anyone what his teaching had been about. He just sat through it, trying to look as if he was concentrating, but in reality his mind was miles away. He'd slumped in his seat with his plastered wrist resting on his knee, reading the messages scribbled on the cast. Some of the missives were dated and that set him thinking. Only two more weeks and the plaster came off. He could be starting his apprenticeship at Hepplewhites in less than three weeks. God, he hoped he'd need some physiotherapy and then the start might be further delayed. But what was he thinking? This was meant to be his chosen path, his career. The trouble was investigating was much more exciting. Maybe joinery and carpentry weren't for him after all. He suspected Blumfield would agree with that.

And so it was in a state of mild distraction that Matt made his way along the quiet corridor at the far end of the second floor. He passed one or two students on the way, but no one with a goatee. Should he pose as a student interested in Islam, or someone looking to buy a car from Mahmoud? The car option was nearer the truth, he decided, and probably more believable. As always, he arrived as everyone was leaving. The door was open and he could see the empty shoe racks by the wall. A tall thin Iranian student saw him and smiled a welcome.

'Hello, can I help you? I'm afraid the midday prayers and meeting have just finished. I'm Mohamed Zahir by the way.'

'Oh hi! Yeah I was lookin' for Mahmoud,' Matt replied and peered past him. He couldn't see anyone still lingering in the room. It was pretty much empty apart from some chairs stacked along one wall.

'Mahmoud Aseed? You look disappointed.'

'Yeah well, I keep missin' 'im.'

'Are you a friend of his?'

'Yeah, kind of,' Matt replied. 'D'you know where 'e's gone?'

Mohamed shook his head. 'Mahmoud doesn't seem to be himself recently, but you've probably noticed that, if you're a friend.' There was a long pause while he looked intently into Matt's face. 'He left today after his prayers. He used to stay and talk things over, you know, religious teachings… anything really, but recently….'

Matt couldn't hold his gaze any longer and looked down at the floor, nodding slowly.

'He reads a lot,' Mohamed continued, 'probably from the internet, and he quotes teachings which seem very…. He seems troubled.'

Matt nodded slowly again and threw in a deep sigh for good measure.

'Withdrawn, maybe that's the word I'm looking for. I haven't seen him with any friends, so I'm glad he's got you. I'm sorry I have no idea where he may have gone. He seemed to be in a hurry when he left.' Mohamed let his last words drift.

'A hurry?' Matt echoed. He'd exhausted the nodding and sighing ploy.

'He didn't stay for the meeting and he didn't speak to anyone. Maybe he was looking for you?'

'For me?'

'Well, you said you were looking for him. Maybe he's looking for you?'

'Oh yeah… for me,' and Matt shivered. The idea was rather unnerving. 'Thanks.'

But what had Mohamed been trying to say? That Mahmoud was depressed and suicidal, or that he was at risk of being radicalised? Did he want to join a gliding club to fall from the air and die in a fit of depression, or have access to the airfield for terrorist reasons? If Matt wanted to top himself and liked heights, he reckoned a multi-storey car park would be easier than gliding. And if he had aspirations to fly with loaded fuel tanks into a skyscraper, well a glider was the wrong aircraft. And anyway, where were the Twin Towers of Suffolk? No, it was more likely he wanted legitimate access to the airfield to steal cars, and failing that, he might simply want to learn to glide. There really were far more questions than answers and it was time to give it a rest. Matt shook his head as he retraced his footsteps from room 259B.

It would have been nice to meet up with Chrissie and Nick that evening in the Nags Head, he thought. Have a chat over a pint or two and run through all the possibilities. But they'd cancelled their Friday get-together the previous evening. They all agreed they'd spent enough money for one week in the Bury Dog and Bone. No, he'd have to wait until Monday and the apprentice release day before he saw them again. Pity, he thought.

CHAPTER 12

By Friday lunchtime Chrissie had completed her phone calls. After a difficult conversation with her insurance company, they finally agreed a rental car for two weeks and authorised the hire of a Peugeot 207 1.4 from Avis. She liked the colour; the blue suited her mood, and when the metallic flecks in the flawless paintwork caught the sunlight, the car's bodywork seemed to come alive. She screwed up her eyes as she looked at the reflected tints. 'Do you know,' she said to herself, 'in this light it almost looks a shade of grey.' So they'd managed to pass her off with a grey car after all – the nemesis of easy recognition in a car park. Great!

It was time to drive over to the Clegg workshops. It might be Friday afternoon, but her mood was low and she needed the distraction of work. She headed the Peugeot in the direction of Wattisham Airfield and drove the unfamiliar car cautiously in the afternoon sunshine. Her missing MG pre-dated such luxuries as power steering, so she had found the hire car surprisingly easy to manoeuvre out of the Avis rental forecourt. Even opening the windows to let in the summer afternoon air was effortless; the Peugeot had automatic electric ones. With just the touch of a switch she watched the glass slide down, letting in a blast of summer air laced with the fruity warm hints of hedge rose and occasional wild honeysuckle. So, no biceps-building effort required to turn a manual window winder then. She was starting to enjoy the little, metallic-blue Peugeot.

Try Sleeping With A Broken Heart, the radio boomed out. *Yes, another hit from Alicia Keys*, the Radio Suffolk DJ announced.

'Oh shut up,' Chrissie shouted and turned off the car radio. Perhaps there were advantages to driving her MG after all. For one thing, she couldn't hear the radio with the windows wide open. Too much wind noise.

She resisted the temptation to close her eyes as she drove along the airfield perimeter lane past the site of the accident. It was better to face your memories, she told herself, to look your demons straight in the eye. So what if the grass verge was still scarred and the tarmac rutted; it didn't mean the crash would rematerialise and happen all over again. She needed to focus on driving, otherwise she might end up in the ditch, and she didn't want that, did she? By sheer force of willpower she pressed on. 'Thank God I've got here in one piece,' she murmured a few moments later as her tyres finally scrunched over the stones on the track leading to the Clegg workshops. 'Just twenty-four hours late, that's all.'

Drawing slowly into the courtyard she immediately noticed a battered old Land Rover. Strange, she thought, somebody's left it at a funny angle close to the barn workshop door. It's almost blocking the entrance. Now who would do that? Someone in a hurry? A customer?

She didn't recognise the Land Rover and still wondering, parked up, glancing around the courtyard before finally switching off her engine. But there was no one about, the place seemed abandoned. And then she spotted the cedar trunk. 'Well at least that's here. There is a God in Heaven after all.' Smiling, she got out of her car and aimed the key fob. With a click the Peugeot was automatically secure, apart from the windows. They were still open.

She pushed the old wooden door to the barn workshop. It swung open with a low creak. She expected to see Ron with the customer, the driver of the Land Rover, but on first glance the workshop seemed deserted. Stepping onto the cool concrete floor she walked further, taking in the familiar smells of wood dust and polish.

'Mr Clegg,' she called. His full mug of tea stood on the bench near his favourite stool. That's most unlike Ron, she thought. If he makes a mug of tea, he always sits down and has a break; to go to the trouble of making tea and then not drinking it wasn't his way of doing things. 'Mr Clegg?' she called again. Perhaps he'd left it when he took the customer to the other workshop, the one across the courtyard with the copper still in the chimney breast. Chrissie retraced her steps and headed out into the sunshine. She was starting to feel uneasy. Something was wrong, but she couldn't have said exactly what. Perhaps it was the sight of the untouched mug of tea that made the back of her neck prickle. There was nothing for it but to look in the other workshop.

This time she approached the door cautiously. Before turning the handle she paused to listen. Were there any voices coming from inside? No, there was silence. Chrissie rattled the door handle as noisily as she could. It was an instinctive act. A bit like a dog might bark and raise its hackles. It made her feel large and ferocious. No, she corrected herself; it made her sound large and ferocious. She opened the door with as much noise and bravado as she could muster and speaking loudly, stepped into the workshop.

'Hello. Mr Clegg, are you ther...?' Chrissie never completed her question. A heavy blow landed on her back, catching her between the shoulder blades. She cried out as the air jolted from her chest. She staggered forwards and fell. Her face hit the brick floor as her handbag flew off her shoulder. Its contents clattered to the ground. She never saw her assailant.

Groaning, she sprawled face down on the bricks. A hard bony knee pushed into her back as her arms were wrenched behind. The sudden pain in her shoulders felt sharp and she struggled, but the knee pushed down harder. It compressed her chest, emptying her lungs so she couldn't scream. She fought to breathe as her wrists were crushed together and something thin and sharp was wound tightly around them. She hoped it was cord and not wire, but she honestly couldn't tell, it was too painful. If it had been her neck she knew she'd already be dead. And so she lay: her chest being crushed, her head starting to lighten and her life slipping away – or so she thought.

She must have lain still for a few moments and then the knee seemed to press down less heavily into her back. As she took a shallow breath an idea took form. She'd read somewhere that playing dead was supposed to work if a brown bear attacked you. Maybe, just maybe, it might work here. She let herself go limp, as if she was already dead. She tried to force herself to relax - not only her muscles but the urge to gasp for breath. The trouble was her heart was beating so hard she was sure it was obvious she was still very much alive. She let the coldness of the bricks soak into her as her pulse raced on. Could this work? Suddenly the pressure eased on her back and the assailant moved away.

Thank God! He must have been reassured by my stillness, she thought. At least she'd got that bit right.

So far she hadn't been able to get a proper view of him. Her head was turned to one side with the bricks pressing into her cheek which burned and throbbed. She dared herself to partially open her eyes and peer through the blue mascara clumping her lashes. For a moment she couldn't see anything and then a grubby trainer and denim trouser leg came into view. Someone picked up her handbag, and as the trainer moved further away she felt safe to look more fully. It was definitely a man and there was something very familiar about him; she was sure she had seen him somewhere before. Sweet Jesus, she thought, it's that strange bloke who was hanging around the Clegg workshops a week or so ago - the one with the goatee. She closed her eyes and willed him to leave the workshop. Yes, thank God, he's going, she thought as he opened the door. The key grated as he turned it in the lock, and then once again there was silence.

Chrissie waited, not daring to move for what was probably only a few minutes but felt like a lifetime. She allowed herself to breathe normally only when she was sure she couldn't hear any footsteps returning. Rolling awkwardly onto her side, she managed to sit up and look around the workshop. There was a bundle of clothes lying in one corner near a stack of old bits of wood. She didn't remember seeing a collection of rags there before, but as she looked more closely, the bundle took form. Ron Clegg lay curled up on his side, facing the wall. His wrists and ankles were tied together behind him. He was motionless.

'Mr Clegg, hey Mr Clegg, are you OK?' she whispered hoarsely. Her face hurt where she'd hit the bricks.

For some moments she watched and listened. No, there definitely wasn't any sound coming from him and she couldn't see any hint of his chest moving. He wasn't breathing. God, he must be dead.

She tried to stop herself from falling into that empty bottomless pit of hopelessness. So what if she was locked in a room with a dead body? At least it was Ron Clegg and not some stranger. Oh God, what was she thinking? She struggled to her feet, and with her wrists still tightly bound behind her back, crept over to Ron.

He lay as still as death, an old duster rag tied across his mouth. No wonder he hadn't shouted a warning, but then of course you can't shout if you're dead.

'Mr Clegg, are you OK?' she whispered again. Her only free limbs were her legs, so she gave him a gentle nudge with her foot, and when there was no reaction, she kicked him.

'Ughhhh.'

'Hey, Mr Clegg,' she said, prodding him with her foot again. 'If you're alive, for God's sake open your eyes,' and then she whispered as an afterthought, 'please.'

Ron's eyelids flickered. He didn't open his eyes, but he frowned and Chrissie took that as a sign of life.

'Let's get that duster out of your mouth.' Her voice cracked as she tried to control her emotions. 'Look, the bastards who've done this… I think they're still out there somewhere. So we need to keep as quiet as possible. Nod if you understand.'

Ron moved his head slightly and tried to pull his arms forward, but his wrists were still lashed together behind his back.

'They've tied my hands, too.' She winced as she moved her elbows. 'God my wrists hurt. But my feet are free. I'll try and ease the duster down over your chin.'

Chrissie balanced on one leg while she tried to work the cloth down with one airborne foot. It reminded her of some wild party game, but without the alcohol. The manoeuvre would have been pretty challenging with bare toes, but with her feet still in sensible summer pumps, well it was nigh impossible. She wobbled as the deep ache between her shoulders bit deeper into her back.

Ron gave a muffled groan as Chrissie lost balance and stood on his face.

'Shush,' she hissed. 'Keep quiet.'

He grunted, squinting at the shoe still resting on his face and then grunted again.

'I don't do Morse code,' she muttered trying to regain her balance.

Ron groaned and screwed his eyes tight shut.

Chrissie sat down. It was easier that way to use one foot at a time to push off her pumps. In the midst of her efforts she heard footsteps crossing the courtyard. They were heading towards the door. She froze, one size 37 canvas partially off. There was nothing for it but to hurry back to where she'd been left, lie down, roll onto her front and feign unconsciousness.

The footsteps kept approaching the workshop door. Then they stopped. The key grated as it turned in the lock. The door opened. She held her breath, closed her eyes and lay like death.

There was silence. An eternity passed as the side of her face started to throb. Chrissie guessed their gaoler was looking for signs of life, and when no footsteps entered and the door closed, she knew she'd passed the test. She looked like a corpse. Only as the key turned in the lock and the footsteps receded across the courtyard did she allow herself a long slow breath. Oh for the lungs of a pearl diver, she thought.

'That was close,' Chrissie whispered as she turned over and sat up in one twisting motion. With a final effort she pushed off her pumps, and surveyed her naked feet. She wiggled her toes as a kind of limbering-up exercise, then tucking her feet under her, knelt and stood up. She felt more balanced without her shoes and moved quietly across the cold brick floor. This time she sat down close to Ron's head, and using both feet like some primitive animal, tried to prize the duster out of his mouth and down over his chin. It was tight and she couldn't work a toe under the edge. It was hopeless. She'd have to use her fingers, but her hands wouldn't move and the pain was excruciating if she bent her wrists. Turning round she tried to feel his face – but her hands were deadened.

'Hmm....' He thrust his head against her useless hands, and as she jabbed downwards, a finger caught in the duster. She pushed, he pulled and then a gasp as the material worked down over his chin.

'Thanks,' he whispered and then coughed.

'Sorry if I scratched your chin.'

Ron tried to sit up but he was too stiff from lying in one position.

'What the hell's going on, Mr Clegg? Are you OK?'

'I don't know....' His voice died away and Chrissie had no idea whether he'd answered one or both questions.

'Who are these people Mr Clegg?' she whispered.

'I don't know, but I've only seen one.' He swallowed, before continuing, 'A young chap with a wispy beard, I think.'

'Ah, sounds like the same bastard who knocked me down.'

'Sorry I couldn't warn you... I....'

'I know, it's OK.' Chrissie paused, reining in the fear which threatened to overwhelm her. 'Look, I'm sure I've seen him before, hanging around here. Maybe two weeks ago. I thought he was a customer, but when I approached him he just vanished.' She waited for Ron to say something, but when he frowned she added, 'To be honest I thought he was probably a bit of a nut, or... a plane spotter.'

'He's a headcase, definitely a headcase,' Ron said under his breath and then winced as he tried to move his arms.

'I'd just made a mug of tea at three o'clock when that... madman came into the barn. All I said was hello and he rushed at me. Before I knew it, I was down. Must have knocked myself out.'

'Good God!'

'When I came round he was standing over me and my hands were tied. I struggled and, well he kicked me and then dragged me here - flung me in this corner and tied my feet.'

'But what does he want? He took my handbag. Is this a robbery?'

'I don't know. He kept muttering about Americans and how they'd killed millions of Muslims. He called me a Suffolk soaker, and then said my Englishness made me guilty by... association, yes that was the word he used.'

'By association?'

'With America. Then he left me in here and locked the door.'

'It wasn't locked when I came.'

'Well no, he came back. He went crazy. Kept asking *where are the helicopters? Why aren't they flying?* I said *it's Friday afternoon. The gliding club flies now till Monday* and... he literally went mad. Hit me around the head and tied this rag in my mouth - said I was *a deceiver, talking filth.*'

'Good God! But you weren't, were you, Mr Clegg?'

'No, no, I just told him the helicopters wouldn't be flying till Monday. He's a lunatic. And then you arrived.'

'Shit! Sorry, Mr Clegg.' Chrissie looked more closely at Ron's face. Grazes and angry red marks already flared on his cheeks and lips. She'd thought they were from the gag, but it seemed the bastard had laid into him as well. 'We've got to get out of here. We need to get our hands untied.'

'I keep some Stanley knives in that filing cabinet near the door. Top drawer.'

Chrissie's heart sank as she looked over at the battered cabinet, dark green with large metal drawer handles. She guessed from the scratches and rust that it too had seen better days. It loomed impossibly tall and she knew her five foot two would be inadequate. She was never going to get her useless painful hands up to the level of the top drawer and pull it open. Not with her arms tied so tightly behind her back. Ron seemed to follow her train of thought.

'If you lie on your back,' he whispered, 'you can do a sort of shoulder stand up against the cabinet and support yourself with your elbows. Then your feet will reach the level of that drawer handle. If you pull with your toes....'

'What?' she hissed.

'Shush, keep your voice down.'

Chrissie closed her eyes and tried to picture the manoeuvre - a bit too acrobatic for her taste. No amount of imagination could transform her legs into the lithe limbs of an athlete with spray on Lycra, just as no amount of skin-tight synthetic leather could turn her into Catwoman. Besides, she didn't have the muscles for stretch fabrics. This was ridiculous. No way. Her legs were deficient, with a hint of cellulite and clad in loose crop-bottomed linen trousers. She felt crumpled, not supple, and her shoulders hurt like hell. Move on, she told herself, move on.

'But if I get it open, how do I get the Stanley knife out of the drawer?' Her quiet words floated on the air, defeated.

'Use your mouth or teeth.' Ron seemed to have all the answers.

Chrissie sighed. The muscles over her cheekbone felt stiff and burned when she spoke. How the hell was she going to use her mouth and teeth to grip something? Even her dentist had never made her feel like this, damn it. She nodded slowly, and summoning all her resolve, walked over to the cabinet. She'd guessed right; the top handle was high and she couldn't grasp it, not with her hands bound the way they were. There was nothing else for it; she'd have to try with her feet.

She lay down on her back. Keeping her shoulders on the ground, she worked herself around so that as she pushed her legs up into the air, she got her back up against the cabinet. Her feet eventually reached the handle and she pushed her toes behind the cold metal, trying to get reasonable leverage. It was surprisingly difficult to pull in the right direction and with sufficient strength. Her first attempt merely lifted her shoulders off the ground.

'C'mon, Mrs Jax, you've almost done it,' Ron hissed from his vantage point in the corner.

Chrissie wasn't at all sure she could do it but one more Amazonian effort and the drawer started to move.

'Remember you've got to open it enough to get your face in,' Ron reminded her.

Chrissie bit back her words and replied with an eye roll. The upside down position was extremely uncomfortable. Her head felt engorged, her cheek ached and her ears buzzed. Five minutes of struggle felt like an eternity, but finally she inched the drawer open to what Ron considered to be her head size. Oh for a smaller head, she thought. With a sigh of relief she swung her legs down and swivelled away from the cabinet. She sat up fast and everything swam. 'Wooah!'

'You OK, Mrs Jax?'

Chrissie nodded and waited a moment for her head to settle. When she stood and peered into the drawer she almost expected she'd opened the wrong one, but Ron knew his workshops inside out and there, neatly stored, were a selection of blades and Stanley knives.

'We're in luck, Mr Clegg.'

'Luck?'

She took care in choosing. She wanted one with only the point of the retractable-blade protruding beyond its handle. When she spotted what she was looking for she ignored the pain in her face and grasped it between her teeth. Ron still lay on his side, but as Chrissie sat down carefully behind him with the Stanley knife in her mouth, he let his head loll back onto the yellow clay bricks. For a moment she thought he'd died. His hands looked blue.

'Try holding it with your feet. It might be safer than your mouth or your hands,' he whispered. 'Then work the blade against the rope.'

It was trickier than she'd expected. The handle kept slipping and it was difficult to get a firm grip between her soles and toes, but at least she could see what she was doing. She tried to keep the blade at right angles to the twine, but it slid and twisted sideways. Shit, she thought, I'm going to cut into his wrists. There's a bloody great artery in there somewhere.

'Just take your time, Mrs Jax. The blade will wear through it eventually,' Ron murmured as Chrissie kept fumbling with her feet.

Frustration, emotion and sheer physical effort gripped and twisted at her solar plexus, catching her breath. She fought back the tears as she worked behind him. 'I will not go under, I can do this,' she repeated to herself through gritted teeth. 'I will not cry. I shall go to the ball.' And that last phrase sparked her sense of the ridiculous as she imagined a pantomime fairy godmother, complete with wand and tutu. Something clicked in her mind and the old plucky self re-emerged. Now wasn't the time to break down. She couldn't afford the luxury of self-indulgence.

'*I shall go to the ball*? Are you OK, Mrs Jax?'

She ignored his question and worked on in silence, focusing on her feet and the Stanley knife. Eventually the strands started to give way and fray. It took a few more moments and then the blade was through. She watched as the binding lost tension and then worked at it a bit more with her toes. At last his wrists were free. He had been bound for several hours and was stiff, but he rubbed and pumped his hands to get the circulation going again. They still looked blue as he picked up the Stanley knife and extended the blade out of the handle so that there were two centimetres of razor-sharp steel exposed.

She felt foolish. It took him less than a minute to slice through the bindings on his ankles and then he turned to Chrissie and cut her wrists free. She couldn't help smiling as, from force of habit, he pushed the blade back into its handle when he'd finished.

'Now what do we do, Mr Clegg?' Chrissie whispered as she nursed her hands and wrists and then tentatively touched her cheekbone.

'Well, the question is, what's the madman going to do?'

'Hmm. Why was he so interested in the helicopters?'

'If he's a terrorist, then maybe shoot them down? Blasting a glider out of the sky in the name of Islam? No. I think he wants an army helicopter.'

'No, but he may have to wait till Monday. We could be here for... two and a half days. Shit! – Sorry, Mr Clegg, but if we don't get out of here....' Chrissie let her words hang in the air. 'Look, if you seriously think he's going to shoot down a helicopter, then he must have a gun. He's bound to be armed.' Chrissie stopped. Christ, he could shoot them. 'So what do we do, Mr Clegg?'

'Well the door is locked and the madman is probably armed with something sufficient to bring down a helicopter. These windows are small and don't open, and to be honest, I'm too old and stiff to climb through one, even if they did. You might, but... if there's more than one of those lunatics out there, well... there's a good chance they'd catch you.'

'And then I'd be dead meat,' Chrissie finished.

Ron nodded. 'As I see it we've got three options; one, we try and escape.' Ron paused.

'Two; we overpower the madman,' Chrissie continued for him. 'But that's risky. He's already had both of us down and trussed up like chickens when he attacked us. And we're not absolutely sure he's alone out there. What's the third option, Mr Clegg?'

'We could barricade ourselves in. There's plenty of wood in here. It's only a matter of time before someone realises you're missing and comes looking for you.'

'I wouldn't bet on it. You do realise, Mr Clegg, if we're still here on Monday and he fires off a missile - well, the army'll retaliate. We're likely to get shelled, particularly if he fires from your courtyard.'

Ron closed his eyes. 'We could of course create our own explosion,' he said.

'So an option four?' Chrissie looked up at the bottles of meths and white spirit neatly standing on shelves above his head. 'Fertiliser or ammonium nitrate in fertilisers, isn't that what you're supposed to use?' Chrissie asked, enthused by the thought of an explosion. 'Do you keep fertiliser in here Mr Clegg?'

'No, Mrs Jax, I do not. We'll have to think of some other way.'

CHAPTER 13

The idea of going to the farmers market became more attractive as the days passed, and by Saturday morning Nick was actively looking forward to meeting Denisa again. He told himself that it was just another opportunity to quiz her about Valko and Jan, but if Denisa had been a Dennis, then there wouldn't have been quite the same pleasurable frisson in anticipating the meeting. He had to admit he was keen to see her.

'How's Chrissie?' his mother had asked, sometime on the Friday evening.

When Nick explained that he hadn't spoken to her all day and her mobile was on answerphone, his mother visibly relaxed and said, 'I hope she's OK.'

Nick had smiled. He could read his mother like a book; Chrissie, on the other hand was much less transparent and certainly not as predictable. He had no choice but to assume she wanted some time and space to herself, and when on Saturday morning she still wasn't answering, he decided it was time to phone Matt.

'Hi, it's Nick.'

'Hi....'

'Look I thought I'd go to that farmers market thing. Remember? I told you about it but....don't suppose you want to come too?'

'Yeah, I remember. Hah! So you do fancy the foreign bird. What d'you call her? The del... deli... delicatessen Delia?'

'Denisa. And it's a fruit stall, Needham Market. I thought we might do a bit of asking about the fruit farm and

Valko. You know, take the opportunity. It packs up at one so we'd better get moving if we're going to make it. Are you on?'

'Yeah. Good idea, mate.'

'I'll pick you up, then. See you – about twenty minutes. OK?'

Nick didn't hang around. He said goodbye to his mother and left the house, though not before she'd asked him to bring back a punnet of strawberries. He smiled to himself. If she'd realised her innocent request might legitimise his visit to the Damson Valley Fruit Farm stall and a hot, red-headed Romanian, she might not have looked quite so relaxed.

It was a warm sunny morning and Nick's mood lightened further as he drove his battered old Ford Fiesta to the Flower Estate in Stowmarket. When he picked Matt up twenty minutes later, he had to look twice to be sure, but there was something distinctly odd about the way he moved. Although he sauntered with his customary languor along the path from his peeling front door on Tumble Weed Drive, he held his upper body uncharacteristically rigid. It was only as he bent to open the passenger door that Nick realised what the problem was. Matt's chest was encased in tightly stretched cotton, the material holding him like a lightweight corset, and as long as he didn't breathe, move his arms or bend, the vice-tight fabric held at the seams.

'See you're wearing one of Tom's retro tee-shirts,' Nick remarked.

Matt grinned. 'Yeah, Grateful Dead.' He tapped his chest.

'Another classic.' The words *GRATEFUL DEAD* were spelt with each letter printed as if cut randomly from a magazine or newspaper. The design was in the style of a ransom note or anonymous poison pen letter, set higgledy-piggledy across the front. The F U and L were larger than the rest, and when stretched across Matt's ample torso, they were eye catching. The word standing out from the rest was FULL - at least that was the trick Nick's brain played, sub-consciously adding a second L.

'Great, aint it?' Matt looked down and surveyed the ransom note from above.

'Just get in the car and try not to breathe or it'll split, mate.'

The route from Stowmarket was reasonably direct. They slowed down to a halt as they waited their turn to creep along Needham Market's bustling main street, lined with ancient timber framed houses. Saturday meant it was pretty busy with cars drawing in and out of parking spaces and blocking the flow of traffic. It took a short while but then they were soon turning into Hawkes Mill Street and crossing the two small bridges where the River Gipping split. This area, tucked away behind Needham Market, was rural and unspoilt; time and traffic had passed it by, leaving a small oasis of beautiful Suffolk countryside. Nick followed the lane to the farmers market where an enterprising farm had maximised its potential, or to use modern language, diversified. There was a small courtyard surrounded by old barns and outbuildings converted to accommodate a small restaurant, bakery, pottery, craft and farm shop. There was even an ancient dovecot tower transformed into a small, though rather odd shaped shop. It could only be described as delightful and the farmers market was an added attraction held there on the third Saturday of every month.

They parked the car and made their way into a court-yard filled with temporary stalls set out on trestle tables covered with brightly coloured cloths. Nick's nose positively twitched with the delicious smells of home baking and the smokehouse aroma of home cured bacon, sausages and salmon. There were cheeses and, if he wasn't mistaken, a stall with bottles of beer from a small independent brewery. The air was filled with the happy background chatter of stallholders hawking their wares. Nick looked around for the Damson Valley Fruit Farm stall.

'Hey over in the corner, there.' It was Matt who spotted the stall first, and it was Denisa who spotted Nick first.

'You come! Is nice to see you,' she shrieked. She was busy serving at her stall, the surface groaning with punnets of raspberries and strawberries. She waved excitedly, almost leaping in the air. Nick was struck by the abundance of hot colour. Her short red hair caught the sunlight and her cheeks flushed pink with pleasure. The scarlet and burgundies of the soft fruits seemed to reflect up into her face. The whole effect was stunning.

'Sh-i-t,' Matt whispered as they walked over to say hello.

'Hi,' Nick said, adopting what he hoped was a casual tone. 'Hi, meet Matt, a mate from college.' He turned to glance at Matt who grinned happily. Denisa stared at his tee-shirt.

'Is very busy this morning. Jan couldn't come, he busy with police. So, just two of us to run the stall!'

'The police? Why the police?' Nick asked as he looked around for the second person running the stall.

'Valko, he had problem with container lorry. He drives to Felixstowe and bang - an accident. Now missing.'

She threw her head back and looked heavenwards before continuing, 'The police found fruit and a Mercedes... SL... AMG in the container. It stolen. Now the fruits gone and Valko gone. The police searching the barns right now!'

'Shit!' Matt finally spoke his first word to Denisa, and then added, 'Searchin' the...? But why?'

Nick shot Matt a warning glance as he felt his cheeks starting to burn. He'd never been very good at lying and he hoped to God it didn't show on his face; after all, he was the one who'd tipped off the fuzz. A little vein of pleasure ran through his mind as he realised they must have taken him seriously when he identified Valko from Chrissie's blurry photo. But his guilty blush, combined with a slight smile, looked rather attractive. Unwittingly Nick had played the unspoken ace and king of hearts. Denisa responded with a coy smile and then pointedly turned her attention to a customer who was trying to choose between several identical punnets of strawberries.

Matt drew Nick to one side and whispered, 'D'you think we should find out more from this Delia bird... or just beat it?'

'Denisa, it's Denisa,' he hissed as he checked his watch. In half an hour the market would be starting to pack up. He made a decision. 'Denisa, do you want to have lunch with us before you go back to Damson Valley Farm?'

'Sure,' she said, shooting him an appraising look from beneath her dark eyelashes. She bent, stretching suggestively to reach a punnet of raspberries. 'We have to pack up first. I ask Peter, he say if it OK.'

'Peter? Ah, I remember... two of you running the stall.' He looked along the trestle table and now noticed a tall young man aged in his late twenties. Why hadn't he spotted him before? Must be Peter, he thought, and judging from the way he's watching Denisa, he must be her boy-friend. Nick felt stupid. He should have guessed there'd be someone like Peter in the equation.

Matt followed Nick's gaze and stared, mouth slightly open.

'Yes, of course Peter as well. Why don't we all have a picnic? Matt and I can buy some things for lunch from the market here. If we're back in about half an hour we'll help you pack up and then we can all have something to eat to-gether. What do you think; good plan?'

Denisa flashed him a brilliant smile. It was a smile to die for, a killer smile. 'That is lovely idea,' she said, glanc-ing at Peter to check he'd seen. 'I think Peter say yes!'

'Great. See you both here in about half an hour then.' Nick steered Matt away from the stall. 'For God's sake Matt, stop staring. You look as if… well as if you've been socked in the face, mate.'

'I was thinkin' that Peter bloke looks like someone I've seen before.' Matt rubbed his head. 'I'm not sure coz of the beard, but I reckon… take away the goatee, and it's got to be one of them Farrow boys.'

'The bloke I was looking at didn't have a beard.'

'No, but this one, 'e's got the same dark hair an' long face. Bet you a pint he's Phillip's big brother. Peas out the same pod, but without a goatee, I reckon.'

'Wasn't Peter one of John junior's mates?'

'Yeah, think so.'

'Well, well, well. This could turn out to be useful.'

'Yeah, and is Delia his bird? I thought you fancied her.'

Nick wasn't sure how he felt. Disappointed? 'Maybe. Bet she's playing some game, you know, trying to make him jealous.' Denisa was spectacularly attractive and Peter already had the advantage; he'd known her for weeks. Nick had only met her a few days before. Did he want to play her game? He wasn't sure. 'Hey Matt, I think I've got a plan.'

'Oh yeah?'

'Why don't you chat up Denisa? Pretend you fancy her.'

'Oh yeah? But I do.'

'No, yes well... it'll take the pressure off me. Peter won't think there's any serious threat. It'll just be a fun picnic if he's not worrying about me. We might get something out of him about Valko or John junior, especially if we load him with some of that beer. Just as well you're wearing your killer tee-shirt.'

'Oh yeah?'

Nick pointed to the stall selling beer. 'Come on, mate. Let's get some bottles of Water-Vole.' He'd spoken, half expecting Matt to be offended by his assumption that Peter wouldn't consider him a serious contender for the hot Romanian. But Matt just muttered something about preferring cold lager and then got side-tracked sampling the smoked ham. It was as if he hadn't picked up the not-so-subtle innuendo, or was he just being a good sport? Nick couldn't tell.

By the time they ambled back to the Damson Valley Farm stall, the trestle table was almost clear; Denisa had proved quite an attraction and nearly every last punnet had been sold.

Nick introduced himself to Peter as they helped pack up the stall. 'I was over at your farm repairing the fruit pickers' accommodation huts the other day,' Nick explained. 'I'm an apprentice with Willows & Son.'

'Oh yes Willows, they're a good firm; you should do OK with them. John, the boss's son, was a good friend of mine. But if you work there you'll know what happened to him. It was awful.'

'Before my time, but yes, I kind of heard. I don't think old Mr Willows will ever get over it.' Nick found Peter surprisingly easy to talk to and they chatted effortlessly as they all strolled from the farmers market car park back up the lane towards Hawks Mill, an old four-storey red brick building.

Nick and Peter carried plastic bags crammed with crusty loaves and bottles. Matt walked ahead with Denisa, swinging his plastered wrist around, as if to emphasise each point he made as he spoke. Unfortunately, with every movement of his arm, the closely fitting tee-shirt rode higher and higher up his back. As they crossed over the small stone bridge, they all paused to look down into the slow flowing water of the River Gipping. Matt lent over the bridge's low stone wall to get a better view, and with this seemingly gentle hunching of his shoulders, the tee-shirt suddenly gave up its unequal struggle. The old cotton stitching ripped with a popping crack. Nick watched, horrified as it split from one armpit, down the side seam, and then finally stopped, halted by the band of fabric which had previously rolled its way up from the bottom. Nick started to laugh. So much for the *Grateful Dead*, he thought. The tee-shirt was proving to be a knockout.

'Shit! I….'

Denisa started to giggle. 'You are the Incredible,' she squealed and then clapped her hands.

'Come on, I'm getting hungry.' Nick pointed to an area of grass close to the bank of one branch of the River Gipping, just as it emerged from beneath the old stone bridge. 'There's a nice spot down there by the river in front of Hawks Mill.' They were in fact walking onto a small island formed by a split in the river and reached by two stone bridges. Matt had already torn his tee-shirt crossing the first one, and with cotton fabric now flapping wildly, led Denisa down to the water and settled on the grass in a shady spot beneath a small weeping willow.

'Time for lunch; let's eat,' Nick said happily.

'Peter, I reckon your brother Phillip's at the Academy with us. Well not with us, right. We're carpentry. I'm sure I've seen 'im with the car maintenance lot.' Matt tucked happily into a bread roll and a slice of cold smoked ham. 'Likes the course, does 'e?' His words were almost swallowed with his huge mouthful of ham.

'I don't really know. I suppose he's enjoying it, but he doesn't say much. You know he's changed his name? He didn't want to be called Phillip any longer.'

'Do you want some beer?' Nick enquired. He knew he had to play it cool and not appear too interested. He shot Matt a warning glance as he passed a bottle across and then asked, 'Why should he want to change his name? Anyway, what's wrong with the name Phillip?'

'I don't know,' Peter said, opening a bottle of Water-Vole. 'Mum can't get used to calling him Mahmoud. None of us can. I mean for God's sake, why Mahmoud Aseed? He didn't even want to keep the family name, Farrow.'

'Maybe he's caught religion,' Matt said to no one in particular before filling his mouth with more bread and ham.

'Well he's certainly got that. Mum prefers to use his nickname you know, Aphid, rather than Mahmoud.'

'Why Aphid, I mean that's greenfly, aint it?' Matt asked.

'Yes, that kind of thing. They're a big problem in our orchards. I suppose it's just another name for a pest, and the name kind of stuck when we were kids. He's our very own horticultural family pest.'

'What is it with you English?'

Denisa didn't get an answer because there really wasn't one. Nick thought she looked puzzled when they laughed.

'So Denisa, what were you saying earlier about the police at Damson Valley Farm? What have you been doing?' Nick asked, still laughing as he offered her some creamy goat's cheese.

'It not me,' she retorted crossly.

Peter was quick to defend her. 'It's Valko they're looking for. He's the chap from Bulgaria who helps Jan with managing the fruit pickers. It seems he's been transporting stolen cars under the guise of exporting our fruit to Europe. The strange thing is the police seem to think Jan has something to do with it all as well. At first we thought it was a raid looking for illegal immigrants, but the paperwork is fine, thank God. That's why I came today, they wanted to question Jan, and Phillip didn't seem to be around either. Dad's pretty upset. He had no idea what was going on. He thinks we should have noticed something was wrong before the police got involved.'

'I think I may have met this Valko character when we came to repair the fruit workers accommodation huts,' Nick prompted.

'He's a strange man. I'm sure they can't all be like that in Bulgaria. One moment he's there and then the next he's gone - creepy. Maybe this stolen car business is behind it all. He's never been particularly friendly with us; don't think I've spoken to him much. Perhaps I should have.' Peter gazed across the river, lost in his own thoughts.

'Did he have much to do with your friend, John junior?' Nick asked.

'Why do you ask?'

'I don't know really,' Nick tried to keep his tone casual. 'I thought he was doing some work for him at the Willows workshop, but I may be mistaken.'

'That'll be the accommodation huts. Willows built the wooden huts, but that was for us, not Valko.'

'That's what it'll have been; as I said, I must have heard it wrong.' But it was clear to Nick he'd unsettled Peter, and his softly worded back down hadn't mollified him. Now why should that be, Nick wondered. There must be something Peter knows but isn't prepared to share with us. But the moment had passed and there was no way he could turn the conversation around naturally to ask more.

The rest of the picnic passed harmoniously and no further information of any sort could be teased out of Peter. There was, in fact, quite a lot of teasing that afternoon, but most of it was from Denisa and directed at Matt who seemed to enjoy it all enormously. It was only afterwards, as Nick drove home with Matt, that he realised he had forgotten something.

'I never bought some strawberries for Mum.'

CHAPTER 14

While Nick and Matt were enjoying the summer sunshine at the Farmers Market, Chrissie and Ron Clegg were experiencing a much darker weekend. By the end of Friday afternoon they had decided that if they were to survive their first night in the Clegg workshop, then option three had the greatest likelihood of success, at least in the short term.

'But how can we barricade ourselves in without making a noise? He's bound to hear us and then he'll be back,' Chrissie had moaned. 'He'll be in here before the door's secure.' She'd nearly added something again about being dead meat, but thought better of it.

'Let's just think for a moment. How does the door open, Mrs Jax?'

She bit back the obvious words that sprang to mind about handles, hinges, and that now was not the time for a quiz. 'What do you mean?'

'The door opens inwards towards us. If we wedge a board up against the door, you know at an angle from the floor, then it'll jam it closed. We can do that quietly, and it'll be quick. By the time anyone hears us nailing wood across the door frame – well, the door'll already be jammed shut. They'll never open it from the outside.'

'Do you really think it'll…?' Chrissie looked across at the wood stacked against the far wall. Most of it was no more than four foot lengths of old timber from discarded draw sides, table tops and chairs.

'Yes, I do. Now we need to move quickly and quietly before he thinks to comes back to check on us.'

And so Chrissie had crept across the workshop and se-lected a sturdy old table leg propped against the wall. Si-lently, she'd carried it to the door. The clay brick floor was uneven and it was easy to lean the leg so that one end wedged against the door and the other caught on a slight ledge in the bricks. Chrissie silently thanked God for the irregular floor as she carried more wood to the door. Ron found a hammer and nails in the bottom draw of the metal cabinet.

'Just hold it there,' he whispered as he prepared to knock in the first nail.

Chrissie held a length of wood across the door frame and winced as the first hammer blow struck the nail. 'Shush,' she hissed, and then felt silly. Ron swung the hammer with surprising efficiency and about ten strikes later a couple of nails were in.

'Christ, I think he's coming. Quick! More wood across here.' Chrissie had mustered all her self-control to stop from screaming as she positioned another piece of wood to jam the handle. Her hands were shaking and her heart pounded as she worked. 'Oh no!'

They heard footsteps running across the courtyard.

'Shit!' Chrissie braced herself. The key grated as it turned in the lock. The handle rattled but it couldn't move. She held her breath. Crack! The old wood almost exploded as the goatee threw his full weight against the door.

'Aah!' she screamed but the wood held.

'Come on, get this next board up quick!' Ron shouted.

Chrissie couldn't remember very clearly all the details of the next few moments. Fear had frozen her thoughts. She'd moved mechanically while Ron gave instructions. Something unseen kicked and threw itself against the other side of the door, shrieking and animal-like in its raw fury. Guttural words of rage and hate vibrated at them through the wood, and then suddenly it was over. There was silence; a lull in the frenzy on the other side of the door. Chrissie looked at Ron and smiled.

'It held. We've done it Mr Clegg, We've done it!' But the smile died on her lips.

'The window - NOW,' Ron yelled.

'Oh no, please no.' Chrissie heaved her practice mahogany board up to the window. It was just about the right size. 'My French polishing....'

They had fixed it there with only seconds to spare as the goatee howled and thumped at the glass. He was terrifying, even with wood an inch thick now separating them. She imagined him foaming at the mouth, spittle flying and droplets spattering the pane as it cracked and then shattered.

'My God! He's a flaming lunatic,' she whispered. 'He must've broken out of a mad house. Someone must be looking for him, surely?'

'I wonder how long it'll take him to work it out.'

'Work out what, Mr Clegg?'

'That we're still his prisoners, more imprisoned than ever.'

'Well thank God he can't get at us… for the moment.'

'That's why he's having a tantrum, or maybe it's a fit.'

'Do you think so?' she sighed. Crack! He kicked the door. Chrissie shuddered.

And he'd done that every hour or so since.

Chrissie imagined it was temper that drove him to keep kicking at the door. It doubled as a psychological game, reminding them he was still out there; at his mercy if they tried to escape. But she guessed it was mainly rage that fed him - and he'd kept it up. All night. Only a fanatic could do that, she thought; a fanatic with a short fuse. She consoled herself with the knowledge that indirectly he was their prisoner as well. For while he kicked at the door at regular intervals, he couldn't leave them, couldn't sleep. He too had to spend the weekend at the Clegg workshops, waiting for Monday when the helicopters started to fly again. They were all prisoners in a way; Chrissie and Ron on remand, the goatee on parole.

By Saturday morning Chrissie sat cold and stiff on the brick floor. She closed her eyes. It was easier that way to weigh up the consequences, the losses and gains of having exchanged her prison for a fortress. It was a bit like auditing a balance book; the habits of her accountancy background ran deep. On the plus side, they were now safe from physical abuse, or worse still, murder. They also had an element of control over their fate. They might not have guns, but their carpentry tools were sharp, serrated and heavy. As weapons they would do nicely, though she couldn't imagine herself using them in anger or on flesh. Above her head were shelves of numerous flammable liquids that could, with ingenuity, be made into explosives.

'So,' she murmured to herself, 'locked, stocked and maybe... two smoking barrels.'

There was another, more basic plus; perhaps it was something to do with the still. The workshop had piped cold water and a cracked basin. She remembered turning up her nose at it when she first arrived, but thank God for the old stained toilet in what, no doubt, had once been an outside privy. Ron must have converted it over twenty years ago to an inside convenience and it was annexed to their prison. They even had electricity. 'All mod cons....'

On the negative side, it was the goatee who would decide the length of their incarceration. They had no food and their electricity could be cut off at any moment if he had a mind to find the fuse box. Chrissie's mobile phone had been taken with her handbag and there was no obvious way of contacting anyone for help. Any foray outside would almost certainly result in injury or, worse still, death. There was another sobering thought. If she, and Ron without his medications, made it through to Monday, then they ran a very real risk of being blown up by a shell. That is if the military helicopters retaliated to the goatee's attack.

'Yes, we're well parcelled and trucked,' she muttered.

And so Chrissie sat on the brick floor, nursing her bruised cheek and aching stomach. Hunger hadn't struck till early that morning, but with every hour that passed, it pulled and gripped at her innards. She'd tried to distract herself by mentally running through the account book of their situation, but to no avail. Each time a kick landed on the door, the sudden jolt of sound released another shot of adrenaline and more acid filled her stomach – burning and all-consuming as she relived the terror of barricading the goatee out.

In the end it was Ron who came to the rescue. He insisted they do a full inventory of everything in the workshop, and at last she had both a task and something else to occupy her mind.

'So Mrs Jax, in summing up, what've we got and how are we going to use it?'

'Well, starting with the chemicals and liquids, we've several bottles of white spirit and some meths. There's: pure beeswax, wax polishes, linseed and Danish oil, some shellac, polyurethane and acrylic varnishes. I didn't know you kept acrylics.' She took a breath before continuing, 'Some water-soluble glues, various paint and varnish strippers, wood filler, wood dyes and - a whole lot of things in jars that aren't labelled.'

'Can you think of anything we can do with it?'

'Apart from restore furniture and French polish wood? It strikes me most of this lot's pretty flammable.'

'Then let's hope to God we're not shelled by the helicopters. We're one huge incendiary device.'

Chrissie shivered. 'Cocktails?'

'Pardon?'

'Molotov cocktails, Mr Clegg.'

'Ah yes, right. Something dramatic… that burns,' Ron nodded.

'I was useless at chemistry at school, but if we want to make anything that explodes, well - we'd have to experiment. We'd probably kill ourselves.' Chrissie closed her eyes. She thought back to a November thirty-five years before. Her brother Simon had a box of indoor fireworks. She remembered choosing a sparkler and he lit it for her. As it spluttered into fiery life, flecks of burning aluminium shot down onto her bare hand. She screamed, flinging her crackling flare back into the box, and then screamed some more when the box exploded into a myriad of colours. No one was hurt; not seriously, nothing lasting. But when she evoked that image and then recalled the sheer force of the Academy canteen explosion, she shuddered.

'I think there's something in here we've overlooked,' Ron said after a long pause.

Chrissie glanced around the workshop. She knew time was weighing heavy, but she really wasn't in the mood for guessing games. I-spy-with-my-little-eye wasn't going to cut it for her. She waited for him to elucidate further.

'I don't know when that copper tank in the back of the fireplace was last used, but I think we could put it to explosive use.' Ron stood up stiffly and limped over to the fireplace. Chrissie thought he looked tired; he probably hadn't slept much and the effort of making the barricade had visibly weakened him. He examined the copper, looking closely at the seams of the tank and then turning his attention to its outlet. 'If we fill the tank with water, block the outlet and light the fire, we could heat the water to boiling point. If the steam can't escape then it'll build up pressure and explode.'

'But if the chimney won't draw, if it's blocked, we'll choke on the smoke. We've already boarded up the window. Anyway, wouldn't it explode through the path of least resistance – into this room, not out through the chimney breast?'

Ron nodded in silent agreement and looked upwards into the chimney.

'I think it was Colditz, but I might be wrong,' Chrissie suddenly said.

'Yes, Mrs Jax, tunnelling to escape. Unfortunately that takes a long time. It's not going to work for us here.'

'No, no. What I mean is, when the allied forces were liberating Europe, the prisoners in Colditz put a Union Jack on the roof so the British and American planes didn't bomb them - so they'd realise they weren't Germans. Apparently it worked. It may not have been Colditz of course.'

'But we're in Suffolk. A Union Jack isn't going to save us here,' Ron reasoned.

'I didn't mean we should put a flag on the roof. We could put a message, like HELP or TERRORIST. Watching you look up the chimney made me think. We've got a roof. When the helicopter pilots fly over, they'll see it,' Chrissie explained.

'Good idea, but I'm not sure the chimney is the best route onto the roof. It gets pretty narrow up at the top.'

'No, no, no. We could get to the roof from inside. It's only a single-storey building. If we get up into the roof space you can take some of the tiles off from the inside. Then you've got access to the roof.'

'Brilliant. You could even throw the Molotov cock-tails from up there.'

'No, no, Mr Clegg. *You* could throw them from up there. I'm no-good with heights.'

'Hmm, Mrs Jax, I'll put my mind to making the Molo-tovs and looking for something to write our message on. You can do the climbing.' And as if to illustrate his point, he sat down stiffly.

'Shit,' she said under her breath. This was getting ri-diculous, but just saying shit reminded her of Matt, and thinking of Matt conjured up the thought of food and…. Good God, she'd forgotten about her stomach pains for half an hour. Action, yes action was the answer. They had a plan and while there was a plan there was a glimmer of hope. But how to get the tiles off without making a noise and drawing attention? If the goatee heard and saw her, well she could get shot with her head poking out of the roof.

'If we do the preparation work now and you remove the tiles during the night, or even early Monday, the goatee might not realise what we're doing.' Ron must have read her mind. He looked up at a small hatchway in the rough ceiling. It was close to the wall opposite the chimney breast. Chrissie followed Ron's gaze. There was no ladder; they were all stored in the large wooden barn workshop.

'How do I get up there?'

Nearly all the decent wood had already been used to barricade the door and windows, and apart from an antique pedestal table waiting for repair, she couldn't see anything to climb on. 'Don't we have anything with more than one leg? That pedestal doesn't look very stable,' Chrissie hissed.

'You'll be fine.' Ron stood up with difficulty. 'Look, at least this chair has four legs.'

'Yes, but they're not all the same length and the seat's split.' Chrissie helped Ron pull the table beneath the hatchway. She watched, biting at the inside of her cheek as he placed the chair carefully so that it was directly over the pedestal. 'What do you mean, I'll be all right? It doesn't look very all right to me.'

'Come on you'll be fine, Mrs Jax. I'll steady the chair for you while you climb up. It won't hold my weight.'

Chrissie stared at the broken furniture tower. It was precarious. Top heavy. It would never hold her weight. This new role of in-house gymnast was getting ridiculous. How could Mr Clegg possibly imagine she could do it? Wasn't it obvious she was just crop-bottomed Chrissie with a huge affinity for the ground? She felt sick. 'I-I....'

'The more you think about it, the worse it'll get. Just do it, Mrs Jax. Here.' He stretched out a gnarled hand.

'OK, but for God's sake don't let me fall off.' Needs must, she told herself as she tried to slow her breathing.

With Ron's help she scrambled onto the table. Then forcing herself to stand, she climbed onto the chair. Everything wobbled for a moment, but she didn't look down and the rickety tower held. Straightening from her crouching position, she lifted her arms until her hands rested on the ceiling and hatchway. She pushed upwards but nothing happened. She pushed again harder, and this time straitened her legs so that she stood almost upright. Suddenly the hatchway gave way. Her centre of gravity shifted. The thrust of her arms flew upwards and sideways; her bottom and legs sailed in the other direction. 'Oh no!'

Ron grabbed the table and let go of the chair. Everything slid away from Chrissie's feet. She made a desperate grab for the sides of the hatchway as the chair skidded off and clattered to the ground. She hung on. Her feet searched for any support. One foot found Ron's head and the other, his shoulder.

'Now come on, Mrs Jax, you can do it. Just pull yourself up into the opening up there.'

Chrissie couldn't find the words to answer; if she had, it wouldn't have been polite. She was going to die. Her hands were slipping and Ron wasn't directly beneath the hatch opening. Straightening her legs just pushed her sideways rather than upwards. Ron shoved the table away and centred himself beneath the hatch opening. Working a hand under each foot he thrust upwards with all his arthritic strength and Chrissie found her head and shoulders propelled through the opening. She pushed her hands down on the rim of the hatchway and heaved the rest of her body up into the roof space. There was no light and she knew the floor wouldn't be boarded. Taking care to only put her weight on the ceiling joists, she shifted herself around and looked back through the hatchway opening. Ron stood in the workshop looking up at her.

'Why're you laughing? What's so funny?' she hissed.

'Sorry – it was from down here. Well done, you're up there now.'

Crack! The door juddered.

'Shush. The bloody madman's heard us. Keep quiet.' Chrissie held her breath. She had no idea why, because no one could hear her breathing up in the roof space. Force of habit, she supposed. She closed her eyes and wished a bloodied toe on the kicking monster. 'Now what do I do?' she whispered.

'Let me find a piece of wood you can rest on the joists. Afraid there isn't much choice. We've used the best bits for the barricade. Don't want you putting a foot through the ceiling when you stand up.' Ron pulled a piece of oak ve-neered plywood from under a pile of oddments near the chimney breast. 'Ah, this should do.'

Chrissie reached down through the hatchway to grasp the piece of wood. Ron winced as he handed it up to her.

'You OK?'

Ron rubbed at his right shoulder. 'I'm starting to stiff-en up, that's all. But don't worry, I'll think of a way to get you down again.'

Her stomach lurched. Swallowing back the bile, she tried to smile. 'Yes, sure you will.' She tugged at the wood, pulling it through the hatchway and then yanked it into po-sition so that it straddled two of the ceiling joists. It gave her a small platform. Crouching on the old veneer, she turned her attention upwards. It was dark. Her eyes took time to adjust. There was no insulation material lining the roof space and she could feel the roof felt between the ex-posed roof trusses. Her fingers disturbed the dust and grime, showering down a cascade of ancient dirt and long-dead flies. 'Christ!' she cried, blinking and rubbing at her eyes and driving in more of the grit.

'Don't disturb the wasps nest.' Ron stood beneath the hatchway, whispering up instructions like an anxious coach on the sidelines.

'What?'

'There may be a wasps' nest up there.'

'Great.' All she needed was a hundred angry wasps buzzing at her. 'Everything up here's dead. Let's hope it's an old nest.' She stared at the roof. Wooden battens would be nailed on the outside to secure the felt and the tiles would be hooked over them. All she had to do was to cut away some felt to expose the battens. Then if she could saw or break through a section of batten, she should be able to lift a tile off and inwards. It all sounded straightforward. And as she struggled to see in the dim light, she spotted it - an abandoned wasps' nest up in the eaves. The yellow and black striped stinging residents must have long since deserted the dangerous roof space. Chrissie smiled. They had more sense than me, she thought. She wasn't even sure which side of the roof faced into the courtyard.

'Mr Clegg,' she whispered, bending down to the hatchway. 'Could you pass me up a Stanley knife to cut away some of this roof felt. Umm... which side is the courtyard?'

'As you're facing now, to your right.' He limped over to the cabinet and selected a knife for her.

'Any suggestions what I can use to cut through the battens without knocking the tiles out? They'll smash down onto the courtyard.' She watched him as he thought. The top of his head seemed strangely sad. No expression, just thinning grey hair with the skin showing. He nodded, but it struck Chrissie as a kind of defeated movement.

'I've got a small padsaw. It's a bit like your Stanley knife but with a saw blade. Or… you might find it easier to use a cutting wire. You can thread it behind the batten, and when you've attached the handles, pull it backwards and forwards towards yourself. It'll be slow hard work. Remember to keep it taut. You've got an awkward angle up there with those tiles in your way on one side.'

'Thanks.' Chrissie leant through the hatchway to take the Stanley knife. 'Will you be OK down there? You seem…,' and when he didn't answer she whispered, 'The cutting wire sounds the best option, if you can find me one, thanks.'

Ron didn't seem himself, but there was nothing she could do and she daren't let herself get distracted. Perhaps he was missing his painkillers and anti-inflammatory tablets. Hunger and unsuppressed arthritis were bound to be taking their toll. There – she was getting side-tracked again. Chrissie turned her attention back to the roof felt and wooden battens.

'How's it going up there?' Ron asked after the next hourly door kick.

'It's getting pretty hot under this roof.' She peered through the hatchway. Sweat trickled down her neck as she pushed her hair back. It stuck in clumps to her damp forehead. She wiped the moisture from her upper lip with the back of one grimy hand. 'I'm through the felt and a section of batten, so I've got some tiles exposed. Now I need to figure out how to lift a tile off.'

Ron smiled up at her.

'Hey you've been busy.' Chrissie blinked as she surveyed the chaos strewn over the workshop floor. Half a dustsheet stretched out beneath her. **HELD - MAD GUN-MAN** was painted across it in huge letters with a dark wood stain.

'That isn't going to break my fall if you're expecting me to jump down from here, Mr Clegg. You'll have to think up something else.'

Ron laughed quietly. 'I wasn't sure how to spell jihadist, and terrorist seemed… just too many letters, so….'

'So, HELD - MAD GUNMAN? It has a certain ring to it.'

'No, HEL**P** – MAD GUNMAN.'

'Ah!' The P looked like a D.

'What did you just ask, Mrs Jax?'

'How to get the tiles off from inside.'

Ron lifted his arms to demonstrate, but winced with pain. 'Where the tile hooks over the batten you've cut away - just pull the tile in towards yourself and then work the tile back into the roof space. The tile above and below will still be held by their battens and shouldn't slide down off the roof. Once you've got the first tile out, you can work sideways and detach more. The ones above and below can easily be removed - just put your hand through the roof to ease the tiles off their battens and then back through the hole.' Ron made it sound almost easy.

'So, the first tile's the key to it.' Chrissie turned back into the hot airless roof space. She didn't like puzzles, particularly the ones with loops of rope entwined around impossibly shaped shiny bands of continuous metal - the type given at Christmas. And this felt a bit like one, but without a huge turkey lunch and a surfeit of alcohol to fuel her.

She'd never been able to get the rope disentangled and free, so how was she going to fare with the tile-and-wooden-batten puzzler? Her stomach lurched. Was it the thought of roast potatoes and stuffing, or memories of family Christmases? 'Just keep focused, Chrissie Jax,' she moaned.

'If you make too big a hole, the goatee will notice immediately. Better do the preliminary work and just take the first tile off. And then the final larger breakthrough on Monday.'

'Yes… sure.'

Ron's instructions seemed to make more sense when she studied the exposed tiles again. It was just a matter of pulling the first tile inwards. Gingerly she grasped one by the lip where it had rested over the batten she'd just cut away. The tile felt warm from the afternoon sun. She gave it a gentle tug and with a little grating sound and a shower of dust, it moved towards her. Using both hands, and taking care not to disturb the neighbouring tiles, she worked it inwards and away from where it overlapped the tile below. Soft afternoon sunlight flooded in through the gap and she felt an overwhelming urge to touch the free air. As she reached out something made her pause. She had an uneasy feeling someone was looking up at the roof. Instinctively she stepped back from the small opening and her movement improved her view. Down below she saw the goatee standing in the courtyard, facing the direction of the Wattisham Airfield, and gazing up into the sky. Luckily his back was turned towards the workshop; he hadn't seen her, and it didn't look as if he had heard her. It was obviously too risky to do any more work on the roof with him standing so close. It was time to get back down into the workshop.

'What time is it? Good God!' The last time Chrissie looked down from her hatchway, the workshop had been chaotic. This time she thought there'd been an explosion, except she hadn't heard one. 'You've taken some of the shelves down.' Bottles and jars littered the floor.

'Those were the longest boards I could find, and of course they were hanging on the wall all the time. What once were shelves is now a ladder... well sort of. Not very long and only a few rungs but it'll get you down and up again.'

'Will it?'

'Yes, and I've nailed the top length of the dustsheet to this wood so it'll hold it out flat when you get it out onto the roof. Easier to read.'

Chrissie nodded. Some twine attached weights to the bottom of the dustsheet. 'You've thought of most things. Well done Mr Clegg. What are all those rags for?'

'They're not rags, Mrs Jax, they're wicks for the Molotovs. Some nice long strips of dustsheet. I've chosen some suitable bottles.' He pointed to a cluster of empty bottles standing in front of the cabinet. 'We've probably got enough meths and white spirit for at least four. It's not an enormous arsenal, I'm afraid, but....'

'When do we assemble them?'

'Nearer the time. While the meths and white spirit are sealed in their storage bottles let's leave them there.'

'Meths sniffing?' The smell or to be more precise, the aromatic hydrocarbons from the meths and white spirit would probably make her ill; best just to get things organised instead, she thought.

Chrissie sat on the edge of the hatchway and swung her legs through the aperture. Saturday had been surprisingly productive, passing more rapidly than expected. She had achieved more, fuelled only by water, than she had ever managed following a hearty breakfast. On the calorie front she was in negative balance, but on the sense-of-achievement and self-reliance fronts, well she was definitely in positive balance. Now all she needed to do was swing down the makeshift ladder like a true gymnast.

Crack! The door shuddered, marking the passing of another hour.

Bugger you, she thought.

CHAPTER 15

Chrissie woke with a start. The familiar sound of her MGB floated through the half-light. The engine had a distinctive note she could have recognised anywhere, even amongst hundreds of tired classics at an MG enthusiasts' rally - a high metallic note every fourth beat. For a moment the sound lulled her into that strange state halfway between sleep and wakefulness; but not for long. Her subconscious kicked in and within a few seconds she was fully alert as she checked her watch; it was five in the morning. Monday morning, and her car was somewhere out in the courtyard. Why?

Her empty stomach lurched and churned with anxiety. Sunday had only served to increase the nervous tension. Most of the day had been spent going over and over the plans with Ron, and the inactivity of waiting was almost unbearable. Now something was happening but not what she'd expected, and not so early in the morning. Chrissie listened again, straining to catch any hint of engine or tyre tread. Silence. There was no mistake, she had definitely heard her car and it had drawn up somewhere outside the workshops. She got to her feet and crept over to Ron. He was still asleep near the fireplace, close to the copper tank he probably dreamed of exploding. He breathed slowly, not quite a snore but heavily. Even in sleep, his bruised face looked haggard.

She shook him gently as she whispered, 'Hey Mr Clegg, wake up. There's something going on outside.'

Stillness filled the room, so dense she felt it should have a colour. Even Ron stopped breathing for a few moments. She touched his shoulder again and this time he opened his eyes. He looked at her without blinking and when she put a finger to her lips, he seemed to understand her command. He half sat up, propping himself on one elbow so he could focus on the room. He didn't utter a sound but she watched him frown as they both heard the creak of the barn workshop door.

'What the hell? Well this is a surprise. *Zdravei!*' The words drifted across the courtyard.

Chrissie didn't recognise the voice. It sounded cold, harsh, and male. She raised her eyebrows, an unspoken question directed at Ron. Another person had arrived, and judging by his greeting, he knew the goatee. But who was he and why was he here? A rollercoaster of emotions looped and spun through Chrissie's head. Hope, then frustration followed by fear; they chased and jostled as her stomach grumbled and ached. This was a turn of events she hadn't anticipated. Up until now the goatee was the only person she'd seen through her roof tile peephole. His wits had been pitched against theirs, and now there was someone else doubling the odds against them.

'Now what in God's name are you doing here?' the voice asked.

'Work, for the glory of Islam.' The goatee's familiar tones cut through the early morning.

'Oh yes?' The voice chuckled, but the tone was arctic.

Clunk! The barn door closed behind the newcomer, shutting out everything but the rhythmic sounds of muffled voices in the barn workshop.

There was a long silence between Chrissie and Ron before she whispered, 'It's starting, Mr Clegg. Monday's starting. Do you think the goatee heard what we were saying yesterday… our plans? I mean we heard them just now, didn't we?'

He shook his head. 'We kept our voices low. Let's hope he was too busy praying.'

Chrissie almost smiled. But if the goatee had heard them, then there wasn't much she could do about it now.

'While they're both in the barn, I'm going up into the roof space to take off some more tiles. There's less chance of being heard while they're still in the barn,' she whispered.

Chrissie looked with trepidation at the vertical makeshift ladder. It was frightening but climbable. Sixty hours of imprisonment had altered her view of fear and risk. The roof space beckoned and as long as she concentrated on visualising the things above her head and ignoring the brick floor beneath her feet, then she could control her phobia for heights. It was a fine balance, this business of risk between the theoretical chance of falling from the makeshift rungs, and the real danger of staying put.

Taking some deep breaths, she set her foot on the first of the rough, wooden steps. A few moments later and she was up in the roof space lit only by a small shaft of early morning light seeping through the gap in the tiles. She peeped through her makeshift window. Luckily the courtyard seemed quiet and deserted. It was the moment to remove a second tile. 'Come on, Chrissie Jax,' she told herself, 'you can do it.' Grasping the tile, she winced as it grated and scraped against its neighbour, sending a shower of dirt and moss scuttling down the roof, landing on the concrete below like a tiny army of ball bearings scattering and bouncing. The sound was heightened by her anxiety. She froze. Nothing happened. The barn door wasn't flung open and the muted sounds of conversation continued. It was OK. Slowly, slowly, she delivered the tile inwards.

'Wow.' She breathed the word softly to the dawn as she stepped back to admire her handiwork. Amazingly the gap created by removing two tiles was more than twice the size of the opening made by one. Of course - the overlap. The tiler's equivalent of compound interest, or was it simple interest? 'Concentrate, Chrissie Jax, concentrate. You're not an accountant now.'

Down in the courtyard below, she spotted the distinctive warm tones of a familiar friend - her red MG. It was parked about 30 yards to one side of the rental Peugeot, and from where she was looking, pretty much in the same state as when it was stolen. Except the hood was now up. Thank God it's OK, she thought as relief flooded through her. But the sudden surge of pleasure was short lived. Cold logic struck home. What's it doing here and why? Who had driven it? There was only one answer. Valko. 'Of course, Valko,' she whispered, echoing her worst fear. He'd stolen her car, so it followed that he....

Her anxious thoughts were interrupted by a grating sound as the barn workshop door opened.

'I've got her handbag. The name on the driver's licence is Chrissie Jax. She drove here in that Peugeot. It's a rental,' the goatee said from somewhere inside the barn.

'*Da!* That explains it. If you've had her locked up here since Friday - well that's why I didn't find her at the address on the insurance certificate. Stupid cow. She'd put it in the glove compartment of the MG. People are so predictable.' The owner of the voice stepped out into the courtyard. 'Of course that's not all I found in her car.'

Chrissie's heart missed a beat. The man's leather jacket was horribly familiar. He glanced up at the early morning sky, and as she caught a view of his face, a chill gripped her. His dark features were unmistakable. It was the same man who had jumped out of the driving cab of the container lorry after the accident. She couldn't see the colour of his eyes from up in her roof turret, but she knew they'd be dark, like black beads. And cold; menacingly cold. Oh God! She looked at his jacket again. The pocket bulged. She knew he carried a gun.

'Valko Asenov,' Chrissie mouthed, moving back from her makeshift window, and almost on cue he looked in her direction, straight at the roof. But those cruel eyes didn't seem to see the break in the tiles.

'This works out well for me,' Valko said, turning to speak to the goatee in the barn. 'I guessed she might work here. Stupid bitch left the address and directions stuffed under the front seat. And it's only a stone's throw from the crash; all adds up. Why else was she on the road?'

Chrissie clapped a hand to her mouth as she remembered; of course, the paperwork from the Academy about her apprenticeship. She'd brought it all with her when she drove out here that first time. The directions hadn't been much use. She'd got lost, but she'd left it all in the car, just in case. Everything must have fallen into the footwell and slipped under the driver's seat, and then she'd forgotten about it. Valko probably found it all when he adjusted the seat so he could drive her car. The bastard. God, she was a fool.

'She's the only one who got a good look at my face. She'll identify me. So I was going to finish her at her home, but this is turning out much better. I thought I'd have to

219

wait for hours to get her when she came to work but you've already got her locked up here ready for me.' He laughed, a strangely metallic sound, hostile. '*Da* - everyone'll think you killed her.'

Chrissie's breathing faltered as tightness gripped her chest. He was going to kill her. She'd seen those stones that passed for eyes; she knew he would do it. Oh God! But Valko was moving again and then the goatee appeared, following him out into the cool early morning air. Chrissie was shocked. The last time she'd seen the goatee's face, admittedly through a haze of eyelashes and blue mascara, it had been Friday. He had looked focused and tough – he'd just knocked her down and tied her up. Things like that tended to colour ones view. But now he was almost pathetic. Matted hair stuck out in clumps. His clothes were crumpled and grubby, and he moved his head in little jerks as he walked. He stopped, close to the Land Rover and stared at Valko. Even from where Chrissie was watching, his face looked sunken, almost skeletal with dark shadowy eye-sockets. She imagined his expression – crazed. He probably hadn't eaten since Friday, although he most likely called it a fast. The goatee was spiralling into a breakdown. She had no doubts of that.

'I've got them both locked up, the old man as well.' He spoke fast, his hand rubbing his forehead, before dropping limply to his side.

'Clegg,' Valko said as he looked at the neatly painted name on the sign above the barn workshop door: 'Mr Ron Clegg, Cabinet Maker and Furniture Restorer. *Kofti*.... Hmm, we'll make sure no one comes looking for him. I'll walk up the track and put a sign: *Closed for the day*. That should do it.'

'Yeah, well don't forget what we've agreed. I'll help you. But remember, you've got to help me.' The goatee tapped the battered old Land Rover.

Chrissie needed to think. Seeing the enemy terrified her. She was vulnerable and exposed and hearing their plans only served to heighten her fear. The malice was palpable. These people intended to kill.

'Mrs Jax?'

For a moment she'd even forgotten Ron. How could she? Bending down, she put her head through the hatchway; it was easier to whisper to him that way. 'Did you catch any of that, Mr Clegg?'

'I heard enough.'

'That other man, I recognise him. He's the driver of the container lorry. The one that hit our transporter. We think he stole my MG when he ran away and now he's turned up here. And so has my MG. And there's more; Nick's seen him before over at Damson Valley Farm. I think his name is Valko Asenov. Bulgarian, I think.'

'He's here to kill you. From what I could hear you'd already be dead by now if you hadn't come here on Friday. And now....'

It was a sobering thought which Chrissie didn't care to dwell on. She had already spent too much time on Sunday thinking about death and the hereafter. For one thing, if as she dreaded, there was going to be a lot of killing, then how would it work when they all met their maker? And what if it was the same maker? That might be a bit of a shock. For a start, there'd be: the helicopter crew, the goatee, Ron and herself. Awkward, while they waited for judgement - dead murderer alongside his dead victims, although the goatee might dispute who the victims were. How would the conversation run? She smiled as she imagined herself asking *so where's Valko? Why isn't he here? How did he manage to get away?*

Chrissie straightened up; all this bending to speak through the hatchway made her head buzz. And thoughts of death, however much they were laced with black humour, didn't lend themselves to optimism. It was time to have another peep through her rooftop window and get on with the business of living while she still could. At least now her cheek only hurt if she touched it.

Down in the courtyard, the back of the old Land Rover gaped wide open. At first it was difficult to make out what the goatee was doing inside it. He crouched over something, and then his hands darted down, a few moments later lifting what looked like a wooden lid. As she watched he pushed and heaved, opened and then closed several oblong boxes. The way he handled them suggested they were heavy, but she knew better than to expect him to lift out gold bullion. She guessed a more ominous content from their colour. He must have been totally absorbed because she heard the footsteps first; scrunch, crunch - soft, but like a pulse beat, rhythmic and incessant.

He froze as the sound finally broke through to him. As if electrocuted, he leapt out of the Land Rover, lips parted in a 12 volt snarl. Chrissie recoiled instinctively, almost stepping off her plywood board, shocked by his sudden movement. But the footsteps never once faltered as a grinning Valko appeared, walking back up the track.

'*Zdrasti* Mahmoud! Time now to finish our two guests. Then we can concentrate on your business. The key, please.' Valko held out his hand and smiled again.

'It's in my pocket, here take it.' The goatee handed the key to Valko. 'You may have a problem getting the door open.'

'Why, it jams?'

'No. They've barricaded themselves in. They've blocked the doorway from the inside. Since Friday.'

'You fool – *glupakut mu s glupak*,' Valko hissed through his teeth, 'Didn't you tie them up?'

In a flash he stepped towards the goatee and struck out like a snake flicking its tongue. Chrissie winced as she heard the crack. A clenched fist must have connected with the goatee's face. Nothing less could have whipped his head back with such force. He staggered and fell. For a moment she was sure he'd broken his neck, but then the goatee put one trembling hand to his face and sat up. He stared at Valko, who turned away. The violent bastard had spared his young friend's neck but probably broken his jaw.

'Well, let's see if we can open the door,' he said with a silky voice and walked towards the distillery workshop door.

'Oh my God, here they come,' she hissed, bending down to warn Ron. She was in such a hurry she nearly lost her balance as she poked her head through the hatchway. And when she couldn't see him, she almost screamed, 'Oh my God, where's Ron?' If she pulled the makeshift ladder up into the roof space and slid the hatchway shut, then…. Chrissie closed her eyes. Hunger, exhaustion and constant fear were starting to turn her mind. She had to hold it together. Breathing slowly, she forced her eyes open. And then she saw Ron. He moved stiffly, his shoulders bent by the weight of a huge wooden mallet that hung from his gnarled hand. He limped towards the door.

'Keep away from the line of the door. He's got a gun,' she shouted, no longer able to control her voice. And then the key started to turn in the lock. It grated and rasped. They both froze, transfixed by the sight of the door handle. It moved and then the door timbers strained.

'God, if the barricade holds,' Chrissie whispered, 'you must amend your notice to *master* cabinet maker and furniture restorer.'

'And if it doesn't then it can read *former* cabinet maker and furniture restorer.'

Bang! An explosive sound reverberated around the workshop. Ron dropped to his knees, but instead of a cloud of dust and debris, the air was clear. The door and barricade looked intact, except for a small rough hole.

'He's fired at the door, the bastard. Are you OK, Mr Clegg?'

The modern bullet had ripped its way through the thick timbers, making easy work of their defences. No doubt they would find its remains imbedded in the opposite wall, while an ugly scar on the door was a reminder of their vulnerability. Thank God it hadn't been a grenade. 'Mr Clegg, it didn't get you, did it?'

'No, no. I was trying to get down on the ground, but my knees wouldn't....'

'Well don't move in case he fires again.'

'Come on let's not waste any more time on these rats,' Valko shouted on the other side of the door. 'I've got a better idea. If we set you up in front of this building, the helicopters will almost certainly shell it in retaliation.' The key grated in the lock again.

'But I - but,' the goatee's thin voice drifted through the ragged bullet hole. 'I was going to set the MANPADS up in the back of the Land Rover. Then I could drive it anywhere here and be under cover as the helicopters fly over.'

'What's a man pad?' Chrissie mouthed to Ron.

'*Ne, ne.* You'll do as I say,' Valko yelled. He must have been standing directly outside the door, because when he spoke softly, they could still hear him. 'With any luck you'll perish with these rats when the helicopters fire at you.' He paused. 'I thought Jan got you a Grom missile from Poland.' Footsteps moved away.

Chrissie shot a questioning look at Ron who shrugged, winced and pointed upwards. She turned back into the roof space, the word missile ringing in her ears. Oh God, she thought, and I worried they might have a grenade. A few moments later she peered through the opening in the tiles. The goatee was back in the Land Rover, rummaging amongst his boxes. He lifted one out.

'Man-portable air defence system; you know: M A N P A D S,' she heard the goatee spell out for Valko. Why couldn't he just call it a man held missile, or something simple? God, they were all the same. Matt would have called it something spectacularly technical as well.

'The Grom is a MANPADS.' The goatee tossed the words over his shoulder at Valko. She couldn't see his face, but she imagined him spitting blood with each syllable. 'Jan told me how the Grom works, but all these instructions are written in… Polish.'

'Ha! Well what do you expect? It was made in Poland. Of course the instructions are written in Polish, you fool.' Valko gazed up at the sky, his face relaxed and almost smiling. 'That's about the only useful thing Jan got out of national service; making contacts to get special equipment.'

Chrissie watched with horror as the goatee lifted a large pipe, maybe a metre long out of one of the boxes. It looked like a common-or-garden conduit for domestic water or waste, except the colour was munitions green. 'Well this,' he spoke with reverence, 'is the missile launching tube.'

Valko turned and sauntered back to the Land Rover. He leant in and pointed to one of the boxes. 'That's the thermal battery coolant assembly unit.' It was difficult to catch all his words. They were unfamiliar; a new vocabulary. 'The gripstock attaches....'

Chrissie couldn't understand what he said next. She guessed, from the number of cases, that the weapon came in several parts and needed to be assembled before use. With any luck, if they made a mistake they might blow themselves up first.

She checked her watch. 7:30 - would Nick and Matt even be awake yet? How long would it take before they realised she was missing, and would they come looking for her? She closed her eyes and shook her head. It was hopeless.

It was time to get the Molotov cocktail bottles up into the roof space and ready for priming. The dustsheet with Ron's painted message still lay on the brick floor. It was no use down there, she needed it up with her. Then she could thrust it out for display at the right moment after she had removed more tiles. Yes, there was still plenty to do. Activity - that was the answer. It wouldn't be much longer before the helicopters started flying.

CHAPTER 16

'Why doesn't she answer, for God's sake?' Nick asked as the ring tone went dead. He didn't know who he was asking: the air, the swirling universe, or simply himself. Frustration and concern drove his question, but he didn't expect an answer. Chrissie would have to switch her mobile on and speak to him if he was ever going to find out. 'Just answer, damn you, answer!'

Nick scratched his head. 'Hmm... just try and be logical. Think like Chrissie,' he told himself. Now that was some joke. How could anyone possibly think like Chrissie?

He pictured the last time he'd seen her, Thursday night, now almost three days ago. She had seemed to be in reasonably good spirits, all things considered. After all, it had been a dreadful day, what with the accident and then having her car stolen. She had been fine when he dropped her off home after more drinks at the Dog and Bone, though the same couldn't be said of Matt. He'd started singing, or maybe rapping, and then he'd tried to pick the logo off his tee-shirt which would have been OK, but they were all in Nick's Fiesta at the time and on their way back from Bury. Nick hadn't said he would phone Chrissie on the Friday and he was pretty sure she hadn't mentioned anything about ringing him. But by Saturday, surely she would have found time to answer his calls? He knew she liked to play it alone - independent and tough, but something about her silence wasn't quite right. And now it was Sunday evening. He still hadn't heard from her and he was worried. Should he drive over to her home and check she was OK? But maybe her mobile had been stolen along with her MG and if that was the case then he would feel really silly driving over to Woolpit.

Sunday evenings tended to breed lethargy and in the end Nick decided it was probably best to wait. He could go to the Academy early on Monday. Chrissie was sure to attend the Monday apprentice release day and he could catch up with her again then.

•••

Matt had also been worrying about Chrissie over the weekend, but he hadn't made any attempt to contact her. He supposed she might want some time to herself, and he knew he wasn't very good at the intuitive, touchy-feely, emotional side of things. His mother told him so. Repeatedly. If he left things for a few days, he reckoned then with luck Chrissie would be back to normal by Monday. That's what he did with his mother – leave her to herself. But a weekend wouldn't be long enough for his mother; she was in it for the long haul. Years, if he considered the time since his father walked out on them. He just hoped it was long enough for Chrissie. He shook his head. How could he think of Chrissie and his mum in the same monologue of thought?

Matt turned his mind back to more practical things. It was Sunday evening and he needed to make his plans for Monday. Should he search out Mahmoud in the morning? There were questions that still needed to be answered, the most obvious being, why was he looking at Chrissie's car so closely that time in the car park? And had he had anything to do with its disappearance? Well of course he knew he couldn't ask the questions quite so directly. He'd need to wrap them up in something about looking for a car himself.

And then there had been the farmers market picnic. That had given him more food for thought. Apart from the obvious charms of the overwhelmingly scarlet Denisa, Valko's name had cropped up just too often to be a coincidence. He was a common thread connecting everything bad that had happened and furthermore, he was still at large. It never crossed Matt's mind to wonder what Valko might do next. He preferred to work out what he had done. To Matt's way of thinking, the past was fact and he liked facts. Predicting the future was - well one couldn't predict the future, could one? And so, as Matt turned in for the night, he set his phone alarm. He decided that if he woke up in time, he'd get the early bus to the Academy and be waiting for Mahmoud at the car maintenance workshop, first thing.

Six hours later, Monday morning dawned warm and windy. Matt heard the alarm tones muffled through the horror of his waking dream. He was back in the Academy canteen, prone on the floor with smoke and dust forcing its way up his nose. Suffocating, he fought to breathe. He lifted his head off his pillow and struggled to sit up as some greater force held him down.

'You must pray, Matt Finch, you must recite the rest of the Koran. All of it, from beginning to end, before I sell you the car,' a voice whispered.

'But I don't know the words.' He flung off his duvet, as sweat gathered in the folds of his neck. 'What'll you do? Another explosion? A bigger nail gun?' he yelled.

Thump, thump! The thin bedroom wall juddered as his mother shouted, 'What you doin' in there? Quiet, you selfish bastard, some of us are tryin' to sleep.'

Matt opened his eyes. His mother's voice cut through the images in his mind and snapped him back into reality. Tired blue walls and retro-posters met his eyes. 6:10am Monday. He lay on his back and breathed slowly. It was a familiar sight, but shite, it was depressing. He checked his phone. He had forty minutes if he was going to catch the early bus.

Matt glanced at the time as he settled himself in the library. 9:30am. He chose his customary place in the corner with a computer, away from preying eyes. He felt disappointed. Despite getting to the car maintenance workshop early and hanging around for three quarters of an hour, Mahmoud hadn't shown up. In the end Matt felt a bit of a turnip and there had been nothing else for it but to slope off. If he'd stayed any longer the tutor would have thought he wanted to join the course – ugh! Monday wasn't turning out too well, so far.

Matt looked over towards the librarian's station; maybe Rosie might be there and he could catch her eye. No; but then the library doors swung open and a familiar figure strode through. Matt smiled, suddenly happy for the first time that day. It wasn't Rosie, but it was the next best thing.

'Hi, over here,' he mouthed as he waved his plastered wrist in the air.

Nick's face seemed to relax when he spotted Matt, but he didn't smile as he made his way across the library.

'Hi, aren't you meant to be in a lecture?' Matt whispered cheerfully.

Nick ignored the question. 'Have you spoken to Chrissie any time since we dropped her off home, Thursday night?' He spoke quickly.

'No, why? Told you on Saturday – wouldn't expect to hear from her over the weekend.'

'You didn't think to phone to see if she was OK?'
Matt shook his head.

'No?' The look on Nick's face was dark. 'Well, she hasn't turned up for our first lecture and she hasn't answered her mobile all weekend. Something's wrong. I've got a bad feeling about this.'

'She could just be late? I mean, like - missed the bus.'

'No. It's not like Chrissie. I'm going to drive over to Woolpit. The Clegg workshops are slightly out of the way, but I thought I'd call in there first.'

'Can I come, if that's OK?'

'Sure.' Nick turned on his heel.

It didn't take a moment for Matt to log out of the computer and follow. 'What's the bloody hurry?' he mouthed as the library door swung in his face. But he was asking the tailwind left by Nick as he took the stairs two at a time. He'd have to make it to the car if he was ever to get an answer. 'Shit!' Matt hissed between breathless wheezes as he rushed towards the student car park. 'Cripes; wait a moment, can't you?'

Matt struggled with his seat belt as Nick threw the Fiesta into reverse. The jolt sent Matt forwards, almost colliding with the front windscreen.

Nick slammed on the brakes, rammed the gear stick into first, let the clutch out with a bang and accelerated out of the Academy grounds. Matt decided to keep quiet and bit back his next expletive. Something about Nick's manner made him feel nervous, and anyway, he needed to keep his mouth shut as the bile rose in his throat. Travel sickness wasn't normally a problem, but this journey was proving a bit of a jaw-clencher. He glanced at Nick's profile before closing his eyes as they swung round another corner. Nick's face was set in concentration and for a moment Matt imagined him with the Stig's white helmet and black visor. All

231

he needed was the soundtrack to some Italian opera with warbling soprano and the scene would be complete. 'Cool,' he said through gritted teeth.

'What?'

'I said cool. Stig-like.' He swallowed hard before continuing, 'You know Mahmoud didn't turn up this mornin' – well not at car the maintenance workshop. Seems Chrissie's not the only one.'

Nick didn't answer. Matt wasn't even sure he'd heard him, but for the moment he didn't really mind. He preferred that Nick concentrate on the road. They might be covering the miles to the Clegg workshop in record time, but it would be nice to get out of the car in one piece and alive at the end of the journey. Matt sensed Nick's urgency was increasing as he got closer to the Clegg workshops. He thought it would have been the opposite, but then he couldn't drive, so how would he know? When the whining roar of the Fiesta engine finally quietened, Matt guessed it was probably safe to look through the windscreen again. The fast moving hedgerows, combined with the rotatory G-force of the cornering had taken their toll, and he pressed his plastered wrist to his mouth. 'Ugh!'

Nick slowed the car as he reached the turning off the perimeter lane. Instead of jolting his way down the uneven track, he paused and then drew to a halt. Matt looked over at Nick. 'Thanks mate. Anymore an' I'd 've chucked up.'

Nick didn't answer.

'Sorry mate. Thought you'd stopped for me.' He let his voice trail, unsure of himself. 'What's up?' He glanced at the petrol gauge, but there was still half a tank showing on the indicator. Matt followed the direction of Nick's gaze.

A makeshift notice had been attached to the board announcing the Clegg Workshops.

Nick slowly read out the words written in bold handwriting across the signboard, 'CLOSED FOUR TODAY.' He turned the ignition off.

'Shall we turn round - go to Woolpit then?' Matt asked.

'Look at the spelling, Matt. Who spells *for* as a number when they mean closed for today?'

'Someone who hasn't got spellcheck? Mind, it can happen with spellcheck.'

'Don't be so bloody stupid. You only make a mistake like that if you can't spell or you're....'

Matt winced as Nick's sharp words punctured his plump pride. Why was Nick being so impatient? Was it because he'd nearly thrown up in the car? He really was starting to feel sick.

'Someone whose first language isn't English,' Nick finished for him. 'And why is the workshop closed for today? Old Clegg never closes. There's nowhere else for him to go. He's probably even here on Christmas day.'

Matt felt his face burn. Did Nick really expect him to answer all these questions? Was this some quiz? 'Best drive on. Check it out,' Matt said quietly.

'No, I think we'll walk. If there's something going on it might be better if no one realises we're here. The engine might give us away. You go ahead up the track and I'll skirt round,' Nick said getting out of the car.

'What, walk the track?' Matt whined, but Nick didn't hear. He was already circling around to one side and heading off in the direction of the workshops.

There was nothing for it but to do as Nick suggested. Matt heaved himself out of the car. It felt good to stand on stationary ground after the gyratory journey, but he couldn't afford to hang around for long. If Nick found him still next to the car… well, it was best to get walking.

So who did Nick think had written the notice, Matt asked himself. Not Mahmoud. He might have changed his name, but he wasn't a foreigner. It went without saying that Chrissie would never misspell *for* and old Clegg never closed the workshop and therefore wouldn't need to write a notice in the first place. Matt scratched his head; he didn't know. As he approached the workshop he caught sight of three cars. There was a battered old Land Rover parked at an angle close to the barn workshop door. A smart metallic-blue Peugeot 207 was parked neatly to one side with its front windows wound down, but miracle of miracles, Chrissie's red MGB was also there, further off to one side. Matt almost stopped dead in his tracks. He looked again to make sure he wasn't mistaken but it really was Chrissie's MG. It could only mean one thing. The police must have found her car. So why hadn't she shared the good news with them?

Matt quickened his pace. It would be good to see Chrissie, but where was everyone? The place felt deserted despite three cars in the courtyard. His trainers scrunched over gravelly stones on old concrete as he headed for the barn workshop door. Grasping the handle, he noticed the warmth on his fingers. The morning sun had already been at work for several hours.

'Bloody right hand, bloody plaster,' he said when the handle wouldn't shift. He turned slightly to make it easier to use his left hand. This time he put his shoulder against the door to add encouragement to the old hinge. As he pushed against the wood, he glanced sideways along the length of the old brick workshop and idly noticed the cedar trunk and a pile of unfamiliar objects. If he hadn't known better, he would have assumed he was looking at the parts of a small rocket launcher - but of course that would be ridiculous. He turned his attention back to the barn door, and this time gave it a more sustained shove as he twisted the handle. Suddenly it gave way and Matt fell inwards through the doorway. Someone had opened it for him. Trying to regain his dignity, he straightened up and looked directly into the face of a man who stood in the shadows, making it difficult for Matt to see his face clearly.

The man wore a leather jacket despite the warmth of the summer morning, and kept one hand ready, as if to reach inside the pocket for something. He didn't say anything, but watched, waiting for Matt to speak. His dark brown eyes threatened and chilled, and as Matt acclimatised to the poor light, he noticed a slight tightening of the muscles around the man's eyes. Matt recognised him. It was Valko Asenov, the same man Chrissie had captured in her fuzzy photo. This was bad; very bad. The silence was oppressive. Matt knew he had to say something - anything to explain his arrival at the workshop.

'Domino's Pizza.' There, it was done. He'd blurted out the first thing that came to mind.

Valko stared at Matt's empty hands and plaster cast, and then back at Matt's face. Slowly he raised one dark brown eyebrow, but only just.

'Wrong address, sorry,' Matt said as he tried to back out through the barn door.

'You appear to have forgotten something.' The silky tones were loaded with menace.

Matt looked down at his empty hands. 'There's a closed sign, so I left 'em in the van just in case it's the wrong address. They stay warmer in their bags, you know. They're insulated… the bags.'

'*Kofti*! I didn't hear an engine. Where's the van?' Valko asked as he finally stepped out of the shadows.

'Just outside.' There was nothing for it but to turn and run. Matt needed to bolt for his life, but with his opening stride a steely pain bit into his shoulder, stopping him from moving forwards. He spun round, unable to control his momentum. 'Ugh!' he screamed. He stared into a pair of cold eyes as Valko's hand gripped his shoulder.

'You forgot to tell me, my friend. What's the pizza topping?'

Matt's mouth went dry. He couldn't read anything from Valko's expressionless face. It reminded him of a shark. 'Pineapple and,' Matt cast about for a suitable topping, 'tuna.'

'*Ne*! Wrong answer; I don't like pineapple,' and the Bulgarian shark almost smiled. 'You're not a pizza delivery boy. Who are you and why are you here?' Valko's grip tightened on Matt's shoulder. He edged his fingers upwards and grasped the side of the base of his neck in the region, Matt later learnt, called the brachial plexus. It was the anatomical name given to the spaghetti junction of nerves leaving his spine to supply his arm. Valko dug in his fingers. It was agony. Matt's knees buckled with the sudden pain. Within seconds he was helpless, immobilised and kneeling on the ground.

'You haven't answered my question; who are you and why are you here?'

The leg of Matt's jeans rode up when he bent his knee, just enough to expose his ankle. There in plain view was the identity band the nurse had attached when he'd broken his wrist five weeks before.

'*Da* - what have we here?' Valko asked as he bent to read the hospital name tag more closely. 'Perhaps you've escaped from an asylum… Mr Matt Finch?'

Matt didn't know what to say. He was in danger, but what were his options? From his position on the ground he couldn't see many. He could either insist he was a pizza delivery boy but without a pizza, or act as if he was just plain mad. But then, under the circumstances he'd have to be mad to pretend he was a pizza delivery boy. 'Sh-i-t,' he whispered. Why, oh why, hadn't he removed the identity tag after Rosie spotted it that time in the library?

'I know that name.' Another voice spoke from the depths of the barn workshop.

Matt watched, his heart sinking as another man stepped out from the shadows. This one was young with dark hair, greasy and uncombed. His eyes darted from Valko to the identity tag and then back to Valko again. Something about his manner made Matt think of a race-horse bucking in the starting pen, full of pent-up energy. The way he kept touching his thin straggly beard and then, when his hand rested still for a moment on his cut lip, a fine tremor gently disturbed his fingers.

Matt knew instantly. It was the goatee. He was the young student who had looked so closely at Chrissie's car in the student car park that time. He had to be Mahmoud, aka the Aphid, aka Phillip Farrow. 'Sh-i-t,' Matt moaned.

'Someone by the name of Matt Finch was asking for me at the car maintenance workshop.'

'Now why would that be?' Valko asked in oily tones and dug his fingers deeper into Matt's brachial plexus.

'Argh! No don't. I wanted to buy a car, and I'd heard Mahmoud was the man to ask.' Matt looked up, pleading.

Nothing registered on Valko's mask-like features. In fact, there was nothing to indicate he was even listening. A muscle flickered close to his eye and then near his jaw. A second later his foot jerked forward. The kick landed with a crack, fair and square on Matt's plaster cast. 'That doesn't explain what you're doing here,' he hissed through clenched teeth as the toe of his shoe struck its target.

'Awh shit!' Matt screamed. He just hadn't seen it coming. 'For God's sake,' he groaned. To be honest, his broken bones were almost healed and well protected by the plaster cast, but he wasn't going to let Valko know that. Matt gave another groan for good measure. 'I told you, I wanted to buy a car,' he whimpered.

'So how did you know Mahmoud was here?' Suddenly Valko turned to Mahmoud. He almost spat out the next words, 'Who else knows you're here, Mahmoud?'

'No one; no one else knows I'm here, Va–'

'Don't use my name,' Valko shouted, cutting Mahmoud off, mid-word.

Matt shrank lower onto the floor. He couldn't decide whether to watch Valko's face or his shoe. He settled for the toe of his shoe. It was closer and probably more expressive than his face.

'Are you alone? Is anyone with you?' Valko asked, reverting to his cold silky voice.

The change in tone frightened Matt more than the words. Valko must have made a decision about him. He shivered despite the sunny summer day. 'No, course not,' he replied to the shoe.

'Well I think I'll go outside and check anyway, just to be certain. In the meantime, Mr Matt Finch, we'll make sure you don't decide to leave just yet. Mahmoud will secure you.'

Mahmoud took a step towards Matt who still knelt on the ground. 'How do I tie him up? That plaster cast on his wrist…?'

'*Idiotut mu s idiot*! Just bind his arms to his chest, tie his feet together and then rope him to something. If he causes any trouble, knock him unconscious.'

'Hah! This pillar drill's got a cast iron base. If he manages to pull that over it'll probably kill him. Will that be OK?'

Matt turned his attention from Valko's foot and watched Mahmoud instead, but what was wrong with the goatee? He held the rope but it seemed to jerk in his hands as if it was alive and writhing. Even the way he kept looking at Valko was strange. Matt knew that look. It was fear. But why?

'Awh! Ff….' Hard fingers pressed deeper into the base of Matt's neck as a deep, tingling pain shot down his arm with the intensity of a red-hot poker. He fought for a breath as he looked up at Valko who smiled, let go of him and stepped back.

'And while you're about it, look for a nail gun.' His voice sounded calm, almost sweet.

Matt watched, mesmerised as Valko turned, and putting his hand inside his leather jacket, pulled out a small handgun. Matt closed his eyes. He waited, trying to control his bladder. The barn door creaked, and when he opened his eyes, Valko had gone.

•••

While Matt ambled up the track to the Clegg workshops, Nick skirted round to one side. The handwritten notice really worried him. He had no idea what he was expecting to find, but he knew something was wrong. As he moved through the rough long grass and stinging nettles close to the overgrown hedge, he decided to work his way past the end of the old brick workshop. Then he could approach the courtyard from behind the far end of the barn. The hedge was ancient and typical of the area. He supposed it was quite a complex structure, consisting of a large ditch which filled with water in the winter, and hawthorn and sloe bushes on both banks. With the passage of time, wild hedge roses, holly and the largest brambles imaginable had sprung up. It struck Nick that anything thorny, spikey or could sting had taken root there.

It was hard going and he realised that if anyone cared to look, he was highly visible. He needed to conceal himself, but how? He decided to get into the hedge. He found if he kept to the base of the ditch, it was relatively clear. He could move forwards slowly, and as long as he crouched down low, he was well hidden. Nick paused and listened. A creak and then a clunk – it had to be the barn door opening and closing. Good, he thought, Matt would have reached the barn by now, even with his slow walk. Nick waited. It was easier to listen if he stayed still, but there were no more sounds. Great, Matt must have gone into the barn; it should be safe to move again.

As he got closer to the barn, he took extra care. It was even more important to remain hidden and silent. His challenge was to negotiate each prickly bramble so that it didn't spring back with a loud rustle and snag into his jeans. He passed the far end of the brick workshop and so didn't see the side of its roof with the missing tiles. It was hot. The air felt humid in his ditch and sweat stuck to his face. A thrush took sudden flight with a smacking beat of its wings. Nick stopped dead. His heart pounded. 'What the hell am I doing?' he asked himself for the first time, but Action Man couldn't come up with an answer. He hadn't thought it through.

Nick thrust on again, only stopping when he reached the point where his hedge-ditch intersected a field boundary. If he clambered out from his cover, there was only a short distance of open ground to cross before he reached the back of the barn workshop. Then he'd be safely out of view of its door and courtyard. Nick straightened up, trying to decide whether to make a dash for the back of the barn but something caught his eye. It glinted in the sunshine. He wasn't certain but it reminded him of the way the light reflected off Chrissie's chrome bumper, after all, he'd followed her car often enough. He moved a little and stood, straining to see, but the angle was wrong and he couldn't get a clear view into the courtyard. Was the heat and the adrenalin playing tricks on him, he wondered. Was he creating a drama, when really she was safe at the workshop and just skipped the lecture? He heard, rather than saw, the barn door open.

'And while you're about it, look for a nail gun.' The words floated towards him on the summer air.

Nick froze. He knew that oily voice; would have recognised it anywhere. His stomach twisted and lurched as realisation struck. Instinctively he ducked down and crouched low in the ditch. 'Christ! It's Valko Asenov,' he breathed, not wanting to believe his ears. 'What the hell's he doing here?' And just as for Paul on the road to Damascus, a blinding light of revelation struck Nick. The intensity of it made him gasp. Of course, Valko must have written the CLOSED FOUR TODAY notice. That would explain the spelling error. But why? Why was he here?

'Shit! Matt's in that barn.' This second revelation almost made Nick vomit. He knew Valko was wanted by the police. He reached into his pocket for his mobile, but he couldn't just ring 999 and ask for the police simply because he'd spotted someone who'd stolen a car and left the scene of an accident. He tried to think. Perhaps he could phone the Raingate Police Station in Bury St Edmunds, but what was the number? What about directory enquiries?

He looked up from his phone and spotted Valko walking slowly alongside the barn. It wasn't the walk of a Sunday afternoon stroll. He took each step as if ready to sprint 200 metres, moving silently like a cat stalking its prey, listening for the slightest sound that might suggest another living creature was somewhere out there and waiting to become dinner. Every few paces Valko stopped and turned his head slowly so he could scan the area. It was almost as if he was sniffing and tasting the air for scent. Even his reptilian-like leather jacket looked predatory in the summer sunshine. But there was something worse. He held a handgun at the ready. Terrified, Nick sank further back into his ditch, and for the first time that day, thanked God for the luscious brambles and nettles worthy of a gold medal at the Chelsea Flower Show.

Nick waited as Valko paused at the end of the barn and then took a few paces towards the hedge – Nick's hedge-ditch. He held his breath trying not to make a sound, conscious that only the dense hawthorn and wild hedge roses growing on the edge of the ditch separated them. He must have seen me, Nick thought, as he huddled lower amongst the stingers and brambles. Crack! A twig snapped as Nick shifted his weight. He braced himself for certain discovery. Something rustled on Valko's side of the hedge, and then Nick caught the unmistakable sound of a zipper. After a moment's pause, the smell of fresh urine pervaded the air as warm liquid cascaded and splashed though the foliage. It seemed Valko had a more immediate matter to attend to than hunting prey. Nick forced himself to stay still, all the while expecting Valko to peer deeper into the hedge, past the dripping leaves and straight into his face. But he was in luck. As is so common with people who foul an area, whether it is litter or excrement, Valko was eager to distance himself from the scene. He simply turned on his heal and headed back to resume his slow circuit of the barn and courtyard, gun held in full view.

Nick let out a long slow breath. His nerves were in tatters. Why was fear described as paralysing? He couldn't imagine being more frightened, and yet he had found it almost impossible to stay absolutely still. Maybe he just hadn't been frightened enough. He didn't know whether to laugh or cry, and then he pictured the gun. 'What's the pissing bastard done to Matt?' he hissed. He still clutched his mobile in his sweaty hand. 'Christ! I never put it on silent. What if…?'

Directory Enquires proved quick and efficient and a few moments later, Nick keyed the number for the Raingate Police Station. He knew he was out of his depth with Valko. The man had a gun. There was no way he could handle this alone; he needed backup. 'I must've been out of my mind sending Matt in,' he whispered, guilt fear and regret mixing a heady cocktail as he waited for what seemed like an eternity for someone to answer. However that seemed short in comparison to the time he spent trying to get past the switchboard operator. Unfortunately the police officer who had taken his statement identifying Valko in the photograph, was not available. He had to satisfy himself with leaving a message with a woman who seemed to interpret his urgency as aggression.

'I'm sorry, sir, but I will terminate this call if you are abusive.'

'No, no… please don't ring off. This is really urgent. I have to whisper.'

'Your voice is breaking up. I can't hear you.'

'Look, I know this call is being recorded. I can't shout. I'm hiding from a man with a gun. For God's sake tell Inspector Merry, *Valko Asinov is at the Clegg workshops off the Wattisham perimeter road, and he's got a gun. Chrissie Jax*, tell him *Chrissie Jax*. He'll remember her,' and then the call went dead. 'Shit! No one's going to come.'

The barn door clunked. 'Valko must have completed his circuit by now,' Nick whispered, 'unless someone's come out.' The tension was unbearable. He didn't know what he could do, but he knew he couldn't hide in the ditch any longer. It was time to brave the short distance out into the open between the hedge and the back of the barn workshop. Summoning his courage and propelled by adrenalin, he pushed his way between the brambles nettles and hawthorn bushes as he clambered out of the ditch, collecting more scratches and stings on the way. A few strides and then he was there; close up against the black-painted weatherboards of the back wall, the side furthest away from the courtyard.

•••

Matt looked at Mahmoud holding the rope. He made a momentous decision. He wouldn't struggle. He feared he might be tied more tightly if he put up a fight. Instead he concentrated on puffing out his chest as his arms were bound to his side, so when he breathed out again, he'd created a little slack in the rope. It wasn't much, but it was better than nothing. As promised, Mahmoud then tied his feet to the cast iron base of the pillar drill. Matt lay face down on the concrete floor, helpless and uncomfortable, watching as Mahmoud searched through Mr Clegg's tools.

'Nail gun? Where's the…?'

'Wha' d'you wan' nail gun for? Are d'you makin' somethin'?' Matt asked, his mouth and nose half-crushed against the concrete floor. His words didn't come out right and Mahmoud ignored him, instead concentrating on his rummaging before finally throwing something onto the floor.

'What have you done to your arm? Why's it in plaster?' Mahmoud asked as he moved closer and bent over Matt.

'Utterly canteen explosion,' Matt answered by way of an explanation, but this time lifting his head away from the concrete so he could speak more clearly. 'Were you involved?' This proved to be a question with double meaning.

'Yes and no, but I've got bigger plans.'

'Shit!' It wasn't the answer Matt expected. He rested his face back on the cool floor and digested Mahmoud's words. A kernel of an idea started to take life - the explosion took place on a Friday lunchtime. At the time,

Mahmoud would have been well out of the way at Friday prayers, safe and praying. Of course he must have been involved. It made sense. Could he really have planted the liquid propane gas cartridge?

'You wanted to blow up the canteen? That's a bit harsh isn't it? I mean, if the chips aren't hal...al....' Lying on the hard concrete was having an effect. Matt focused his thoughts.

'What did you say?' Mahmoud resumed his search.

'Said the chips are OK, you know, in the canteen.' Matt craned his neck trying to see what had been thrown on the ground. There didn't seem to be anything obvious other than a lot of loose nails. 'Why're you chuckin' nails on the floor?'

'So it'll look like an accident when they find you. It'll be obvious to everyone the nails became airborne in the explosion and imbedded in your neck.'

The shock of his words made Matt's stomach lurch. He rested his face back on the cold concrete and if he hadn't already been sprawled on the ground, he was sure he'd have fainted. With a huge effort he took some slow deep breaths and calmed himself. There were so many questions he needed to ask, but he wasn't too sure if he wanted to hear the answers. 'But why?' he finally asked into the floor.

Mahmoud ignored the question as he pulled more drawers open.

'You won't find no nail gun. Old Clegg's a traditionalist.'

'Traditionalist? Mr A is a professional.'

'What's that s'posed to mean?' Matt had already guessed the A stood for Asenov, Valko Asenov.

'The nail gun worked last time. He probably wants to avoid using bullets. If you're shot with a civilian one… well, questions would be asked. This way it'll just look like another accident and *case closed*.' Mahmoud had been directing his words to the cupboards, shelves and drawers as he searched; anything rather than look at Matt. But suddenly he stilled and turned to face him. 'You shouldn't have come here, mate. You shouldn't have come.'

There was no point in going over the old ground of why he'd come to the workshop. It had already earned him a kick and Matt didn't want another one. 'What you mean a nail gun worked last time?' Matt asked as the barn door creaked open and Valko stepped in.

'You ask too many questions, Mr Matt Finch,' Valko said smoothly. He stood and surveyed the scene, taking in the nails strewn on the floor as he put his gun back into the pocket of his leather jacket. He nodded slowly and smiled at Mahmoud. Matt thought the smile was more a baring of teeth than pleasure, and his heart sank.

'Find anyone?' Mahmoud asked.

Matt held his breath, bracing himself for the reply, but Valko said nothing and shook his head, a strangely elegant movement. Matt silently thanked God, Nick was still at large.

'I can't find a nail gun,' Mahmoud said, his eyes darting about excitedly.

Valko held up his hand, as if for silence or stopping traffic. '*Kofti*, but we can improvise.'

'Shit!' The word *improvise* conjured up terrifying images. Matt had watched too many American gangster movies and the thought of the nail gun was, quite frankly, preferable to his vivid imaginings. 'Shit!' He needed to keep

247

talking and playing for time, but even he realised one-word expletives were hardly conversational. In desperation he settled for, 'Why can't you just let me go?'

'*Da nye si lood*? Because you've seen me here,' Valko's words cut through the air like a falling icicle.

'Mahmoud has business here with Allah and wants everyone to know it, but my business must remain secret.'

'I could promise not to tell.'

'Don't make me laugh. You wouldn't like me when I laugh.' Valko showed his teeth in the semblance of a smile.

'But what's Mahmoud doing here?'

'Too many questions. But maybe Mahmoud might like to answer that one.' Valko turned, and with his teeth still exposed, gestured to Mahmoud.

'The helicopters; I'm here to blow them from the sky!' Mahmoud's words darted through the air, staccato and harsh as he shuffled his feet in some bizarre dance of death.

'But why?' Matt waited for more as Mahmoud touched the cut on his swollen lip, all the while looking at Valko. He seemed to have run out of words.

Valko finished the explanation for him. 'It's Mahmoud's jihadist terror attack. He's going to strike down an army helicopter in retribution for the West's treatment of Islam, and then - it's *dovizdanye* and straight to Paradise.'

'But how does he get to Paradise? He's blowing him-self up too?'

'*Ne*, he's only got one Grom missile and he's saving that for an army helicopter.' Valko laughed before continu-ing. He spoke slowly, as if explaining something to a child, 'Remember - one missile; only one helicopter gets shot down. There'll be plenty of other army helicopters still at the airbase and… once they get airborne he'll be a sitting target down here.'

'Shit!'

'I anticipate a shelling of this workshop site, and when they strike, well its bull's eye and straight to Paradise for Mahmoud.'

Matt's mouth was too dry to say the word shit again. To be honest, he felt sick.

'You, Mr Matt Finch will be, what shall we say, caught up in the collateral damage,' Valko concluded with obvious relish.

Matt looked across at Mahmoud with new respect. The man was mad; he had to be to carry out some half-baked attack on an Apache helicopter. To be honest, he didn't look well. His greasy hair and wispy beard framed a thin sunken face. He looked as if he hadn't slept or if he had, it was in his clothes – they were crumpled and grubby. A bit how Matt felt lying on concrete, and bound and tied to a pillar drill. Mahmoud's eyes flicked restlessly from Valko to Matt and then back to his watch. Sh-i-t, Matt thought. He's unstable. Valko, by contrast, appeared to be getting calmer and more composed.

Suddenly everyone in the barn workshop froze. The deep hum of a distant rumble filled the air. It was unmistakable - the sound of a helicopter still far away but flying in their direction. Mahmoud sprang into action, almost as if an electric shock had galvanized his legs. He ran to the barn door and wrenched it open. Without even pausing to check it was safe for him to go outside, he almost flew out of the barn.

'Wait! It's only the first helicopter of the day,' Valko shouted.

CHAPTER 17

Nick waited, pressing his back against the black wooden weatherboarding and tried to control his breathing. He knew he was taking a risk, but if he assumed Valko had completed his outside checks and returned to the barn workshop then it should be safe to creep along the barn's back wall. Nick considered the word *safe*. He couldn't imagine anything less safe. It was a stupid word to use.

He made good speed along the length of the barn, paused, listened and when he was certain he couldn't hear any voices or footsteps, rounded the far end. He wanted to reach the door on the front wall, but that meant exposing himself to full view from the courtyard. Crouching low, he kept moving, half expecting to be seen and challenged at any moment. Finally he reached the door and squatted with his ear pressed to the old wood. Relief flooded over him with surprising intensity as his friend's muffled voice drifted through. Matt was still alive, thank God. As he listened, Valko spoke, cold and threatening, and then a third voice replied. It had to belong to the name being bandied around - Mahmoud. Could this really be Damson Valley Farm's youngest son, Phillip? And anyway, why was he here? Coldness gripped the pit of Nick's stomach as the conversation continued and the sheer audacity of Mahmoud's mad plan slowly unfolded. Were they really going to fire a missile at one of the Apaches?

The sudden rumble of a distant helicopter engine shifted Nick's attention from the voices inside to the cloudless blue above. He never heard the quick footsteps moving towards the door just before it was wrenched open. Almost falling into the barn, he jumped sideways. A man sporting a goatee rushed out, looking ahead and up at the sky. Nick didn't wait to be discovered and darted back to the side wall. If the man had turned his head just a fraction, Nick was sure he'd have registered him in his peripheral vision. Nick tried to look small, pressing close to the weatherboarding, not daring to move. That must be Mahmoud, he thought, and then his heart missed another beat as Valko stepped out through the doorway. He walked purposefully, watching for any sign of trouble. If he'd looked back, he'd have spotted Nick, but his attention was on Mahmoud.

It was only as Nick watched them cross the courtyard that he noticed something for the first time. Propped against one end of the cedar trunk, close to the brick workshop, was a green metal tube. He knew he wasn't looking at an automated tennis ball launcher. The green was more army than Wimbledon and the collection of objects lying close to it didn't look like racket bags.

'Fuck,' he whispered.

The deep, thumping rumble from the helicopter engines was getting louder. Nick counted to three and ran. He crossed the front of the barn and ducked in through the open doorway. He crouched low, waiting for his eyes to acclimatise, not knowing what he expected to find. The light was poor, but the sunshine flooding in through the door illuminated a grubby pair of trainers. He looked more closely. They were attached to legs encased in baggy jeans. A rope bound the ankles, anchoring them to the base of a pillar drill. Nick could have recognised that mix of faded and grubby denim anywhere. It was Matt, face down on the concrete floor.

'Christ, Matt! Thank God you're here. You OK?'

'Just about, mate. Can't feel me feet though.' Matt's voice sounded croaky. 'You took your time.'

Nick glanced around the workshop. 'I was lucky to get past Valko. The pissing bastard nearly spotted me. He's got a gun, for Christ's sake! Where's old Clegg?'

'Don't know. Haven't seen 'im.'

Nick looked at Matt's suspended ankles. The weight of his legs pulled on the rope, tightening it and digging into his flesh. Nick turned towards a rack of saws, but in his haste, stepped on the loose nails. He skidded on the concrete floor, just managing to regain his balance as he grabbed at a bench top stacked with glass jars.

'Keep quiet. What you playin' at? Action Man? Batman? We've got to get outa here. Stop arsin' about, will you.'

'Oh shut it, Robin. There's bloody nails everywhere. What the hell's been going on in here?'

'Come on, you're wastin' time. They'll be back any moment. Untie me an' I'll explain.'

Nick set about freeing Matt, all the while ducking lower than the bench tops in case Valko or Mahmoud returned. He knew he had to work fast and concentrated on keeping his hands steady. The saw had sharp teeth and it only took a few moments to cut through the rope's coarse fibres.

'You know they're goin' to shoot a 'copter? Called it a Grom missile.' Matt rubbed at his feet and ankles.

'Shush, keep your voice down. I know. I think I saw it in the courtyard.'

'What we goin' t'do?'

Nick glanced around the barn again. There was nowhere secure to hide; they'd be sitting ducks for target practice. 'We've got to get help. Here, take my mobile. The Raingate Station number is on there. Quick, phone them and also 999 for help.'

'Yeah, but what you goin' t'do?'

'I can't stay here. I think I'll take my chance, see what I can…. God knows if you're safer staying in here, or getting the hell out.'

'But where you goin' now? Hey, take somethin' with you as a weapon.'

Nick didn't hang around to answer. He had more urgent things on his mind. But Matt did have a point, so he paused briefly as he headed for the doorway and picked up a large chisel. Then he was gone.

•••

While the drama of Matt's capture had been running its course, Chrissie kept watch from her rooftop lookout. Earlier that morning she'd heard footsteps on the track and when Matt briefly came into view she managed to suppress an overwhelming impulse to shout. Instead, she tried to catch his attention by throwing a segment of roof batten, something she'd cut out earlier. But it was too light and awkward to throw, and like a poorly folded paper dart, it landed short. Matt didn't even notice. He stared at the cars, oblivious to the rest of the world. Why was he alone, she wondered. It wasn't in his nature to walk if he could hitch a ride and the workshop wasn't on a bus route, so… he must have come by car and that meant Nick's Fiesta. So where was Nick? And come to that, where was his Fiesta? She didn't dare call out. Valko and Mahmoud would have come running out of the barn, and then what would happen?

Chrissie watched, torn between horror and indecision. She waved frantically, trying to attract his attention as he struggled to open the barn door, even pushing with his shoulder when he thought it was sticking. And then he was gone, swallowed up by the barn, and she was filled with guilt. She had strained hard to listen, but just as before, it was impossible to hear what was being said inside the barn. She comforted herself with hope. Harmless bumbling Matt wouldn't be seen as a threat, surely? He'd talk himself out of the barn again, but when the door creaked open and she heard the words, *and while you're about it, look for a nail gun*, her heart sank. Matt didn't come out. Valko emerged, gun held at the ready. Her heart pitched lower into the depths.

Chrissie kept an uneasy silent watch from her limited viewing point, but when Valko returned after five minutes and went back in through the barn door, she turned away. She never spotted Nick; she was too distracted when she heard the distant rumble of the first helicopter. It was her cue for action. She didn't dare mess anything else up. The plan she'd worked out so carefully with Ron had to work.

Chrissie ducked back into the roof space and gathered up the dustsheet with its painted message. She pushed it through the gap in the roof tiles as the throbbing engines approached and just as the barn door flew open. The material caught on the sides of her makeshift window and dislodged a tile. It slithered down, gaining momentum, but somehow landed in the guttering – steadied but waiting to fall. Her attention was on the tile, willing it to balance as Mahmoud burst out of the barn. She hardly noticed Valko follow. Her hands were full and her view obstructed. She certainly didn't see Nick; she was too busy securing the sheet.

'Have you attached the battery unit?' Valko's voice rose to her vantage point.

Oh my God, she thought. They're right below me. Chrissie craned to get a view. Mahmoud and Valko bent over their boxes, oblivious to everything but the contents. The metal tube stood propped against the end of the cedar trunk as Mahmoud tried to lock something onto it.

'I can't get this hand piece on.'

'Here, give it to me. You won't get the gripstock onto the launching tube like that. *Idiotŭt mu s idiot!*'

'Launching tube?' Chrissie echoed as the thudding grumble of the helicopter's engines swelled.

Mahmoud pulled excitedly at the awkwardly shaped weapon, but Valko put a hand on his shoulder and bent down to point at something still in its case. The helicopter was now directly overhead and Chrissie felt the crescendo of sound as the motors drove the rotating blades above. A moment later, and the noise was dying, no longer palpable as the Apache circled away from the workshop complex. Could it have seen the written message on her dustsheet?

'The battery unit – remember?' Valko's voice was audible once again. 'Yes, I know there's a battery inside the missile to work the guidance system, but first you've got to launch the bloody thing. That,' he pointed into the case, 'is the second battery, the one to work the pre-flight firing systems. I told you you've got to attach it. They don't operate by clockwork. You don't understand, do you? *Glupak - glupakut mu s glupak!*'

Chrissie watched Mahmoud as he tried to hold what she assumed was the gripstock. His arms were puny. His hands shook. At this rate she wouldn't need her Molotovs.

Valko seemed to be enjoying himself. He laughed and pushed Mahmoud to one side. With a few slick moves, he connected the battery unit to the gripstock and handed it back to Mahmoud. 'Remember, *magare* - you don't need to aim accurately. The infra-red guidance system will lock the missile onto the exhaust and engines, and then you have your helicopter. Boom!'

Oh my God, she thought.

'Whoa, this can't be right,' Mahmoud gasped, struggling to hold up the assembled Grom and balance it on his shoulder. He stood with legs apart and Chrissie thought he looked, from all his grimacing and straining, as if he was about to give birth standing up.

'When the missile's fired there'll be tremendous recoil. That shoulder buffer should fit against you here,' Valko explained, thumping Mahmoud's chest and pushing at the Grom so the buffer rested against his upper body. Mahmoud buckled under its weight. 'It's only 16 kilo. You'd expect to carry that sort of weight in a backpack for training. You're pathetic. Look at you - your legs aren't even strong enough to stand while you fire.' Valko almost spat out the words.

'I'll pray that Allah may give me strength.'

'Well on the off chance he doesn't hear you; you'd better lie down on your front to fire it. *Pabarsaï*!'

'Or I could just rest it on this tree trunk?'

'Not my cedar trunk,' Chrissie whispered under her breath. The distant drumming of the helicopter's engines started to get louder. Oh God, she thought. It's completed its first circuit of the area and it's coming round again. Had someone read her notice from the air? Could the pilot see anyone on the ground, she wondered. The helicopter was approaching from behind the barn. It would be right on top of Mahmoud before it spotted him. The Molotovs; she needed to light her cocktails now.

She ducked her head back into the roof space where the glass bottles and jars waited. They were arranged in neat rows, filled with meths or white spirit and with the dustsheet wicks poking cheerfully out at her, giving an air of seaside frivolity to the lethal containers. She knelt down and using a box of safety matches, lit her Molotov cocktails. 'It's time, Mr Clegg,' she hissed through the hatchway as she stood up.

'Has Matt come out of the barn?' he asked.

She didn't answer, she couldn't find the words.

'Poor Matt. Just get those bastards if you can. Remember to make sure the wick is burning well before you throw the bottle, otherwise it'll blow out mid-flight. Now go on and give it your best shot. Use enough force. The glass must smash on impact.'

Chrissie couldn't help but smile. Ron was ever the teacher, and she the apprentice. It was good to be doing something after all the waiting, even if she might be shot.

•••

Nick crept out of the barn workshop door, gripping the chisel. He looked across the courtyard at the collection of boxes and launching tube where Mahmoud crouched low. At first Nick thought something might have happened to Mahmoud, but as he moved forwards, he realised Mahmoud was kneeling, his chest bent forwards, head on the ground, no doubt making a reservation for his place in Paradise. Valko stood with his back to the praying figure and gazed up into the sky. All his attention was focused on the approaching helicopter and he failed to notice Nick.

'An Apache,' Mahmoud pointed out as he stood up, no doubt satisfied with his early booking confirmation.

'Yes. Better than a Sea King search and rescue,' Valko agreed.

'What?'

'I said, a Sea King – unarmed, bad publicity.'

'They're all Western pigs!' Mahmoud shouted. 'He appeared invigorated by his prayers.

•••

Chrissie popped her head out through her rooftop window, holding a Molotov cocktail in her hand. She felt empowered by the warmth of its burning wick and the smell of meths. She was just in time to see Mahmoud pick up the Grom. Valko bent over it and pressed a sequence of buttons. She guessed he'd primed it for firing before stepping back out of the way. As he straightened up, she caught sight of Nick. He appeared out of nowhere, down in the courtyard. Surprise, relief, fear; one followed the next on the helter-skelter of her emotions. But Valko saw Nick at the very same moment. His response was instant and physical. He sprang into a semi-crouching position ready for combat. He reached into his leather jacket for his gun.

Something snapped in her mind. Adrenalin surged through her veins and she sprang into action.

'Look out, Nick,' Chrissie yelled with the loudest shriek she could muster and hurled the Molotov bottle at Valko. Her voice was swallowed by the helicopter above, but the glass smashed at Valko's feet spraying up fine droplets of methylated spirit. The flame from the wick ignited the spirit. A sudden flash and then a ball of fire almost enveloped his shoes. It didn't hit him, but he was taken by surprise. He jumped back from the burning spirit, his attention on the flames at his feet. It gave Nick time to break into a run. He literally launched himself past Valko and towards Mahmoud. Valko looked up at Chrissie and fired. She instinctively ducked down, reached for her second lit Molotov, and standing up briefly, flung it at Valko who still faced her squarely. It smashed on the courtyard, this time landing a little short as a bullet struck a tile above her head. She felt the ricochet of dust and tile fragments.

'You bastard,' she yelled as helicopter engine noise filled the air.

Chrissie reached down for her third Molotov cocktail, heady on adrenalin. Almost instantly she was back at her post and ready to throw, all concern for her own safety blown out the window. As she took aim at Valko, she saw Nick throw himself at Mahmoud's legs in a perfect flying-tackle. But Nick was too late. Mahmoud must have pressed the fire button because, as he twisted and fell forwards, the missile flew out of its launching tube. The recoil smashed the Grom's handle-buffer back into Mahmoud, striking him across his chin and knocking him unconscious. He fell to the ground with Nick's arms still locked around his legs.

The missile launched horizontally, four feet from the ground. It flew straight and low, bellowing out yellow-white flames and exhaust from its rocket. It failed to lift. It hadn't been airborne for long enough to allow its guidance motor and secondary flight rocket to engage. Chrissie watched as it sped directly towards the hired Peugeot. It passed clean through the open front windows and flew on.

'Oh no, please no!' She knew what was going to happen. Her MG was parked on the far side of the Peugeot. She felt rather than heard the massive explosion as the missile detonated on impact. Her car erupted, spewing shards of metal, black smoke and fire.

Chrissie dragged her eyes away from the pyrotechnics and looked for Valko. He was already sprinting towards the barn workshop. With one huge, final effort she hurled her third Molotov cocktail, still lit and ready in her hand. It sailed through the air in a great arching lob and smashed on the courtyard, just to one side of Valko as he ran. He neatly side-stepped the flames as the spirit droplets ignited. In another second he was out of view, disappearing into the barn workshop.

The engines rumbled and thudded overhead as the Apache wove to one side and accelerated away, all the time keeping low. Chrissie watched as it headed to Wattisham Airbase. The pilot must have seen the explosion. Christ, what was going to happen next?

•••

Nick rolled over and rubbed his knees. He felt dazed. Mahmoud's inert body had partially shielded him from the worst of the explosion. At least he'd been lucky with that. He checked Mahmoud had a pulse - yes, the bastard still lived, but where was the chisel? For a moment Nick wondered if he'd somehow managed to stab Mahmoud when he fell. And then he spotted it, clean and bloodless, lying on the concrete where it must have landed when it sailed from his hand in the flying-tackle. He staggered to his feet and picked it up, expecting to see the wreckage of a helicopter belching black smoke somewhere nearby, but - he blinked and rubbed at his eyes – there wasn't one. He was pretty sure he was looking at the remains of a car. The burning tyre and hubcap were the give-away.

'Christ, Valko!' For a moment he'd forgotten him. Immediately he cast around, looking for any sign of where he'd got to, and then as he raised his eyes, he noticed a dustsheet flapping on the tiles like a fallen sail on the waves.

'Hey Nick! Up here.'

'Good God.' He couldn't believe it when he saw Chrissie's head poking out through the rooftop. Earlier, when he crept from the barn and faced Valko, he hadn't noticed her looking out from her hole in the tiles. When the Molotov cocktail smashed at Valko's feet, he thought it was fired by the Apache. He simply reacted, taking advantage of Valko's surprise. It was only while he lay on the ground, gripping Mahmoud's legs, that he thought it a bit old fashioned - a glass bottle incendiary device in a modern army? But as he looked up at Chrissie now, he couldn't for the life of him think what she was doing with her head sticking out between the tiles.

'What the hell…? How long have you been up there?'

'Since Friday. Don't just stand there; take cover.'

He frowned as he tried to make out her reply. His ears felt blocked and her voice sounded muffled; bloody explosion. He could have sworn she'd said Friday, but that meant three days with her head poking out of the roof.

'Watch out, Valko's in the barn,' she shouted, waving in the direction of the barn workshop door.

The name, Valko and the words, watch out cut through the fuzziness in Nick's ears. Chrissie's traffic cop arm movements only added urgency but no details. Just like Chrissie, he thought. It felt good to have her back, but hearing Valko's name had an immediate and dramatic effect. Nick dropped down onto the concrete and crouched behind the cedar trunk, his pulse racing. A chisel was no match for a gun. And as if to underline his feeling of hopelessness, a moan escaped from Mahmoud's motionless body where it lay face down nearby.

•••

While the drama played outside, Matt had not been idle in the barn. Armed with Nick's phone, he moved to the far end to get a better signal. The reception was patchy around Wattisham and although he didn't want to admit it, he felt safer being as far as possible from the door. First he phoned the Raingate Police Station, but he got nowhere. What was it with switchboard operators? Why were they so suspicious? Finally he called 999. It took forever and he was still on the line pleading when the missile exploded. The sound bounced around the courtyard, reverberated over the satellite airwaves and finally galvanised the operator into action. Having been about to dismiss the call as a hoax, she changed her mind and finally insisted on sending all three services: police, fire and ambulance.

Matt sank down onto the concrete floor exhausted and defeated. He was too late. Mahmoud had bagged his helicopter after all. But as he listened, the engines continued to rumble and thump without a pause. That could only mean one thing. The helicopter was still flying. Maybe something else had been hit instead? Matt didn't like guessing. He'd heard the explosion and his emotions were shredded. To be honest, he didn't want to go out there again; not until it was all over.

As he cradled his head in his hands, someone burst in through the open door. Footsteps echoed through the barn, urgent hurrying. Matt held his breath and tried to make himself smaller. Was it Nick? Whoever it was, stopped.

262

They must have seen the pillar drill, but without his trussed up body.

'Where are you Matt Finch?' Valko shouted.

Matt swallowed his scream and curled tighter into a foetal position. If he closed his eyes, would Valko's disappear? A metallic crack rang out. It answered his question. Sh-i-t, he's shot the pillar drill, he thought.

'Hah! *Vij* - the bitch's handbag. The keys will be in there somewhere…. *Da*!'

Of course, Matt thought, Valko must have Chrissie's handbag from when he stole her car. But why bring it here? Wouldn't he have got rid of it, taken what he wanted and then ditched it? Did Valko have a taste for ladies handbags? His thoughts were interrupted as Valko started moving again but not, thank God, in his direction. It sounded as if he was making his way to the door. Matt reckoned it was safe to open his eyes again. He peered round the workbench. Valko stood at the barn door, half crouching and looking out, gun in one hand, handbag in the other. Matt wasn't particularly arty, but this particular view of Valko framed by the doorway, struck him as ridiculous and edgy. And then Valko raised his arm, aiming at someone out there. The picture of a drag queen had gone; the psychopathic killer was back. Something clicked in Matt's mind. He only knew of two people outside: Mahmoud and Nick, and Matt cared about one of them. He had to do something. Now.

Driven by pent-up emotion and a desperate bid to escape, Matt hurled himself through the full length of the barn workshop, accelerating as his trainers gripped on the concrete floor. He let out a yell as one sole skidded on the nails Mahmoud had scattered earlier. Valko, taken by surprise, turned and fired into the barn. His bullet went wide of its mark as Matt lost his balance and fell forwards, putting out his left hand to break his fall. He screamed as he felt his left wrist crack against the hard floor.

'Shit!' Matt moaned. His cry and fall must have sounded as if the bullet had reached its target because Valko had gone.

•••

Chrissie watched as Nick ducked down out of sight behind the cedar trunk.

Bang! A shot rang out and someone in the barn screamed.

'Look out!' she yelled as Valko ran from the barn, weaving and firing his gun as he headed across the court-yard towards the Peugeot. 'Keep down, Nick!' Bullets sprayed everywhere, but she got the distinct impression he was mainly aiming at her. 'He knows I've got another Mol-otov,' she called to Ron, silent in the workshop below. She had no choice but to take cover in the roof space; she just hoped Nick was all right.

'What the hell?' she asked herself, the roof tiles and Ron. She was sure she'd seen Valko carrying her handbag. What was he after now? And then she remembered the hire car keys. They were in her handbag. The one Mahmoud took when he attacked her. She was so cross she stood up and leaned out of her rooftop window, no longer caring if she made herself an easier target.

'My Peugeot!' she shrieked as Valko wrenched open the driver's door and leapt in. The Peugeot was parked at least thirty yards from the MG and had survived the nearby explosion. She watched, shouting with rage as he rum-maged through her bag. 'No, you bastard, stop!' But he didn't and the car started first time. He revved the engine hard, almost as if he to say *and two fingers to you, mate.*

The car had been rocked by the blast. It was covered in dust and the paintwork blistered on the side nearest the explosion but it was still in some kind of running order. The heat must have softened the tyres though, because as he accelerated away, he left rubber on the concrete courtyard.

'I hope the seat's bloody hot and your hands weld to the steering wheel.'

There was no point in hurling a fourth Molotov. The Peugeot was well out of her throwing range and Valko was already escaping. Even the hateful leather jacket was no doubt working for him, shielding him from the worst of the heat. She watched as he accelerated out of the courtyard, taking her handbag and her hire car. Why hadn't they scrambled the helicopters from the airbase? Couldn't anyone help? Well; four X to you, she thought. Where was an Apache when you needed one?

CHAPTER 18

The Peugeot was out of sight, but Chrissie could still hear its engine whining and screaming in first gear as Valko accelerated down the rough track and away to the perimeter lane. From her position up in the roof, she thought Nick might be dead; he lay so still in the courtyard below, behind the cedar tree trunk.

'Nick, Nick! Are you OK? Hey Nick.' Chrissie felt her panic rising as she shouted. And then she saw him lift his head from the ground. 'Thank God. Are you OK? Have you been hit? A stray bullet?' Chrissie didn't know why she used that term. If Nick had been shot, Valko wouldn't have considered his bullet a stray; and then in case Nick hadn't heard, 'It's all right. Valko's gone.'

The sound of the Peugeot's engine faded into the distance and for a moment there was silence. And then all hell broke loose. Chrissie heard the sirens.

'Are you OK, Chrissie?' Nick sat up. 'Is… who else?'

'Yes, I'm fine. Valko's gone. That leaves Mahmoud and… quick, I think I just saw him move.' Chrissie heard the sirens getting louder. Perhaps the airbase had sent out an alert after all.

Nick stood up. 'I thought he was out cold but….' Nick made his way to Mahmoud's prostrate body. There was a low moaning sob, almost animal-like, and Chrissie watched as he crouched to take a closer look. For a moment Chrissie wondered what he was doing as he pulled off his belt. But then Mahmoud started to move.

'Look out; be careful, Nick.' Chrissie watched as he tied one end of his belt tightly around Mahmoud's wrists.

Grabbing the other end, he drove the chisel through the buckle ring and into the cedar tree trunk, but by then the sirens were shrieking out a cacophony of sound matching the loudest helicopter engine, even when directly overhead. In fact a police helicopter had been scrambled from Wattisham Airbase and was soon illustrating just that point.

The noise was too loud to hear Nick speak. Chrissie gazed out, numbed as the police cars rocked and rattled their way up the old track, stones and gravel spraying against their bodywork as they travelled as fast as they dared. Brakes squealed as they turned into the courtyard, doors sprang open and armed police jumped out. Chrissie thought they were dressed in a rather fetching shade of midnight blue, with full body armour, helmets and visors. They held automatic rifles at the ready with the sights trained on her head, still poking out of the roof. The loudhailer was difficult to hear against the sirens.

'Put down your weapons and come out slowly with your hands above your head.'

'I don't have any weapons,' Chrissie shouted. She looked down at the dustsheet, flapping on the tiles below her roof window. The painted message announced her as the **HELD – MAD GUNMAN**. Did they think she was the mad gunman?

'Put down your weapons and come out slowly with your hands above your head,' the loudhailer repeated.

Chrissie watched in horror as two armed police officers approached Nick, who stood near Mahmoud.

'Lie flat on the ground. Put your hands behind your back,' the loudhailer commanded.

Chrissie watched, speechless as Nick silently followed the instructions. One armed policeman held his gun to

Nick's head while the second bent over his body. They seemed to be checking he wasn't rigged with an explosive vest. They must have been satisfied because they soon got close enough to snap handcuffs on his wrists. Chrissie bit back some tears as they dragged him away towards a waiting police van.

'No, you're making a mistake,' she shouted. 'He's one of the good guys.' Couldn't they tell they were arresting the wrong person? She shook her head. 'Look, there's someone still in the barn. Matt Finch. He may be… injured.' She didn't want to use the word dead. Chrissie resisted the impulse to wave her arms in the direction of the barn in case they thought she had a weapon and shot her.

And then something snapped inside her head and she lost her temper.

'Now look here, just you listen to me for one moment,' she said eyeing up the policeman holding the loudhailer. 'I have been held prisoner and locked in this building since Friday. It has taken me days to cut my way through this roof.' She kept her voice firm and her words clear. 'Do I look as if I know one end of a gun from the other? Do you seriously think I'm a terrorist? Take a reality check.' She paused for breath. 'I have had enough! Radio the Raingate Police Station in Bury St Edmunds this instant and ask for Detective Inspector Merry. Your jihadist terrorist is lying down there.' She pointed at Mahmoud. 'And that was my beautiful MG.' She crushed the sob in her throat as she pointed to the burning wreckage in the courtyard.

'Now calm down, madam, and keep your hands still and out on the roof where we can see them.'

'Don't you tell me to calm down, officer. I have been attacked, held prisoner, shot at and starved. And now I've seen my car hit by a missile and you people are training guns at my head. The man you want is called Valko Asenov and he just drove off in my hired metallic-blue Peugeot 207. He is armed with a handgun and extremely dangerous.'

She held up one hand, showing the palm - not as a sign of peace, but to indicate the loudhailer was to remain silent. She had more to say.

'Now I'm going inside and down into this building's workshop. You will hear hammering and splitting wood. Mr Clegg, the owner of these workshops, is also held prisoner in here. We had to barricade ourselves in to stop that man....' She paused to point at Mahmoud. The police marksmen tensed on their triggers but she continued, 'And Valko Asenov from killing us.'

'Keep your hands still, madam,' the loudhailer commanded.

'You will find the keys to this workshop door in that man's pocket.' She pointed at Mahmoud in a final act of defiance before continuing, 'Or somewhere in that barn workshop. You will need to let us out, or break the lock.'

Chrissie guessed the policeman with the loudhailer must have attended courses on anger management, dealing with aggression, and hostage negotiation. She also supposed correctly there wasn't a course on how to talk a starving, angry, middle-aged, female, carpentry apprentice down from a hole in the roof. She watched as someone scribbled a message and then held it up on a clip board for him to read.

'Now Chrissie, try and stay calm,' the loudhailer advised soothingly.

Chrissie's head nearly exploded. Did they think she was a fool? It was obvious someone had given him her name in that message. Did he really think that by using her first name she would be soothed and reasonable? Little did he know her.

'Don't call me Chrissie, my name is Mrs Jax. And I am completely calm,' she responded, her voice rising.

Chrissie had had enough from the loudhailer, and putting both hands above her head, dropped back into the roof space. She bent down and peered through the hatchway to see Ron sitting hunched up in the corner, well away from the door and window.

'Well that went well with the police, then,' he said.

The noise from the sirens filled the pause while they both considered the situation.

'They think we're the terrorists don't they?' Ron observed, weakly shaking his head.

'I don't think they're thinking, just reacting. Look on the bright side - it won't look good in the papers if they shoot us and then discover we're unarmed. We haven't any weapons in here, so it should be obvious we're not terrorists.'

'What about the Molotovs? They're weapons and probably illegal. We'd better dismantle the one's you haven't thrown, just to be on the safe side. It won't take a moment to put the bottles back on the shelves and get rid of the evidence. The ones you've already used will be considered self-defence rather than assault.' Ron stood up stiffly and limped over to stand under the hatchway.

Chrissie handed down the unused Molotov cocktail, the box of safety matches and the empty white spirit and meths containers. She waited where she was, watching Ron as he moved slowly, dispersing the bottles and losing the evidence. What had all this done to him, she wondered, apart from the obvious effects of missing his arthritis medication for three days? Chrissie climbed through the hatchway and turned her attention to the barricade across the door.

Ron was too stiff to help her dismantle the solid construction. It was funny, but for a moment she didn't want to pull it down. For three days it stood firm, between her and certain death. It was like a comfort blanket, and now she had to cast it aside and expose herself to men-in-blue with flak jackets and guns. She looked at Ron and he nodded. In the end, it took all her remaining strength to ease out the large nails. With the help of a claw hammer, crowbar and wrench, she pulled the fortifications apart, splitting and cracking the old wood.

'You can unlock the door now,' she shouted, sweating and grimy as she thumped it to get outside attention. The bruise on her cheek already stained one side of her face.

'Stand back from the door Mrs Jax, we're opening it now,' the loudhailer responded.

The key grated as it turned in the lock. The handle twisted and the old door slowly swung open. Sunny fresh air streamed in, and Chrissie breathed deeply.

'Come out slowly with your hands above you heads,' the loudhailer commanded.

'I can't get my hands above my head, my shoulders have seized up,' Ron whispered. 'Do you think they'll shoot me, Mrs Jax?'

'Most probably, Mr Clegg, but knowing my luck, they'll miss you and hit me instead. Like my car.' Chrissie didn't move, she wasn't sure about leaving her fortress. 'Do you think my car insurance will cover it, or say they're not liable because it's an act of God?'

'And who's God would that be?' Ron asked.

Chrissie followed Ron as he limped out into the summer sunshine. As she gazed around the courtyard she felt strangely distant, as if she was an observer present at a crazy scene but not part of it. If she'd been able to feel more connected, she would have said *hey it's a carnival* with everyone dressed in costumes of midnight blue or white and green, yellow reflective jackets and hard hats. The fire crew hosed what remained of her MGB with something suspiciously like cavity wall insulation foam, while the cedar trunk also got a dousing for good measure, suds lifting in the air and falling like huge clumps of snow.

It was all madness, someone else's madness. Even the hazard crime scene tape fluttered like bunting. But her isolation seeped deeper as she imagined Nick already marched off and bundled, no doubt, into a dark blue van with a metal grill and small window. And then she caught sight of an unmistakable form – Matt. He was alive, but the paramedics obstructed her view.

The policeman with the loudhailer stood in front of her. Seeing him was like a red rag to a bull. A pink haze descended. She headed straight for him with a purpose in her step that belied her hunger and exhaustion. Out of the corner of her eye she saw an armed police officer as he shadowed her path, but no one stopped her. The loudhailer took an involuntary step back.

'You can put that loudhailer thing away, now.'

'Keep your distance, madam. Stand still.'

'The man who got away is called Valko Asenov. He's already wanted for leaving the scene of an accident and stealing my MGB last Thursday. He's just made off in the Peugeot 207 I hired on Friday and he may use my house keys. They were in my handbag. He has a gun and has already tried to kill us. He even shot through the door you've just unlocked for us. Check, if you don't believe me. You can see the bullet hole from here. And old Mr Clegg - he hasn't had his medications since Friday morning.' Chrissie turned to look at Ron. A paramedic threw a blanket over his shoulders, despite the summer sun.

'You seem to have had a lot of dealings with this Valko Asenov.' The policeman paused, letting his words hang in the air before continuing, 'It would be helpful if you'd tell us the colour and registration number of the Peugeot, madam. Of course, you know you should never leave your handbag and keys in an unlocked car.'

Chrissie felt her cheeks flush. 'This is not the moment for community policing. For your information, I was carrying my handbag when I was attacked, tied up and imprisoned by that madman, Mahmoud. I'll have you know I locked the Peugeot. My mistake was leaving the windows open.' Chrissie was about to say more but changed her mind.

The pre-requisite female police officer had been located and approached. She was flanked by ambulance crew and carried a blanket held at-the-ready, as if to throw over a wild cat. The bulletproof jacket made her look enormous. Chrissie almost stepped back, but despite her slight frame, even trimmer since shedding a few pounds on her enforced water-only diet, she stood her ground.

'This woman police officer will accompany you in the ambulance. We would like you to be checked over at the hospital before we take your full statement. Now please, go along quietly,' the policeman said as he held the loudhailer, lifeless in his hand.

Chrissie hesitated and then thought better of saying more. She could tell, by looking at the police officer's expression, that any resistance would result in a loss of dignity that would be hers, not the officer's dignity. She felt her energy drain away as she realised she had no choices left and reluctantly she submitted to a superficial body search. It was more of a patting down for concealed weapons and an explosive vest than anything more aggressive or probing.

In true equine spirit, she allowed herself to be led, with the horse blanket draped over her shoulders, to an awaiting ambulance. And so one nightmare ended and another began.

CHAPTER 19

'C'mon, he's in here somewhere.' Nick led the way. He had no idea where exactly he was going, but someone on the front desk had said Butterfly.

'Butterfly?' Matt queried and then resumed chewing.

'Yes. She said Butterfly Ward, second floor.' Nick headed for the lift, and Chrissie followed. It was Wednesday evening and they were in the Ipswich Hospital, searching for Ron Clegg.

Matt chewed noisily as he walked. 'Why'd they bring him here, not Bury?'

Nick looked back at Matt. A large corridor stretched behind, seemingly for miles. 'Same reason they brought you and Mahmoud here. Difference is they let you out.'

They got in the lift and Nick found himself jostled and nudged to the back wall. The doors slid across, barring the exit and everyone stilled. He closed his eyes and for a moment pictured the cell he'd been held in for thirty-six hours.

'Anyone pressed for the second floor?' someone asked, and suddenly he was back being interrogated. Sweat broke out on his face as the anti-terrorist officer leant in close. *You were the one who fired the missile, weren't you? You smashed up that young man's face, you lying bastard.* Nick felt hot. His throat was dry and he couldn't speak. The image came again as the words repeated, over and over in his mind. And then just as suddenly, it stopped. *You can go now.*

The lift juddered to a halt. 'I think this is the second floor,' someone said. Nick opened his eyes and saw Chrissie watching him. He felt embarrassed.

'Are you tired, mate?' Matt asked and Nick nodded, not trusting himself to explain. How could he tell them he'd just relived part of the worst experience of his life? Facing Valko, had been nothing compared to being questioned by the anti-terrorist squad.

They eventually found Ron Clegg in a side room on one of the general medical wards. Only two visitors at a time, the nurse said, but Nick flashed one of his smiles and launched his charm offensive. She blushed and said she recognised his face from the picture in the local paper. Another smile and then they were in, all three of them. The orthodontics had paid off.

Nick wasn't sure what he'd expected to find, but he was relieved to see Ron looking much the same as ever, thinner and tired but still the same old Ron. 'Hello, Mr Clegg,' he said, hoping he'd conformed to the hospital visitor etiquette.

'They nearly didn't let us all in. Only two visitors at a time,' Chrissie added, and then grinned. The bruising on her cheek had changed colour and spread down to her jaw like a five-o'clock shadow.

'Well, they've made a dreadful fuss of me. The physiotherapist said something about being in the papers. I can't think why. Now sit down, don't stand there hovering over me. Makes me uncomfortable.'

'You made it to the nationals, so that makes you a celebrity, Mr Clegg.'

'Did I really, Mrs Jax? They wouldn't let me see a paper till I'd made my statement. That explains it.'

'So why the drip?'

'Ah Matt, there you are. They said something about dehydration and electrolytes.' Ron smiled before continuing, 'I thought they'd send me straight out. You know, part of the mark-'m-up and move-'m-on culture but unfortunately I proved too stiff. They weren't able to sit me up, let alone send me home. The physiotherapist said something about unlocking joints, at least twenty of them.'

'Sh-i-t.'

'Matt!'

'It's fine, Mrs Jax.' Ron beamed at them. 'You have no idea how pleased I am to see you all. And you, Matt; for a time we thought they'd killed you. But didn't you only have one arm in plaster last time I saw you?'

Matt nodded and held up both forearms; one sheathed in a rather grubby plaster cast and the other in a back slab and crepe bandage.

Nick started to laugh. This was just like Matt - a slapstick artist with brittle bones?

'It's only a hairline break this time. Radius, or did they say ulna? Anyhow, I've got to go back to the clinic.'

'But what happened?'

Nick's attention wandered. He'd heard it all from Matt earlier, and anyway he'd been in the barn for part of the time. He gazed around Ron's small room: the white basin in the corner with its shining chrome taps, the suction unit on the wall near his bed, and... *you were the one who fired the missile, weren't you? You smashed up that young man's face, you lying bastard.* The voice reverberated in his head as he remembered his thirst, the cell, his…. His pulse raced. Christ, he thought, it was all my fault. If I'd driven over to the Clegg workshop sooner, things might have been different, none of this need have happened.

'I still don't understand why Mahmoud was throwing nails around in the first place.' Ron's voice drifted into

Nick's consciousness, bringing him back to the present and the hospital side room.

'You OK, Nick?' Matt stared at him and then started chewing again.

'Yes of course. Stop asking, will you.'

'Sorry, mate.'

Nick gave himself a mental shake. What the hell was he doing snapping at Matt? Of course he wasn't OK. None of them were OK, for God's sake. He closed his eyes for a moment and composed himself. 'Shall we start from the beginning?' Nick asked, breaking the silence as they all stared at him.

'Yes please,' Ron said quietly.

They drew the wipe clean plastic chairs closer and huddled around Ron's bedside. Nick glanced at Matt; he looked almost as pale as Ron and his attention seemed to be on a bunch of grapes on the locker. It was easy to read his mind but with both wrists handicapped, he didn't rate Matt's chances of plucking one from the bunch and popping it in his mouth unnoticed. He'd have to content himself with his gum. He seemed to be making a meal of that anyway.

'We've found out a lot from Detective Inspector Merry,' Chrissie explained.

'No, you've found out loads from DI Merry.' Nick was surprised to see her blush.

'After the crash,' she continued, ignoring Nick and directing her attention on Ron, 'the police couldn't trace the owner of the container. They opened it up and found fruit for export, and that led them to Damson Valley Farm.'

'Yeah, but that's not all they found. You've missed–'

'Thank you, Matt. They found a false partition and a 2010 Mercedes SL AMG.'

'Is that something special, Mrs Jax?'

'It's in the Absolutely Stunning category, Mr Clegg.'

'It was stolen to order and Valko was transporting it to sell in Europe,' Nick explained. Chrissie seemed to be making a bit of a meal of it all; he couldn't think why. It would take forever to explain everything at this rate and Ron looked restless. 'He was in the business of stealing top-end sports cars,' he said, hoping he'd wrapped it up neatly for Ron.

'Is that why he took your car, Mrs Jax?'

Nick struggled to keep a straight face. 'No. Chrissie's car would best be described as bottom-end of the market.' Nick almost felt the withering look she flashed at him.

'My car just happened to be there when he needed to escape. Mine was never taken for export.'

'I still don't understand how any of this explains why Mahmoud threw nails around. Am I missing something?' Ron frowned and moved his hand with the drip taped to the back, and tried to get comfortable.

Nick kept his mouth closed. He'd read Chrissie's unspoken message loud and clear. Best keep the peace and leave it for her to explain.

'Sorry, Mr Clegg, you're getting tired. To understand it all, you need to…. Well it helps if you understand Damson Valley Farm is the key to it all. Jan Kowalski and Valko–'

'Jan Ko who ski?'

'Jan Kowalski. He's the fruit pickers' manager and Valko is his right-hand-man. They've been running a stealing-cars-to-order scam for ages. John Willows junior was–'

'Me second cousin–'

'And one of the carpenters who worked on the fruit-pickers' accommodation huts. He also made the false partitions for the containers used to smuggle out the cars. Are you following this, Mr Clegg?'

Ron looked from Chrissie to Matt. 'That dreadful business with the nail gun a year or so back? He was found dead wasn't he?'

Chrissie cut in before Matt could answer. 'We think Valko killed him with the nail gun and in some way Mahmoud was part of it. He'd have known them all. He's one of the fruit farmer's sons, a Farrow boy. They were going to do it again, you see. Kill Matt with a nail gun.'

I don't think I see at all, Mrs Jax and you're starting to sound like Miss Poirot.' Ron lay back on his pillows.

'I think we should go,' Nick mouthed, raising his eyebrows while secretly thinking *Herculette* Poirot; good name for her.

'Already?' Chrissie mouthed back, frowning.

'You can take the grapes if you like. Oliver Blumfield brought them for me; kind of him. I'm starting to feel rather tired. Sorry….'

Matt stood up and reached for the grapes, but Nick was faster. He'd guessed what was in Matt's mind and with lightning speed whisked the bunch off the bedside locker. With one deft move they were safely in his hand.

They said their goodbyes and threaded their way back towards the lift, Matt never more than a pace behind the grapes, and Chrissie silent and in her own thoughts. Nick suggested they took the stairs instead of the lift when they passed the stairwell, and no one disagreed.

'There's some kind of visitors' coffee place near the main entrance. Maybe it's only a machine but I need something,' Nick said when they reached the ground floor.

They sat at a table across from the hospital shop and drank from waxed paper beakers in silence. Nick felt uncomfortable. There was something between them, something unspoken like an elephant in the room they didn't want to acknowledge. Chrissie seemed distracted and now, as she rested her hands on the table, he caught sight of her fingers. The tips looked bulbous and she'd bitten her nails down short. He couldn't recall ever seeing her bite at them before. Poor Chrissie with her bruised face. And Matt seemed to be chewing continually; first the gum, and now the grapes. He kept popping them in his mouth, slowly stripping the bunch and leaving behind the thin twig-like branches pointing skeletal fingers accusingly at Nick.

Chrissie finally spoke. 'What's wrong, Nick?'

'I was going to ask you.'

'No. You haven't really told us what happened after the police took you away.'

'No.'

'C'mon mate. I want to hear.' Matt turned his attention back to the grapes.

'Another time.' Nick watched Chrissie as she traced the lettering on her beaker with her thumb. There were cracks in her dry skin and the tip was fissured and sore. He wondered what Chrissie was building up to. She usually just backed off, sensing when he didn't want to talk. Anyway, he'd thought she was the one who had a problem. 'What happened to your fingers, Chrissie?'

'What?' She looked at her hands. 'Oh that - it was difficult making a hole in the roof, that's all.'

They sat in silence for a moment. Nick sensed Chrissie was making a decision and waited for her to speak.

'I told them what happened, you know gave my statement. The police know you aren't a terrorist, Nick and... DI Merry believes me,' she said, this time not blushing.

'Yeah, I told them too; said you saved me life.'

You smashed up that young man's face, you lying bastard. The words echoed in Nick's head.

'But what if Mahmoud lies, says I attacked him and broke his jaw? I'll be done for assault. They said they'd charge me with grievous bodily harm.' Now it was out. He'd said what he heard over and over in his mind.

'Look, use your head,' Chrissie said quietly. 'The bruises and marks on Mahmoud match the shape of the missile handle buffer, not your knuckles. I expect if they look really closely they'll even make out the imprint of the letters Grom on his face. And another thing; his fingerprints will be all over the missile launcher, not yours.' Chrissie smiled and then sipped her coffee.

Nick thought through what she'd just said. Maybe it made sense. 'So what's happened to Mahmoud? They wouldn't tell me. Have you heard?'

'Well, Mahmoud expected to die and go to Paradise. Instead he came round in a NHS hospital bed with a male police escort for company. That's what happened.'

'Hah! Not quite the seventy-two virgins then.' Matt swallowed the last grape and coughed.

'DI Merry says he's been talking - singing like a bird since he's woken up. Shame about his broken jaw, must be very painful for him.' Chrissie fell silent for a moment and then slowly smiled. 'Seems he's discovered his conscience.'

'Oh yeah?'

'No, after you gave your statement, Matt, DI Merry questioned him about John junior and what he'd said to you about the nail gun. Apparently Mahmoud wants to set the record straight and point the finger fairly and squarely at Valko and Jan.'

'Strikes me you should be calling DI Merry by his first name by now. I assume he has one,' Nick observed. He couldn't help but laugh when she blushed.

'What you mean? Mahmoud's in loads of shit so why'd he say anythin' 'bout John junior now?'

Chrissie took her time before answering. 'If he can demonstrate remorse by giving evidence against the other two, including Jan's part in providing the Grom, well then he may gain some leniency along with a plea of diminished responsibility.'

'Shit! That's a load ol' squit. Lookin' after your own skin, I call it.'

'Exactly, Matt. He'll allege he was brainwashed into being a jihadist terrorist; that he was vulnerable, isolated and naïve, and... he was the real victim.' Chrissie almost spat out the word victim.

'Hmm. You know the letter I found from Wattisham? Their glidin' club? I gave it to the police, the same one that questioned me after the canteen explosion. 'E came back from Martlesham Heath to see me. Don't know if your DI Merry's seen it.'

'What letter? And he's not my DI Merry, Matt.'

'Yeah course, you never saw it did you? It proves Mahmoud was askin' 'bout the glidin' club. Has to be pre-meditation; tryin' to infiltrate Wattisham Airfield.'

'And I've given DI Merry the photocopy of the plans we found in the files at Willows. I bet they match the exact dimensions of the false partition in the container. And Valkos's initials are clearly written on them.' Chrissie fell silent.

Nick watched in disbelief as Matt put a ball of old chewing gum back in his mouth and worked it around, his jaw muscles clenching and relaxing rhythmically.

'I been thinkin'.' Matt spoke slowly between chews, 'Bet Mahmoud was there the night John junior died. 'Spect he's got somethin' incriminatin' on Valko.'

'Valko certainly made sure Mahmoud was exposed out in the courtyard when he fired the missile. He hoped the Apaches would shell us all, including Mahmoud. God, he's a bastard,' Chrissie added.

Nick suddenly realised what was eating at Chrissie. Valko; it must be Valko. 'Have the police found him yet?'

'Yeah, what's Merry said?'

Nick watched as Chrissie bit at one of her fingernails before she answered. 'They've found the hired Peugeot in one of the short-stay Dover Port car parks. The number plates had been changed, but the scorch marks on the paintwork and seats were unmistakable.' A muscle close to Chrissie's left eye started to twitch. 'They've checked the CCTV showing all the passengers boarding the ferries that day and… well there were several men of similar build. They're looking at the images more closely. He could have been disguised.'

'He might have turned the infamous leather jacket inside out – you know, a coloured lining or something,' Nick suggested and pulled a face.

'Reversible jacket. I never thought of that.' Chrissie frowned. 'The bastard! Anyway, they've alerted the French police and Interpol. The Border Agencies are on the case, so there's nothing more we can do for the moment.'

'So is it safe to go home?'

'They've put a police guard on my house for the moment but... it'll be OK.'

'Are you sure? You can always stay over at mine if you're worried. I'm sure my parents wouldn't mind. There's loads of room.'

'Thanks, Nick but I'll be fine.' The muscle flickered again and she rubbed at her left eye.

They tossed their empty paper beakers into the waste bin. It was time to leave the hospital and go home.

Nick felt slightly better. What Chrissie had said made sense. The air had been cleared and more importantly, the elephant was no longer in the room. There'd been quite enough mention of DI Merry for one evening but tomorrow he'd check if Matt had said anything to anyone about Peter Farrow; the way he'd reacted a bit strangely when they'd asked him about Valko being friendly with John junior. Perhaps someone should suggest to the Inspector he interview Peter about it? Chrissie could do that. And then he smiled.

CHAPTER 20

It had been four weeks since the attack at the Clegg work-shops and although Matt's right wrist was out of plaster, he sported a new plaster cast on his left wrist and lower arm. The doctor said it hadn't been such a bad break as the first, the one from the canteen oven explosion, but it was still enough to stop him taking up his apprenticeship at Hepple-whites until it healed. Mr Blumfield said if there were any more breaks, then he'd have to repeat his apprentice year. Matt reckoned he hadn't even started it, so how could Blumfield talk about repeating it? He certainly didn't want to spend any more time on the Planning & Communication module, so when Nick suggested they all go over to the Clegg workshops after the Monday apprentice release day, Matt leapt at the idea. Well that wasn't strictly true because he was taking extra care after what old Blumfield had said.

It was the first time he'd been back since the incident, as Chrissie liked to call it, and he wasn't sure what to ex-pect. Nick talked about getting flashbacks, but for Matt nothing happened while he was awake, only in his dreams so he expected to feel pretty much as he always felt when Nick drove up the rough track and into the courtyard.

When he stepped out of the Ford Fiesta and looked at the barn door, he felt his stomach lurch. He assumed it was just the journey. Nick had taken most of the corners at speed and like the last time they'd driven to the Clegg workshops he felt queasy.

Matt followed Nick through the old barn door. The cool air and slightly dim light should have transmitted a feeling of calm order as he stepped onto the concrete floor.

So why was his heart racing? It thumped against his chest and his face felt hot.

He gazed around the workshop. As he looked at the benches, tools and the pillar drill, some of the memories came back; a bit fuzzy around the edges, like a black and white photo degrading to washed-out shades of brown. He tried to focus but everything continued to fade until all he saw was an empty film set. The main players had gone, leaving behind nothing but echoes. It was only in his dreams that the film played out in full colour and the characters were real. Matt reached into his pocket for some gum. It helped if he kept working his jaws.

Matt glanced down at the plaster cast, popped the gum into his mouth and chewed hard. Yes, it had all really happened. He hadn't said much since he'd arrived, but then he didn't know how to explain what he felt. No one seemed to want to talk about the incident so he sat in the barn with Nick and Ron Clegg, drinking mugs of tea while Chrissie chatted about looking for a car to replace her MG. It all felt rather matey, almost as if they were the cast gathering for a new production and the action scene in the horror movie had been forgotten with the last roll of the credits.

'I didn't notice the old wreck when we arrived,' Matt interrupted. He'd half expected to see burnt-out metal welded into the courtyard, a kind of Suffolk Picasso, but all trace of it had been removed.

'They took it away. There's nothing left but a charred metal frame stored in a police warehouse as evidence,' she explained. 'My insurance company were a bit tricky but they're still going to pay up. Technically it was stolen at the time it was shelled.' Chrissie smiled, but a muscle beneath her left eye flickered rapidly like a butterfly fluttering beneath her skin. Matt had noticed it kept happening recently.

'And you, Nick - how are you?' Ron asked.

'Good, Mr Clegg. I'm good. They're not going to charge me with assault and,' he turned to Matt and added, 'I haven't had a chance to tell you this yet but I've had an invitation from the Wattisham Airbase.'

'What? You're kiddin' me.'

'As a reward for deflecting the missile, I've been invited for a flight in one of the helicopters.'

'You jammy bugger.' Some people have all the luck, Matt thought

'Good for you. Did the police ever get to the bottom of John junior's death?' Ron asked, but before Matt could say anything, Chrissie butted in.

'DI Merry interviewed Peter Farrow, the oldest Farrow boy, about John junior's death. I'm not really supposed to know this but – well it's pretty incriminating for Valko. Stop me if you've heard this before.'

'No, no, Mrs Jax, carry on.'

'John junior was a friend of Peter Farrow. They'd known each other since school days. He told Peter he was interested in buying a car and at the time he'd been working on constructing the fruit pickers' accommodation huts at the Farrows' family farm, Damson Valley. Peter put him in touch with Jan Kowalski, the fruit pickers' manager who was always talking about cars and seemed to be car mad.'

'The brains behind the stealing-cars-for-export scam,' Nick added.

'Valko asked John junior to do some extra work making partitions for the containers transporting the fruit from the farm. There's no suggestion he knew anything about exporting the stolen cars. But then John junior came across Mahmoud in one of the outhouses on the farm changing number plates on a Mercedes SL600. He thought it suspicious and spoke to Peter, Mahmoud's older brother.'

'Yes but I still don't understand. What do they think happened to John junior?' Ron asked.

'Well John junior put two and two together and became suspicious. Remember he was working on the farm site. He saw the containers being loaded with fruit and the amount didn't even begin to fill the containers. He reckoned he'd seen a stolen car; and he was making wooden partitions. He drew the obvious conclusion. He told his friend Peter who thought it was all nonsense and said if he was so worried, he should speak to Valko.' Chrissie shook her head. 'And soon after that Mahmoud was caught and arrested for stealing a car.'

'Why didn't Mahmoud point the finger at Valko or Jan? It sounds like he wasn't the only one stealing cars,' Ron asked, shaking his head.

'DI Merry thinks Mahmoud was easily led and intimidated by Valko. He was probably terrified of going against him. I mean we've all met Valko and he's a psychopath,' Chrissie explained. The muscle started twitching beneath her left eye again.

'So what happened next, Mrs Jax?'

'We have to assume John junior made the mistake of speaking to Valko rather than going to the police. They arranged to meet at the Willows workshop in the evening after work. Mahmoud apparently said in his statement that Valko told him to come to the meeting as well.'

'Shit! I guessed as much.' Matt almost bit his tongue as he worked the chewing gum around his mouth.

'DI Merry thinks Valko wanted to show off to Mahmoud; you know, demonstrate how powerful he was and what happens if anyone crossed him. A not very subtle warning of what would happen to Mahmoud if he went to the police. And of course it was a kind of initiation into the gang. Anyway Mahmoud says they both went to the Willows workshop. There was an argument between John junior and Valko. You know how Valko can suddenly lose his temper and become violent. Well that's apparently what happened, according to Mahmoud. Valko picked up the nail gun and simply fired it into John junior's neck. They both stood and watched while he tried to pull the nail out of his neck. He bled and choked to death.'

'Sh-i-t, that's… that's murder. Did 'e just stand there and do nothin' to save 'im?' Matt felt his face flush as his ears buzzed.

'Apparently it affected him quite badly.'

'I bloody hope it did.'

'He didn't dare speak to anyone about it at the time. It explains why he was so isolated and vulnerable while he served his prison sentence, and why he was open to conversion and then targeted for radicalisation.' Chrissie paused before adding, 'Well, that's how they've explained it to me.'

Matt didn't buy any of that. They'd all been affected by the incident four weeks ago but it hadn't made them rush out and join a jihadist group. So Mahmoud had been upset and that made everything all right?

'Poor bloody Mahmoud, my arse. An' John junior, what about 'im?' But it was what he didn't say that weighed heavy in the air. No one spoke for a while.

'And significantly on the anniversary of John junior's murder, Mahmoud planted the canister in the canteen ovens.'

'So that makes the Utterly explosion OK, do it, Chrissie? An' Valko,' Matt blurted out, 'does he get away with it too?'

'I don't know.' Chrissie nibbled at a fingernail as she stared at the floor.

The silence was broken by the sound of tyres scrunching up the rough track and the muffled noise of a well-tuned engine in low gear.

'What now?' Nick stood up. 'Visitors?'

Matt wasn't listening. His mind was filled with a red mist. He closed his eyes and a kaleidoscope of shapes and colours swirled into something. Gradually an image of strawberries materialised. It was as if he could see Valko smirking, delicately wiping strawberry juice from his lips as he watched John junior cough up blood and claw at the nail in his neck. An idea took form. He spoke, keeping his eyes closed to hold the image.

'There's somethin' buggin' me - the punnet of strawberries in the Willows workshop. Valko liked 'em – even had a punnet in his drivin' cab. Chrissie, can you ask your inspector to ask Mahmoud: did Valko take strawberries with 'im when they killed me second cousin?'

Chrissie didn't answer immediately. Matt was conscious of some commotion around him and heard the barn door open. Oh God, he thought, I've summoned up Valko.

'You can ask him yourself, Matt,' she said, and he opened his eyes to see her blushing.

She stood smiling as she looked in the direction of the door for a moment and then sat down again. 'Come in, come in, Clive. Everyone's already met Detective Inspector Merry, I think.'

'Hello Chrissie. Sorry to intrude like this.'

'Well, I aint met 'im,' Matt said whirling round and staring at the stranger. His pulse raced as he assessed the visitor. For a moment he was convinced this was Valko in disguise, except Valko was dark haired and swarthy, and his eyes were expressionless – like a shark's. This man was much taller and smiled; even the skin near his eyes crinkled when he smiled but – sh-i-t, Matt looked again, yes – he had red hair. A ginger cop.

'No, I haven't either. You'd gone home when we went back to Raingate Police Station – when we left a message about identifying Valko in Chrissie's photo. I'm Nick, by the way. Nick Cowley.'

'Yeah, an' I'm Matt.'

'And this is Ron Clegg.' Chrissie blushed again.

'Well sorry to intrude, but I felt I had to drive over and deliver the news to you in person, Chrissie. Well – it's on my way home.'

Matt watched as all the colour drained from Chrissie's face. She's not the only one seeing ghosts, he thought.

'No, no it's good news. Valko's been picked up in a stolen car as he crossed into Germany.'

'Thank God!'

'Sh-i-t.'

'When they caught him he was wearing a grey linen jacket with thin black stripes and a leather lining. So your theory was right, Chrissie.' The Inspector grinned and looked at them all in turn. 'Seems he's wanted for violent crimes in Bulgaria. The Bulgarian police have first call on bringing him to justice. So it'll be some time before he's extradited back to the UK for his Suffolk crimes.'

'So the police guard on your house isn't needed any longer, Mrs Jax?' Ron got up from his stool, smiling. 'Good news, Valko behind bars. Well, life can return to normal at last. Now I think we've done enough talking and its time we all got some fresh air and you three started on the totem pole.'

Matt eased himself down from his seat and followed the others outside. It was a chance to steal another glance at Chrissie's inspector. Clive, did she say? He looked much the same age as her; middle aged and a bit on the thin side. He wore his shirt open at the neck and without a tie. Matt reckoned his trousers were the bottom half of a suit; the jacket was probably in the Ford Mondeo parked in the courtyard. No doubt he put it on when he arrested people. However, instead of saying goodbye and going straight to his car, he ignored it and walked on with them all. Matt was surprised.

The cedar trunk had been stripped of it bark and the fire fighting foam had long since disappeared. Matt could still see the scorch marks – charred evidence of the searing heat when Chrissie's car exploded. They were mainly on one end. But it was the bullet holes that really grabbed his attention. They were massive. Chrissie walked over to him as he stared, fascinated.

'The police dug the bullets out for evidence. That's why it resembles a Swiss cheese.'

'Ah! That explains it. But what we goin' to do 'bout it?'

'I thought we could use it as an excuse to make the totem pole shorter.'

'No, I think we should try and incorporate the damaged wood in some way,' Nick suggested as he stood and gazed at the cedar trunk.

'We could use those holes to represent the drainage of the fens,' Chrissie said.

'I think it'll just look like we think Emmental cheese comes from East Anglia.' Matt looked up to see Ron laughing. 'What's funny 'bout that?'

'You three. You've got a lot to learn about carving. Most of the time I've no idea what you're talking about, but at least I can teach you something about wood and carving and….' He looked up into the sky.

They all heard the distant rumble as another helicopter took off from the Wattisham Airbase.

The End.

Lightning Source UK Ltd.
Milton Keynes UK
UKHW020915150320
360356UK00006B/135